RESIDUE

STEVE DIAMOND

PRIMORDIAL PRESS

Paperback ISBN-13: 978-1-960244-18-5
Hardcover ISBN: 978-1-960244-19-2

"An intense, high-energy, what-lurks-in-the-shadows tale of monster, both men and otherwise. Steve Diamond can make you shiver." —**Terry Brooks,** *New York Times* **Bestselling Author of the Shannara Chronicles**

"Residue is a fast-paced, fun read with great characters and the best prom scene since Carrie. Steve Diamond writes kick-butt mutants, psychics, and guns. I love it!"—**Larry Correia,** *New York Times* **Bestselling Author of the Monster Hunter series**

"I really enjoyed Steve Diamond's novel, Residue. Steve Diamond is not just a writer to watch... he's a writer to read. Give yourself a treat and look for Residue! I look forward to Steve's future works."—**Robert McCammon,** *New York Times* **Bestselling Author of** *Swan Song* **and** *Boy's Life*

"Residue will scare you—that's its primary goal—but along the way it will touch you, shock you, make you laugh, make you cheer, and make you think. Horror has been waiting for Steve Diamond."—**Dan Wells,** *New York Times* **Bestselling Author of the John Cleaver series and the Partials Sequence**

For Jenny, Logan & Alyssa

Acknowledgments

I'll keep this short.

For this modified, author's edition of *Residue*, my earliest alpha readers still deserve their due. You all are awesome. Tom Lloyd, James Barclay, John Brown, Bryce Moore, Shawn Boyles, Dan Smyth, Vanessa Christenson, Don Darling, Rob Code, Nick Sharps, Alan Bahr, and Dan Wells.

If you know me, you know I'm heavily influenced by a bunch of authors and artists. Brian Lumley, F. Paul Wilson, Bob Eggleton, Joe Lansdale, Jonathan Maberry, and Richard Matheson. Without those folks, I wouldn't be writing what I write.

And I'll give a special mention here to Terry Brooks and Robert McCammon for the incredible cover quotes. McCammon, specifically, is probably the most important author to my writing. Thank you.

And for Larry Correia, the best friend, co-author, and mentor a guy could ask for—well, thank you doesn't cover how grateful I am to you.

I have amazing parents who got me reading early and often. My mom and dad are awesome.

And to my wife Jenny, thank you for supporting my dream to get this book done and for helping me not give up on it. I love you more than anything.

Last, but certainly not least, the patient readers who have stuck with me during all these publishing changes and adventures. Thank you for picking up *Residue*. Keep reading, and read everything.

—Steve Diamond

CONTENTS

PROLOGUE

Alex

Illuminated in the harsh, red light, bodies lay twisted and bent in shapes the human figure was never meant to experience. Their faces—where they still had them—were locked into final screams of pain and terror. The scents of coppery blood and gunpowder filled the air.

Alexandra Courtney shook her head to clear the noise. Each time the red light pulsed, the piercing wail of an alarm accompanied it, making concentration impossible.

Alex's boots lost traction in a smear of blood, and she fell hard on her shoulder, nearly losing her grip on her gun. The red liquid seeped through her light jacket. She found herself staring into the face of a dead guard in a Helix Corporation uniform, his head twisted around to face backwards, fresh blood still leaking from his nose and mouth.

A bestial roar and the sound of gunfire from ahead refocused her attention. She pushed herself back to her feet, shoving away an offered hand of help from one of the guards that had filed into the hallway behind her. They were nervous. Alex was pretty sure one of them had pissed his pants at the sight of the half dozen mangled corpses in the hall.

Weak, she thought.

She ran towards the gunfire, glass crunching under her boots.

To her left was a holding cell, now with a gaping hole smashed through the reinforced glass. The red alarm light pulsed again, and through the hole she saw more dead guards inside, ripped to pieces.

Alex motioned for the two nearest men to secure the cell. The door, standing untouched by the violence, read 213.

Her mouth went dry.

The Leech's cell.

More gunfire sounded from up ahead, accompanied by the screams of the dying.

She sprinted toward the sounds, hurdling bodies, blood pounding in her veins in time with the pulsing red light. A crash ahead of her echoed over the shrieking alarm, and she barely registered movement ahead in the emergency lighting. She turned a corner, finding more bodies, and just caught sight of a misshapen silhouette illuminated in the light outside the building's fire exit. Whatever it was, the form couldn't be the Leech. It was too big.

She jumped over a crumpled, lacerated corpse and burst through the open doorway after it.

Instantly, the building's outer floodlights blinded her, and she lost precious seconds blinking to adjust her vision.

Stupid, Alex berated herself. *I'm a sitting duck.*

Her vision cleared, and the light, nighttime breeze carried away the odor of violence from behind her.

Across the grass clearing she caught a glimpse of a boy-sized figure fading into the woods on the opposite side of the electrified fence enclosing the building. The Leech. Closer, and just now passing through the ragged hole in the fence through which the Leech had escaped, Alex spied the bulky creature that had set the Leech free and killed the guards.

Alex's instinct kicked in before her mind reacted. Her arms snapped up and she pulled the trigger on her pistol four times in the span of a heartbeat.

The creature bellowed, staggered, then fell.

The guards behind her were already forming up to track the Leech. *Good.* Alex had read the thing's case file. *If we don't find it...*

She approached the creature she'd shot, gun poised to put the remaining rounds in its skull if it so much as twitched. It still lived, gasping for air, but its hide was riddled with a dozen bullet holes. Far more than the four she'd made.

At least my guys went down shooting.

Up close, Alex recognized what she was looking at, though she'd never seen one of these beasts in person. Bony spikes stood like quills on the back of a heavily muscled form that had once been human. Claws jutted from fingers and toes, and its teeth looked impossibly sharp. Its arms were elongated to accommodate loping on all fours. The beast's face appeared to have been frozen in mid-transition from human to the were-wolf it was patterned after.

This was one of Whyte Genetics's abominations. A Hound. Genetically mutated pack animals.

Where there was one, more would follow.

This was far worse than just the Leech getting away.

Alex pulled out her phone and dialed Helix's head of security.

He answered after the first ring. *"Bishop here."*

"This is Alex. We've got a situation."

"What happened?"

"We've got a lot of dead people here—"

"How many casualties?" Daniel Bishop interrupted.

"I don't know," Alex replied. The Hound at her feet gasped for air. "At least a dozen. Hard to tell. A lot of them were... in pieces. The work of a Hound. We stopped it—it's dying now—but not soon enough." She shook her head. *How could this happen on my watch?* "It looks like some sort of screwed-up rescue mission. Something was set free."

"What do you mean it was a rescue mission? What was set free?"

"The Leech."

Bishop didn't speak for several moments, and when he did his voice shook. *"I'll be right there. Just... put the Hound down. They can't be turned back to humans. And Alex..."*

"Yeah?"

"I'm sorry," Bishop said. *"You shouldn't have to deal with stuff like this."*

The age thing again. "No worries, sir. Better this than normal college crap."

"Yeah," Bishop said. He didn't sound convinced. *"I'll be right there."*

The call ended.

Alex slipped the phone back in her pocket and looked down at the Hound. Blood leaked from the Hound's mouth, and it gasped for breath. She'd only seen one actual werewolf in her young life, but at least it had looked natural. This thing was the test-tube version of that beautiful beast. A weapon. She wondered if the creature could even think.

Alex looked into the thing's eyes. All she saw was animal fury.

She aimed her Sig P226 and put two rounds into its head.

CHAPTER I

Jack

"We think your father is missing," the deputy said. "We found his truck abandoned several miles outside of town. Can you to tell me if he came home last night? If so, is he still here?"

There are a few things I never expected to hear in my life. That was one of them. For a moment, I stared blankly at the man—his name tag read "Deputy Path"—and wondered if this was some sort of joke. A really bad one.

"Mr. Bishop?" the deputy asked. "Jack? Are you hearing what I'm saying?"

I almost laughed in the man's face. "Who put you up to this? This doesn't really feel like something my dad would put together. He doesn't have much of a sense of humor. Was it Barry? He can be an ass sometimes, but this is excessive, even for him."

"No one put me up to this, Jack. If your father's here, I need to know right now."

"This isn't a joke?" I rubbed my eyes, trying to clear the cobwebs. I'd been sleeping soundly on my living room couch when the deputy knocked on my front door.

I was a bit annoyed getting yanked from the sweet dreams I was having. I'd dreamt about who I would take to Homecoming. I'd already graduated from Calm Waters High earlier this year in the summer, but the local tradition meant guys and girls like me went back and attended the dance anyway.

I was at the part of the dream where one girl had just said yes, and then two more lovely ladies came into the picture, fighting over who would be my *second* date to the dance. I offered to take them both, of course.

They'd been fawning over me when the pounding on the door ripped me from that moment of bliss.

"Look," I said with a weary sigh. "My dad left last night after a call about some security thing at Helix. I couldn't hear much of what he said. I was waiting up for him, but I must have crashed on the couch. He's probably upstairs, sprawled out on his bed."

"Would you mind checking for me, please?"

"Seriously?" I shook my head in annoyance. "Sure. Take a seat. I'll only be a second."

Deputy Path nodded and stepped inside, but made no move to sit down. Something in his expression made my heart beat faster.

Dad *had* gone out last night, after getting a call about some security thing at Helix. I fell asleep before he got home, but surely he'd actually come home. He probably saw me asleep on the couch and tiptoed past, not wanting to wake me.

I glanced over my shoulder to the stairs leading up to the second floor of our home, then back at the Deputy. Seeing him standing there, expression grave, forced my tired mind to catch up to the situation and all its possibilities. A cold lump of anxiety settled in my stomach.

I tried not to hurry as I went up the stairs, reassuring myself as I climbed. My dad would be up there. I'd open the door to his room, and he'd be lying there, snoring like usual. Maybe he'd even still be in the clothes he'd worn last night.

Yeah.

His truck was abandoned outside of town.

That stray thought floated through my mind as I reached the top of the stairs.

Now I was worried.

I stopped at my dad's bedroom door, and when I reached out to turn the knob, I realized my hand was shaking.

I steadied myself and opened the door.

The bed lay empty, made, and undisturbed.

I walked through the room to the adjoining bathroom and it was empty.

Panic clenched in my gut.

I ran out of the room, shouting for my dad. I threw open every door on the second floor. Every closet and bathroom. I even checked under the beds, the rational part of my panicked brain knowing he wouldn't be there. It didn't matter. I had to check.

He wasn't here.

Unexpected helplessness clutched at me. I couldn't *do*

anything. There wasn't any magic pill or wand to make my dad appear. I threw a glass I didn't even realize I'd picked up. It shattered against the wall in the hallway, spraying glass everywhere.

Deputy Path pounded up the steps and burst into the hallway. "You okay, Jack? What's going on?"

I gestured with a vague wave down the hall. "He... he isn't here. My dad's gone." I tried calming myself with a few deep breaths. "Where do you think he is? Is... is he alright?"

My cell phone buzzed in my pocket. Probably my dad, apologizing for all the worry. I checked the phone and it showed five missed calls from my friend Barry and one of his texts.

Dude. Call me ASAP. Things are crazy.

Whatever. Barry could wait. He'd left me hanging more than once. After all, *his* dad wasn't potentially missing or anything. There was nothing from my dad.

It took all my self-restraint to not hurl the phone at the wall like I had the glass.

"Talk me through it, Jack," Deputy Path said. His voice held that false calming tone all cops had to be pros at. "What exactly did your dad say last night?"

I took a few more deep breaths and resisted the urge to sink to the floor. No. I wasn't going to embarrass myself any more than I already had.

"He got a call last night from someone at Helix," I said as calmly as I could manage. "I only heard part of the conversation. He asked the person on the phone about casualties or something."

I closed my eyes, trying to remember the words. It had all happened so fast. One minute we were eating root beer floats while watching *The Raid,* and the next he was on the phone, tense like I'd never seen before.

"He said..." How had he put it? "He asked something like, 'What do you mean it was a rescue mission?'"

"Are you sure that's all he said?"

"Look," I said. "From the moment he got the call, to when he flew out the door was, like, three minutes. He said he'd be back later, and we'd have some things to 'discuss' when he got back. Whatever that meant."

"Do you remember what time he left? Any chance you know who he was speaking to?"

"He ran out fairly late. Maybe... a little after eleven? We were about halfway through the movie. But no, I don't know who called. Seems like maybe you should ask the people at Helix."

Deputy Path scribbled something in his notepad, and I felt a little bad that I'd briefly lost my cool. He was just doing his job, asking the types of questions he had to ask. He gave me a practiced smile and asked, "Anything else you remember?"

Again my impatience bubbled to the surface. I wanted to reach out and strangle him. *Other than that? Nothing.* "I don't know what else you want me to say. You came to *my* house, remember? How about you tell me what the heck is going on?"

"Calm down, son." He put a hand on my shoulder. "Just calm down."

I pushed his hand away. Probably not the smartest thing to do to a cop, but I was sick of his patronizing attitude. "Don't touch me," I said through clenched teeth. "And I'm not your son. Now how about you actually give me a little bit of information?"

His eyes briefly narrowed, but then he nodded, as if finally appreciating my situation at the moment. The change in his expression calmed me for some reason. I wasn't normally the combative type. This wasn't me. I was just so... so...

I was just so worried.

Was my dad okay? He had to be.

"Your dad called Helix last night and told them he was being followed. Then his phone cut out. We tracked the GPS on his cell and found his truck a few miles from the Helix offices. We found his phone in the vehicle, but he wasn't there, so we wondered if he had come home. I'm sorry, Jack, and this is a terrible question to ask, but do you have any other family in town? Anyone who can keep you company until we sort this out?"

Oh man. This guy was dead serious. "I have an aunt in town. Martha Thompson."

"Care if I call her up?"

"That's fine. Do you need her number?"

"That won't be necessary, Jack."

"Any... any idea where my dad is?" It was a stupid question. The deputy wouldn't be here if he knew. But I had to ask anyway. The deputy shook his head. Of course not. Pity showed on his face and in his posture. I didn't want his pity. "What's going to happen now? With my dad, I mean."

"We'll coordinate with Helix's security people. From what I understand, they already got some of their people together since his truck was found on land they own."

"Great," I said. "Let's get going." A search would at least give me something to do. I wasn't going to sit here twiddling my thumbs.

He hesitated. "Jack, it would be better if you waited here. In case your dad comes home and—"

"Not gonna happen," I interrupted. I needed to be out there. I needed to *do* something.

The deputy held up his hands. "Look, how about we sit down for a second—"

"I am *not* going to sit down!" A flush of embarrassment crept into my cheeks, and I lowered my voice. "You can either drive me to Helix, or I'll drive there myself."

"All right," he said after a moment. "Let's go."

CHAPTER 2

Jack

We rode in silence. The trip to Helix didn't take long, but once we reached the corporation's land, Deputy Path took dirt roads for another thirty minutes. I didn't even know these roads existed.

What was my dad doing driving way out here? His words repeated themselves in my mind. *What was set free?* Had he gone to look for something out in the woods? What did a company like Helix even possess that *could* be set free? None of this made any sense.

Deputy Path's phone rang. "This is Path. Oh, hey." His eyes flicked my way. "Yeah, he's in the car with me. He's going to join the search party. Uh-huh. Uh-huh. Alright. Will do, thanks." He hung up and tossed his phone in a cup holder next to him. "That was the acting head of Helix's security with an update. She said to let you look around your father's vehicle. See if anything seems out of the ordinary to you."

"Okay," I said. That made some sense, at least. "What about the search party?"

"They already got started."

"But—"

"But nothing, son. They aren't waiting on one kid. Helix knows this land far better than you do. Let the pros do their thing."

A short while later the dirt road opened up to a small clearing, and I saw my dad's F-150 smashed into a tree. I was out of the deputy's vehicle and running for my dad's truck before the deputy had even come to a complete stop.

I ran around to the front of the F-150, praying I wouldn't see an impact mark in the windshield where my dad's head would have struck it when hitting the tree. I let out a ragged breath I didn't know I'd even been holding. The windshield was fine. I looked inside the cab but didn't see any blood. Since I didn't see his phone, I had to assume that Helix's people had taken it. Even though the front of the truck had smashed pretty hard against the tree, everything else in the truck looked normal.

My dad had wrecked his truck, and now he was missing. But he wasn't dead.

Probably.

Crouching down, I looked back in the direction of the main road, noting the furrows in the ground made by my dad's tires. It looked like he'd swerved off the road—maybe *forced* off?—but I couldn't be sure. I certainly wasn't a professional. Resting my back against the nearest tree I slowly sat down on the ground. With my hands in my armpits to ward off the cool October temperature I asked myself the obvious questions. *What was I doing? What did I think I could really accomplish by coming out here?* There were professionals out here searching for my dad, and here I am thinking I can help and do what they can't. It was so absurd.

That was when I noticed the tracks.

I'd gone hunting with my dad before, and he'd taught me the basics of tracking. He'd gone on and on about the legendary tracking skills of my grandfather, Wyatt, and how maybe I had a little of him in me. I'd always laughed the words away. But now as I stared down at the depressions in the dirt, I was grateful for my dad's lessons.

The tracks started at the truck's door, leading away deeper into the forest. If I hadn't been sitting down I might never have seen them. The early morning light caught the moisture trapped in those tracks, giving them a weird purple sheen that made them easy to follow.

I walked wide of the tracks while following them deeper in the woods. Somewhere in the distance, I heard the chatter of what had to be the search party looking for my dad.

Maybe the worry for my dad had my nerves on edge, or maybe it was walking alone through the forest, but I found myself dreading every tree and giant fern I passed. I kept imagining I'd suddenly stumble across my dad's body, half-covered by the foliage. Maybe he would be leaning against a tree, slumped over and dead. Maybe covered in blood...

I stopped walking and tried to steady my breathing. I squeezed my eyes shut and shoved away those thoughts.

The tracks took a sharp turn, diverging from the path taken

by the Helix search party and their constant chatter. The further away I got from their calls for my dad, the forest quieted, revealing the sounds of birds and insects. Ageless redwoods towered over me.

The tracks led further and further into the trees. At times the tracks seemed to fade into the shadows, but I would pick them up again a few feet farther along. In time they entered another clearing, ringed by ferns, and what I saw on the ground brought me up short.

There were tracks everywhere. I spotted my dad's jumbled in the clearing, but mainly I saw other imprints... strangely long, and almost animal looking. Almost. Here, too, the tracks shimmered in the light, almost purple in color. The tracks looked like elongated and misshapen human hands and bare feet. But their ends reminded me more of animal prints, and I could even make out where claws came from them.

They were everywhere. The ground and the plants in the area were torn to pieces. Noticing the sap oozing from broken branches, I could tell that whatever had happened here had happened recently.

Panning my gaze across the scene, it looked like something —several somethings—had surrounded my dad. Animals of some kind. Not that I was a professional tracker or anything, but the marks didn't bring to mind any animal I was familiar with. All kids growing up in a town like Calm Waters knew at least what deer and cat tracks looked like. Even wolf. The tracks mixed with my dad's were completely different from anything I'd ever seen.

But as I stared, the word *animal* felt wrong.

Something. Something *else*.

They led away from the small clearing, off into another part of the forest. I wasn't really sure if I should follow the tracks, and I didn't see any more of my dad's footprints leading away. Had these animals *taken* my dad? Dragged him away? I didn't see any blood. The whole scene brought more questions to mind than it answered.

"You aren't supposed to be out here."

I spun at the voice. It belonged to a girl—eighteen or nineteen, my age—standing near where I'd entered this clearing. It took me a moment, but I recognized her.

"Alex?" Her face was partially obscured by the gloom of the forest. "What are you doing here?"

Alexandra Courtney. She was in most of my classes at Calm Waters Junior College, and like me, she worked at Helix on the weekends. I didn't have a clue what she did. Probably something important. She was the kind of girl who effortlessly aced everything even though she never seemed to pay attention. The kind of girl most other college students hated out of jealousy.

She was also drop-dead gorgeous and way out of my league. Though at the moment, instead of the fashionable clothes she regularly wore, she had her blonde hair pulled back in a ponytail under a hat, and she had on a plain, black shirt over cargo pants tucked into boots. The whole ensemble looked strangely... military. Is this what she thought trackers wore? Maybe she'd been watching too many Tom Clancy movies.

Then again, what she wore looked more practical and comfortable than the jeans and windbreaker I wore.

"Oh, hey Jack," she said. "I didn't realize that was you. I'm out here looking for Mr. Bish—uh, your dad. Like everyone else."

"Right. Sorry. That makes sense. Thank you for helping out."

"No problem." Alex smiled for an instant, then stared for a second before saying, "So?"

"Yeah?"

"What are you doing out here? You're supposed to be looking over your dad's truck, seeing if anything sticks out to you since you've been in that vehicle more than anyone else. Didn't Deputy Path tell you?"

Of course. My head was all over the place. I rubbed my eyes before answering and tried to steady myself. "Right. I'm sorry. He did tell me. I did look in the truck, but didn't see anything out of the ordinary inside. But then I spotted some tracks and followed them here."

"Tracks?"

"Yeah."

"What tracks?"

I frowned. Was she blind? If they were as clear as day to me, how could anyone else have missed them? "Isn't that why you're here? Didn't you follow them?"

"No. I followed the sound of you crashing through the woods." She glanced around in confusion. "What tracks are you talking about?"

I sighed and pressed my fingers against the side of my head where a sharp ache was developing. At this rate my dad would never be found. I pointed behind her to the boot prints my dad had left. "Look, right there—"

I stopped. There were no tracks. "That's weird," I mumbled. They'd been crystal clear before. Now they were so thoroughly gone that I didn't even see any obvious depressions in the earth.

"I followed them here to this clearing," I continued, almost talking more to myself than to Alex. "To all these other tracks..."

I looked around. The prints in the small clearing were gone too.

Alex looked at me curiously.

No. Something was wrong. "I don't understand... they were here. I *saw* them! A bunch of them that looked like they belonged to some weird four-legged animals. Footprints *and* pawprints."

At that moment, my vision swam, and before I knew what hit me, I lay sprawled on the ground. Nausea and pain spiked in my skull. The beginnings of a migraine. Perfect. Just perfect.

"Take it easy, Jack." Alex crouched down next to me. She appeared concerned.

My vision blurred, and my head throbbed harder, the pain growing until it felt as if my head was about to split open.

"Jack? Are you okay?"

Her voice seemed so far away. My vision tunneled until I couldn't see anything. Pain burned away any ability to think until there was only pain and darkness. I drowned in them. Suffocated in them. I let myself sink until the merciful darkness claimed me.

CHAPTER 3

Alex

Alex Courtney stared into the clearing as paramedics carried Jack Bishop's unconscious form back to the main road. They had concluded he'd passed out due to the stress of the situation.

Alex suspected that wasn't the case.

Jack's words replayed themselves over and over in her mind, and though she couldn't see the large number of tracks he'd described leading here, she knew he hadn't been lying. He had been genuinely confused. She could always tell when someone was holding the truth back. Alex had a sense for these things. Always had, going back as far as she could remember.

It was her gift.

The other thing confirming Jack's story was the clearing she stood in. Well off the beaten path and with evidence a struggle had taken place here. Jack was right, something had happened here recently. She couldn't see any clear tracks the way Jack said he had, but the other signs were clear. Scuffed ground. Trampled twigs and leaves. Obvious if you knew what to look for.

She located the spot at the edge of the clearing where the creatures—probably Hounds from Whyte Genetics—had departed. How many were there? Five? Six?

She walked further into the clearing, examining the ground for any further clues. Jack had been surprised to see her, the doubt in her abilities or qualifications clear. The truth? There wasn't a person in the city who could do what she could. Her hand went to her side where her Sig P226—chambered in 9mm—usually rode, but it wasn't there. Alex shot better than any firearms instructor she had met so far—an area of pride for her—but her superiors had given her strict orders not to wear her sidearm in public. The higher-ups in the company, her father included, thought her carrying in public would make people feel *uncomfortable*. That it wasn't *normal*.

Normal, she scoffed. *I'm not even close. Thankfully.*

Alex knew what *really* existed out there in the world, hiding in the shadows.

But instead of being allowed to devote her complete attention to developing *useful* skills like hunting, shooting, and tracking, she had to continue with *college*. Her *other* skills got her through school without a hitch, but still. It all seemed like such a waste.

Now, deep in the Redwoods without her gun, she knew it would be suicide to follow the Hounds. What were they doing here? Just sending one to free the Leech seemed... off. Alex let the thought go.

She'd call it in. Let the clean-up teams deal with the situation for now. She had more important things on her plate.

Alex's thoughts returned to Jack Bishop. Something definitely had happening with him. She couldn't put her finger on what the "something" might be exactly, but it was there. The way he'd acted, and the way he'd rambled on about the tracks he saw... well, that meant she'd have to watch him more closely. More closely than usual, anyway. Classes over at the Junior College would resume after the weekend. She nodded to herself.

Yes, Jack would need to be watched *very* closely.

CHAPTER 4

Jack

I woke up in a hospital bed and found myself, wearing only a creepy, backless hospital gown. My head still hurt, and so did my eyes. Constant pressure pulsing behind them, but nothing like the world-ending pain from before. I had some wires coming off of me, leading into a machine that occasionally beeped. I shifted to my side and noticed a tube running from my arm up into a bag filled with clear liquid.

My mind raced back to the last thing I remembered, and it was Alex Courtney staring at me like I was some sort of mental patient while I raved about tracks she couldn't see. But I knew I wasn't crazy. I *saw* those tracks. Something freaky was going on.

Taking it slow, I sat up and swung my legs over the side of the hospital bed. *So far so good.* A clock on the wall over my bed read 4:00 PM.

"Glad to see you're up."

I glanced up to see a nurse standing in the doorway to my room. The backless nature of my "robe" left me feeling... well, exposed. I clutched the back of it together.

"You gave some people quite a scare," she looked over at the machine I was hooked up to and asked, "how are you feeling?"

"Okay, I suppose. I guess I must have gotten dizzy." I pointed at the wires and tube running out of my arm. "Is this all necessary? I feel okay."

"Your BP is back to normal, and the rest of your vitals look okay. You were probably just dehydrated and your blood pressure dropped a bit, leaving you light headed." The nurse smiled. "It's not that unusual. You just need to keep drinking fluids and make sure it doesn't happen again. I'll just check a few things before clearing you to go," she said. "Your aunt is here, and she can take you home. You've been under a lot of stress today. More than anyone your age should ever have to deal with."

The nurse prattled on and on, her tone never veering from cheerfulness as she removed the wires from my chest. It seemed like everyone knew my dad was missing. Oddly, I didn't feel as worried now as I had earlier today. Whatever had taken my dad—I hadn't seen any blood in that clearing, so I had to assume he was still alive. He was out there somewhere, I was sure of it. But what had taken him? Animals? No. No matter how I sliced it, those *other* tracks hadn't been animal. But had they been human? Again, no. Regardless, whatever they belonged to, why cart my dad off and *then* kill him if you could have done that in the clearing where he got caught?

Was I fooling myself? Giving myself false hope? Maybe. But what else could I do? My dad and I had talked about this sort of thing before. *Son*, he had said, *when a parent's kid goes missing, all they can do is hold out hope. Once they let go, it's the beginning of the end.*

The beginning of the end.

No, I wouldn't go there. I wouldn't give up on my dad being found. Ever.

"Jack, did you hear me?"

Oh, she was talking to me. "I'm sorry, was thinking about... what was going on. What's up?"

"Let me take out the IV."

I held out my arm as the nurse removed the white medical tape holding the IV in place.

"Hold your breath, this'll feel weird."

I did as she asked and she pulled at the clear tube sticking out of my arm. The odd slithering sensation of the plastic tube withdrawing from my vein sent a shiver of revulsion through me.

The nurse pressed a piece of gauze onto the spot where the tube had been, and she used some medical tape to hold it in place. She gave me a smile and said, "You're all set to go home and your aunt is in the lobby. I'll leave you to get dressed."

She winked at me. Geez. I was pretty sure that was illegal somehow. At the very least it was just wrong.

My aunt waited for me in the lobby like the nurse had promised. The lights in the hospital struck me as overly bright and the sounds inside the building were amplified. I'd had migraines before, and the after-effects always sucked, but never to this extreme.

Luckily my Aunt Martha was the quiet type. She'd always been that way as far back as I remembered. At the few family gatherings we had when I was growing up, sometimes you didn't even realize she was there.

"Ready?" she asked.

I nodded, surprised she'd even said that much. I winced when the lobby door slammed shut as another patient left the hospital. Our hospital hadn't upgraded to sliding doors everywhere yet.

My aunt wordlessly handed me a water bottle and a couple of pills, as if she had been expecting me to be in pain.

The drive home was mercifully quiet and uneventful. Martha turned the radio off and kept her eyes focused on the road. She didn't offer any condolences about my dad, and she didn't ask what happened in the forest, which I appreciated. The last thing I wanted was another person giving me sympathy—false or real.

We pulled into my driveway a little after 5:00 PM. Martha popped her trunk and walked back to pull out two bags, both of them small; I guess she didn't plan on being at my place long.

Walking back into my home was strange. Without Dad, the atmosphere felt colder and less welcoming. Martha went upstairs to the spare room, and I went to my own. I didn't peek in my dad's room. I knew he wouldn't be in there no matter how much I wished it so. He was gone. Taken.

I heard Martha walk back downstairs, followed by the sounds of her pulling out some pots and pans. In my house for less than five minutes and she was already cooking. She might not talk much, but she knew exactly what was needed.

I lost myself in thoughts of how I would go about finding

my dad. I didn't have anything to go on other than those tracks in the woods. Of course, my dad would never have been out there anyway had he not received that phone call. Several things about the call nagged at me. The fragments of his side of the conversation replayed in my head, but it was the vague hints that something kept at Helix had been set free that grabbed my attention. My dad mentioning a rescue mission. And what bothered me most of all, was his fear.

I pulled out my phone and plugged it in. The battery had died while I was in the hospital. It was evening by now, time for the news, so I flipped on the TV in my room, hoping to find some sort of press release about the incident with my dad. The first story mentioned a series of mysterious pet disappearances. The poor reporter, this must have been her first assignment. She managed to appear absolutely devastated.

The next story railed about rising medical costs. Even with all the worry, I shook my head at the report. My recent visit would probably cost us a fortune. My dad always complained Helix's health insurance wasn't all that great, and we weren't exactly swimming in cash. I never did understand why my dad was so undercompensated as the Chief Security Officer at Helix.

Finally, the news I'd been waiting for came on.

"Tragedy struck Helix Corporation's Calm Waters location last night," the news anchor said. Her dark hair was perfect, her teeth blinding white. Every line of her face gave a crispness and directness to her words. The whole package looked so neat and tidy I wanted to reach through the TV and slap her. My dad had instilled a few basic beliefs in me over my nineteen years of life. First, there were only three real Star Wars

movies. Second, don't trust the government, and especially don't trust the media. But I didn't really care for the lies the anchor surely would tell. If she had any good information about my dad or the Helix incident, she'd be worth listening to.

"An equipment malfunction resulted in the injury of several employees and the deaths of ten others," she continued. *"The identities of the victims have not yet been released by the company while they conduct an internal investigation."*

They cut to one of the PR guys at Helix. He looked familiar, but it was hard to say if I had ever personally met him while doing my filing gig at the company. A small text border appeared on the screen naming him, and the chyron listed him as "Mel Smart." Another day I would have laughed. Of course his last name was Smart. I wondered if it was his real name.

"As most people in the country know," he said, *"Helix Corporation utilizes the most cutting-edge equipment in the surveying of the environment. Late last night, one of our newest machines, used in the prediction of weather patterns, experienced a power surge and exploded. This terrible incident claimed the lives of ten employees."*

Smart paused, no doubt trying to delve deep into his bad acting roots for a tear or two. I could easily tell from his mannerisms that he was full of crap. He was fidgeting, and even though someone had applied makeup on him, he was sweating through it, and that smile of his was as fake as a three-dollar bill. The absolute falseness of it all sickened me. How could anyone believe this joker's lies and insincerity? Worse were the people I could see on camera buying his story without question.

"The hearts of every person at Helix Corporation—we are a

family—go out to the loved ones of those who were tragically taken from us in this terrible accident."

The anchor then moved on to another story.

"That's it?" I said aloud. "Unreal."

No mention of my dad. Nothing about anything being rescued or anything escaping.

Why were they lying? Was this a cover-up?

No. I wasn't going to let it all be swept under a rug. Whatever had *really* happened at Helix last night had somehow gotten my dad abducted.

My eyes fell on a badge half-buried under college textbooks. I moved the books to the side and picked up the small piece of plastic. My face stared back from the shiny surface, looking bored like most entry-level employees do when having their picture taken. It was my Helix Corporation ID. I didn't have access to much at the building, but I did have access to a huge selection of old files. It might be a Hail Mary, but maybe something in them would help me out.

CHAPTER 5

Jack

School. The bane of my existence. College sucked under the best of circumstances. Especially Mondays. When you add all the extra crappy conditions on top? Unbearable. I didn't want to be here. Maybe I couldn't do much to find my dad, but I was positive I wouldn't learn anything about what happened at the local junior college.

But I kept telling myself to stay busy. I knew myself well enough to know that staying home and wallowing in the frustration, anxiety, and fear wouldn't get me anywhere. So this morning I'd made the call. I made what my dad would call the "best bad decision." Would I regret going to classes? Probably. Would I regret staying home more? Maybe.

After graduating from Calm Waters High School, I'd been under the impression life would improve. Classes at Calm Waters Junior College—CWJC—would somehow be *better*.

More useful. My dad had laughed when I'd shared these hopes with him.

Instead, I now dealt with pretty much the same kids from high school. The same pointless busywork. Teachers trying to brainwash us with their propaganda. Even the links between the high school and CWJC basically made this "thirteenth grade." Plastered on every wall were gaudy posters advertising the Calm Waters Homecoming dance. I'd originally planned on giving in to the local tradition of going back to the high school dance, but with everything going on... well, even the thought of the event annoyed me.

Each class was more of a chore than usual. I found myself staring at the clock, watching the minute hand tick. Every minute here was a minute I wasn't trying to find my dad. And in between classes I walked through the school, from class to class, feeling like a bug under a microscope.

Other students literally stopped walking to stare at me. Conversations turned into hushed whispers. The layout of CWJC was made up of several uniform, multi-floor, red brick buildings set in a large circle. The area in the middle of the classroom buildings was a field of grass dotted by trees we called the quad. It wasn't uncommon to have to cross the quad between every class.

With everyone staring at me like a two-headed goat, those walks seemed even longer than normal.

My calculus teacher decided the weekend had been a fantastic opportunity to study, and gave us a pop quiz. I blankly stared at the sheet of paper in front of me. It all seemed like gibberish now. The thing was, I was actually pretty good at calculus. I should have been able to at least put down some good guesses, but this time I couldn't even lift a pencil to put my name on the paper.

The teacher walked by collecting our papers, and stopped when he saw my blank sheet. He shook his head and patted me on the shoulder. The girl to my right saw it all and burst into tears. You'd have thought my father had been murdered by a serial killer. Everyone around me seemed so fake. Later she would talk to her friends and they would all one-up each other over who felt worse about my situation.

The rest of the class passed in a blur as I zoned out. Suddenly people were sliding out of their seats and heading for the door. I waited until everyone had left, then got up. Only one class left. Music Appreciation. Then I could go about trying to find some real information on my dad's disappearance. All I had to do was keep my head down...

"Hey."

Crap. Not what I needed. Some girl actually wanted to talk to me and tell me how sorry she felt for me. I looked up to tell her where she could shove her false sympathy, and found myself face-to-face with Alex Courtney.

"Uh, hey." Not my smoothest response ever, but I was pretty sure this was only the second time she had spoken to me —the first being yesterday in the forest.

"Looks like you checked out okay after yesterday," she said.

"Yeah. The folks at the hospital said something about being dehydrated or something."

"I'm really surprised you're here."

I'd already worked up an excuse for this observation, and it wasn't too far from the truth. "Needed to keep busy," I replied. "Dwelling on what's going on just makes it worse."

Alex didn't look convinced.

We walked to the music building as slowly as possible. I realized I didn't want to sit through another class with people —the teacher included—giving me pitying looks.

"I'm sorry about your dad," Alex said.

"Thanks." I glanced at her from the corner of my eye. She seemed like she actually meant it. I stopped walking.

"What?"

"I think you're the first person to say that and actually mean it," I said. "Everyone else seems to be making it into a contest or something."

"Who can be the most devastated and weepy?"

I barked out a short laugh. The first one since this whole mess started. "Yeah."

Something about Alex made me want to talk to her. Maybe because I thought she was hot, or maybe because she was the only person around here who even seemed to care. I decided to take a bit of a risk.

"Did you see the news report last night?" I asked her. "The one with Mel Smart?"

It was hard to keep a smile down as she rolled her eyes. "I personally loved his whole 'We are all a family at Helix' garbage. It's a dysfunctional one at best."

"What was that nonsense about an explosion?" I watched carefully for any reaction from her. "We both know an explosion didn't cause my dad to drive out into the woods and then get taken by something."

Alex took a step closer and lowered her voice. "What did you want them to say? They can't say the truth of it right now.

At least not until it's all been managed internally. And maybe not even then. It's been complete chaos there."

"I heard..."

I trailed off. This was stupid. Why did I even trust her with this? Even as I doubted myself, I already knew the answer. I *needed* someone to trust, someone to talk to. My dad was usually that person, but he was missing.

"What?" She took another step forward. I could smell the herbal scent of her shampoo. We were almost the same height —I had her by an inch if I was being generous, and I was just over six feet tall—and I looked right into her eyes. She appeared legitimately concerned.

"I heard my dad on the phone the night he disappeared. And what he said wasn't even close to the stuff being put on the news."

"What did you hear?"

"He talked about something being set free. Mentioned a rescue mission. I don't know what any of it means, but I know he certainly didn't say anything about an explosion."

"Do you know who he was talking to?"

I shook my head. "Nah. He was spooked though."

"So what are you going to do?"

The bell rang for class. I glanced around at the emptying quad and shook my head. "I can't stay here right now. I just don't think I can deal with another class. I just want to go to work. Maybe look around while I'm there and... I don't know. I just need to do something, and going to classes isn't going to accomplish anything."

Alex nodded. "You work at Helix. In the archives, right? You think you can find something there?"

"I don't have any better ideas," I said. "I figure if Helix has some secret stuff going on, then it didn't just start recently. There might be some old documents that will get me going."

"How can I help?"

The question shocked me. I had hardly ever spoken with Alex before yesterday, and now suddenly she was offering her help? It seemed odd. A bit suspicious.

"Why are you offering to help?" I asked. "It's not that I don't appreciate the offer, but I don't get why you want to help me."

"I want to help you because you're right," she said quietly. "There is something going on at Helix—and not just at this location, but at *all* the locations. I've heard things. Things that might seem crazy to other people. To normal people."

She stuffed her hands into her pockets and looked embarrassed. Nervous. I got the feeling she was holding something back... but whatever. Alex had her reasons for wanting to help, and I'd be stupid to turn her down.

"Well," I said, "I'm not exactly normal anymore, am I?"

I tried to pass off my comment as a joke with a smile, but all Alex did was stare at me and reply, "No, I guess not."

We stood there for a few minutes looking at each other. It was finally quiet and calm. I took a deep breath and let it out slowly. The quiet was good. Refreshing. Soothing.

"I like the quiet too," she said, as if reading my mind. "Helps me think. You want to know what I'm thinking?"

"Sure."

"What I think," she said, walking past me, "is Music Appreciation is a stupid class anyway. We only take it for the easy 'A', right? Let's get out of here and see if we can't get some answers at the office."

She headed for the parking lot, and I had to jog a few steps to catch up. "What exactly do you do at Helix anyway?" I asked.

She gave me a sly smile, the kind that seemed almost flirtatious. My heart beat a little faster, and I knew I wasn't the type of guy that normally got to see it. I suddenly felt a little more hopeful.

"I do a bit of everything," she said.

We talked about our game plan on the way to Helix. We drove slowly and stopped for a late lunch. Talking with Alex and driving around with her was an odd experience. We instantly clicked, and our minds worked the same way. She knew right away the direction my mind was traveling, and she seemed to come to similar conclusions as if we were on the same wavelength.

She didn't dwell on my dad being missing, and didn't shower me with pity. Most importantly, Alex seemed genuinely certain my dad was alive. The glass-half-full attitude was just what I needed.

"Helix has been here since the Cold War," she said. "If there's anything weird going on, you might be able to find the beginnings of it in the papers you're making digital backups of. This company doesn't throw *anything* away."

"Well, we know what I'm doing. But what are you going to

do?" I asked. "You can't just walk around asking if there are any conspiracies going on that you should know about."

"Sure I can." She grinned, never taking her eyes off the road. "You just have to ask the right questions, and know how to listen the right way."

I shook my head. "You really aren't like all the other people around here, are you?"

Her face took on a serious expression. "No." She shook her head. "I'm really not. You see, Jack, I've learned that everyone is a liar. It makes a girl think about things a little differently." She pulled her silver Honda Civic into one of the staff parking spaces.

I tried to lighten the mood. Things were too depressing at the moment, and the last thing I wanted was for her to feel as crappy as I did. "Not everyone is a liar," I said. "I'm not."

"You're lying right now."

"Nope. Not possible. I'd know."

She did smile a little at that. Mission accomplished. Kinda.

"I can tell when a person lies," she said. "I swear people lie almost every time they open their mouths. Drives me crazy. I just want people to tell the truth."

My first impulse was to crack a joke, but I held back, not wanting to make the wrong one and risk the tentative ally I now seemed to have. My dad was missing, my life on the brink of disaster, I was a wreck, and here I was trying to make Alex feel better. She smiled at me, and it felt like a sincere gesture, and that was enough. Without any further exchange of words, she seemed more at ease, and I felt better too.

"Ever since I woke up in the hospital yesterday," I said, "it's been weird. I just want to find my dad and have things go back to normal. Maybe it's stupid, but I'd almost rather people tell me what they really think about the situation rather than the canned 'I'm *so* sorry.' So maybe I think I know how you feel." I looked at her and shrugged. "Am I telling the truth?"

Alex smiled back at me. "One hundred percent." She stuck out her hand. "All right. Let's do this. Good luck on digging up something useful."

I took her hand and was surprised at the strength of her grip.

"Right back at you."

CHAPTER 6

Jack

No matter how much momentum I had going into the search for a conspiracy at Helix, it was long gone after only a few hours.

My workspace at Helix consisted of little more than a small storage room with a computer and a scanner. Rows of identical metal shelves lined the walls, and on each of those shelves were stacked boxes of old documents. The left-hand wall held incoming boxes ready to be archived, and the right-hand wall was where I put the documents after I'd scanned them into the huge database of information Helix maintained. I'd worked in this room for two years now, and during that time I'd never seen the incoming boxes section empty.

Today, I examined every paper as I fed it into the scanner. The majority of them were old expense reports, old weather data, and other useless crap.

Why did they even keep all this stuff?

The task quickly became tedious, and I knew despite my good intentions, I was getting nowhere.

I pulled out my cell phone and checked the time. It was already 8:30 PM. I usually only worked a couple of hours on Monday nights, but I couldn't envision heading out now. Somewhere out there, my dad counted on me.

The next paper was a travel reimbursement for a trip to Los Angeles in 1976, same as the last five reports. I set it aside and pulled out the next hand full of papers. They all had the same date on them too.

I dropped them and rubbed my eyes. I saw double, and I hadn't found anything relevant. I needed a break, which meant it was time for a Dr. Pepper.

The door to the room locked behind me as I made my way to the main cafeteria. Helix boasted a full-service employee cafeteria on the ground floor. During the day a group of chefs worked constantly to provide the workers with breakfast, lunch, and sometimes dinner during the busy weeks. No one prepped food at night, but a refrigerator full of beverages remained available to those working long hours.

I grabbed a can, cracked it open, and the delicious carbonation burned going down my throat.

I knew I was stalling, but I now knew the answers to my questions wouldn't be found searching through some old papers. I'd assumed I'd start looking through them and answers would miraculously appear in one of those documents. My audacity would have been comical if it hadn't been so pathetic.

With those thoughts crashing down on me, the flavor of the

Dr. Pepper wasn't quite as good. I threw the can away without finishing it.

Alex said she would give me a ride home at nine, so I still had some time to kill.

I'd have liked to spend the time hunting for information with Alex rather than on my own, but she'd been clear about the necessity of keeping our distance while at Helix. *People are always watching here*, she had said. *If we are seen together too often, they might start thinking we are working together, which would make it harder for me to ask questions about your dad.*

Her logic still didn't make a ton of sense to me, but being cautious seemed like the way to go right now.

When I reached the door to the archiving room I noticed it stood open a crack.

Odd. I always closed the door behind me when I left. Always.

I pushed the door open carefully, willing it not to make any noise. My heart hammering in my chest, and all those scenes from crappy horror movies replayed themselves in my head.

The room was almost exactly the way I'd left it.

Almost.

A new box sat on the desk near the computer. Its size and coloring were different from the uniform boxes I'd gone through for two years. While the normal boxes lining the walls were all white and identical, this one was blue, and about half the size of the others.

I glanced quickly from side to side to see if anyone lurked about. The door clicked shut behind me, the sound unnaturally loud.

I crossed the room quickly and yanked the lid off the box.

The pessimist in me imagined it would be full of even more useless forms. But as I pulled out the first paper, I realized the pessimist had the wrong of it, and muttered, "What the heck?"

Bizarre symbols covered one side of the page, filling every inch of space. There weren't even margins. Some symbols looked like unfamiliar swirls, while others resembled the letters of the English alphabet stretched and skewed. The other side of the paper was blank.

After staring at them for a few moments my vision swam and my head started pounding. I put the first paper aside, face down on the computer desk, then pulled out another handful. Only a few more remained inside the box.

Every paper showed me more of the same. One side covered in gibberish symbols, the other side blank. The ink used to write or print the symbols—I couldn't tell which—was an odd shade of purple that seemed to change to black or silver depending on how I held it. *Weird.*

I wanted to toss the papers back in the box and get out of the office, and yet... something in the symbols called to me. They seemed familiar somehow.

Maybe if I had time, I could make sense of them.

The thought came from nowhere, and I immediately recognized how stupid it was.

Because you can just pick up a paper of odd symbols and decode them, I told myself. *Right. Last time I checked, you weren't some code-breaking genius.*

But the thought stayed and felt more right with every passing moment. There was something here. Something *important.* Whoever put this box in here—probably Alex— thought it would help me. It was too much of a coincidence the box appearing during the ten minutes I was out of the room.

There were maybe a couple hundred sheets of the symbol-filled paper. I grabbed them and stuffed them all in my backpack. I couldn't risk leaving them here.

"You ready to head out, Jack?"

I nearly jumped out of my skin and let out a strangled yelp. I turned to find Alex in the doorway struggling not to laugh. Her smile was contagious. *Beautiful.* Soon I was laughing along with her.

She shook her head and beckoned me to follow. As soon as we were outside I edged closer to her.

"Thanks for that box of papers," I said.

"Huh?"

I smiled at her. "You don't have to act all evasive. We aren't in the building anymore."

Right at that moment my phone rang. I let it buzz in my pocket. Probably Barry calling for the hundredth time. Sometimes people need to know when to back off.

Alex stopped abruptly, forcing me to leave her behind as I kept walking. "Jack, what are you talking about?"

"The box of papers? In the archiving room?" All the back-and-forth had given me a headache. A *bad* headache. "I went and got a soda, came back and found a new box in the room. I assumed you left it there."

"I didn't leave anything for you, Jack," she said, shaking her head. "I was busy doing my own stuff. The first time I came down was on the way out. What papers are you talking about?" She hurried over to me and lowered her voice. "Did you find something?"

I opened my mouth to reply, only to be interrupted again by my phone. "Seriously, Barry," I muttered, pulling it out of my pocket. "When are you gonna get that I need some spa—"

My words died as I looked at the caller ID. It wasn't Barry. It wasn't anyone. There wasn't even an "Unknown" on the display or anything. Just the phone ringing.

With a frown, I answered it. "Hello?"

"*Jack Bishop,*" a voice answered. "*Thank you for finally answering your phone. Would* texting *have attracted your attention sooner?*"

Alex caught my eye and mouthed, *Who is it?* I shrugged.

"Who is this?" I asked.

"*I am the generous man who just gave you a box full of answers forty-two minutes ago,*" he replied. "*The real question is, who are you?*"

What in the world? "You obviously already know who I am, so tell me who you are and why you are calling, or I hang up."

The voice *tsked* on the other side of the call. "*If you hang up, I won't help you find your father.*" He paused for a moment before continuing. "*Well. Since I didn't hear you hang up, I assume you are willing to listen for a moment, yes?*"

I nodded, unable to find my voice.

"*Jack,*" the voice said. "*I suggest you do more than nod when you are on the phone. I can't read minds.*"

He could see me. I spun in a slow circle scanning the parking lot for anything that would give the man away. A running car. The light from a cigarette. Anything. "I'm listening."

Alex appeared as confused as I felt.

"*Let's back up a few steps, shall we?*" His voice reminded me of a grandfather. Old, dry, and expecting to get his way. *"Yes, I know who you are, Jack. I know your father, Daniel. I personally knew your grandfather, Wyatt, and I know he died the day you were born. I know more about you than you do. I need you to understand yourself, to know who you actually are. Because you won't ever find your father until you do."*

"Where is my father?" I managed to say. "What have you done with him?"

"Me? Don't be absurd." The man laughed briefly. *"I'm not some idiot villain calling you to brag about my 'caper' and monologue at you. I'm the one trying to help you. Do I know where you father is at this very moment? No. But do I have a general idea who took him? Perhaps."*

"Then spit it out."

"Why should I? It seems unfair for me to be the one giving you all the answers when your little friend there knows most of them herself."

CHAPTER 7

Jack

The phone almost slipped from my hand. "What do you mean?"

"I mean, Alexandra Courtney is keeping information from you," he replied. *"She hasn't been completely honest with you as to her reasons for wanting to help you find your father. Ask yourself this; isn't it far too coincidental that she suddenly is around to talk to you and help you out?"*

I wanted to hang up right then and there, but I realized he was right.

A strange expression crossed Alex's face. As if she knew what the mysterious guy on the phone was saying. "Everybody holds back information." I said. "Why would she be any different?"

"Because people can't *hold information back from her."*

I laughed into the phone. This was just ridiculous. Whoever

was on the call was implying that Alex could *always* tell what people are thinking. As if she could read minds.

My laughter died when I saw Alex's expression morph into one of guilt. Like someone whose secret had been found out.

Holy crap. Impossible.

"I don't believe what you're telling me," I said. My voice lacked any shred of conviction. Things had been... weird lately. But still. There was weird, and then there was *mind reading*. No way it could be real.

"Of course you do," he laughed. *"Or at least, you should. Think hard on it. I'll call you back in a day or two. We can chat more about your progress then. Until then, take a good, hard look at those papers I gave you. They were made by your grandfather. They should... unlock a few things for you."*

"My progress?" He acted like he was a scientist and I was a research project. "What do you mean the papers were made by my grandfather? Why are you helping me?" I didn't actually believe anything this guy was saying about Alex, nor did I think he was really helping me, but that was certainly the implication of his call. Frustration burned in my gut. But this guy might have some real answers, and I wasn't going to let him distract me by putting the focus on Alex. "Hello?"

The line went dead.

He'd never even given me his name.

I glanced from the display on my phone to Alex. I didn't even know where to start. "Supposedly we have an ally."

"We?" she asked quietly. The tone of her voice spoke volumes, it was almost like she was particularly vulnerable, which didn't fit her personality. Or at least, not the one I was familiar with.

"...isn't it far too coincidental that she suddenly is around to talk to you and help you out."

The man's words repeated in my mind and forced me to focus on Alex. She and I had never really talked before our encounter in the woods yesterday. Having grown up in the same small town, you couldn't avoid constantly running into the kids your age, but every time I had seen her, Alex always seemed so self-assured and... in control.

That's not the behavior of a typical teen. Most of us are giant bags of insecurity, but for her it was like...

Well, it was like she always knew what people around her were thinking. Like she always knew what a person was going to do next.

"Yes, *we* have an ally," I said. "But I need you to be honest with me."

"Can you promise you'll never lie to me?" she shot back.

A loaded question, that one. Could I promise that? Unfortunately, no. "I can't promise I'll never lie to you, Alex," I said. "Though if what this guy on the phone said about you is true, it hardly matters, does it?"

"It matters to me."

"Fair enough." I paused for a long moment before speaking again. The temperature was dropping, and Alex hugged herself against the chill. I took a step, closing the distance between us until we weren't even a foot apart. When I spoke again my voice was quiet. Could anyone else be listening to us right now? "Is what the guy said true? Can you... read minds?"

She nodded.

Oh, man.

Did I believe it? I wanted to believe, but not blindly. There was only one way to find out.

"Okay... I'm not sure that I can believe in something like that with no proof. You have to see this from my perspective." I held up my hands to keep her from jumping all over me. "Look, I believe you. I just... I need proof of this one thing."

"I'm not a carnival act," she snapped.

"Never said you were," I replied before adding, "and I never *thought* it either, did I?"

She shook her head grudgingly.

"Come on. I gotta know."

She turned her back on me, leaving me staring at the back of her head. Finally she sighed and said, "Fine. Go for it. I'll keep my back to you so you don't think I'm cheating somehow. I can even wave my hands around like all the bad psychics in the movies if you want."

She loves her sarcasm, I thought.

"I wasn't being sarcastic."

Whoa.

Okay then.

I thought of one of my favorite desserts. A root beer float with cookies-and-cream ice cream instead of regular vanilla.

"Wow." She shook her head in disbelief. "Why would you ruin a classic like that?"

"Because it's delicious," I muttered, and paused as I realized what she'd just done. "No way!" Could that have been a lucky turn of phrase?

And then another thought ran through my head, and I smiled. I deliberately pictured Alex in a swimsuit. In my imagination she was stunning, of course.

Alex stiffened, spun around, and shoved me, an expression of shock on her face.

Any doubts I'd had were now gone.

I couldn't help but laugh at her outrage, and soon she laughed along with me. The laughter felt good. She seemed to need the release of tension as much as I did.

When our laughter died off after a minute, she said, "You aren't angry." It wasn't a question, though. She knew.

"Not really. Come on, how can I be mad about something like this? It's amazing! What am I supposed to do? Storm off? Scream and yell? And all because some mysterious voice on a phone tells me something super personal about you? Look, I'm just trying to wrap my head around the fact you can hear what everyone is thinking and see what's in their mind's eye."

"But how can you trust me? I know *I* wouldn't trust me. It's why I don't tell anyone. Ever."

"Who else *can* I trust?" I asked, my voice barely above a whisper. "The only family I have is an aunt that hardly strings two words together, and my friends won't understand what I'm dealing with right now. Heck, I don't understand it myself, and I'm *living* it." I ran a hand through my hair and sighed. "I need to trust you, Alex. But that means you've got to trust me too. We could work together with me constantly wondering if you are judging my thoughts, and you trying to catch me in a lie, but I'd rather we not have to resort to that. What do you say?"

Alex stared at me for a long moment. I wondered what she was thinking. Or if she was just reading my thoughts to see if they were sincere.

"All right," she agreed finally. "If you want to know the

truth—the *full* truth—we're going to need a place to sit down. You hungry?"

"Always."

"Good, because I'm starving," she said. "Let's get a bite while I explain. Plus I want to hear what the guy on the phone said."

"You didn't hear? I mean, you know, in my head?"

Alex shook her head. "Just bits and pieces. Mostly when you would repeat something. I can't hear thoughts through phone, or from a great distance."

"Unreal. I can't believe I'm having a serious discussion about this."

"I can't believe someone told you about my ability," she countered, real anger in her voice. "There aren't too many people who know. This is a serious breach of security."

I frowned. What an odd thing to say. "You say that like you're part of a security team or... something..."

She stared at me.

I realized I knew nothing.

"Let's go," she said. "I've got a lot to tell you."

CHAPTER 8

Alex

Alex kept her eyes on the road ahead as they drove. She had so much to explain to Jack, but they both needed a breather from the revelations they'd already discussed. Although the need for a break benefitted her own needs more than Jack's. He viewed the world in a completely different light now, and was dying to take it all in like a firehose to the face. Her, not so much.

For Alex, she didn't know the world in any different way. She had always lived in a world where she could hear what other people thought. Monster-like creatures were normal. Things like the Hounds which had set the Leech free, and taken Jack's father were just another part of it. Hardly anyone knew about what really went on at Helix, or in the world at large, but Alex had always been one of them. Special. Gifted.

And now, to have one of her secrets casually thrown out there for another to hear and judge...

She would have told Jack eventually, if the need arose. But to have the choice of that decision yanked from her hands infuriated her. *How had the guy on the phone known?* She already knew she couldn't trust him. She couldn't trust anyone. But still...

And who was the man on the phone? How could he know so much about me?

In the back of her mind Alex heard Jack's thoughts bouncing from topic to topic. In her experience, she'd found most people's thoughts had no real structure. Jack's were no different. Scrambled one moment, predictable the next. And with the phone call he'd received from their supposed "ally," coupled with the realization of her own ability... well, his brain seemed to be working overtime. She half-expected to see smoke pouring from his ears.

Jack had mentioned papers, and now she wondered what they were. His mind wasn't thinking on them at all. It was one of the frustrating aspects of being able to hear thoughts: not being able to direct them without asking leading questions.

Just after 10:00 PM she pulled her Civic into the parking lot of a local diner. It was one of the few places in town open twenty-four hours. Jack was thinking eating fast food this late was always a bad idea. The burgers would be cold, the fries rubbery. Alex agreed... or at least, she *thought* she did. Sometimes other people's thoughts rubbed off on her, making it hard to distinguish her own opinions from those of the person she listened to.

They went inside, ordered some food, and found a back corner where they could talk.

After a few silent moments, Alex went first. "There are a

few things you need to understand. I was going to tell you about... what I can do. Eventually. I just didn't want to freak you out."

"It's fine," Jack said. "Can we just start with the basics?" He panned his gaze across the restaurant and leaned forward. "This mind reading thing... it's got to drive you nuts hearing thoughts even when nobody is saying things."

"I've learned to tune out most of what people are thinking around me." Alex frowned. "You might think that mind-reading is a gift, but it's actually sort of... let's just say it has its ups and downs. You'd be surprised what's crawling around inside some people's heads, it's not pretty. Almost everyone is tainted with thoughts that they keep hidden away, ashamed of who and what they are, and it's sometimes the most angelic faces that veil the most hideous beliefs or perverted fantasies."

Jack sat back, his mind chewing on what she'd just said. "Well, since I can't read your mind, can you tell me the real reason why you offered to help me? Also, what do you know about my dad? Oh, and can other people do what you do?"

Alex nodded. "I'll start with the last bit since it all goes toward why I'm helping you. Can other people do what I do? Yeah. Last I heard, every Helix Corp location has a person who can read minds. And reading minds isn't the only crazy thing people can do. Some people have exceptional strength, others speed. A lot of times people don't even realize they have a special power. They just think they have natural talent in something—sports, for example."

"You're saying that people in the world are born with these... abilities? Can they do more than one thing?"

Alex shrugged. "Born with them? Sometimes. More often

these days, they are given to people in experiments. I've never heard of a person with more than one ability. There may be something about the brain not being able to handle any more. I don't really know. Not my area of specialty."

"Is that what Helix does?" Jack asked, leaning forward in his chair. "Are they experimenting on people?"

"It's *one* thing they do. Though as far as I know the experiments are all pretty tame. Mostly Helix hunts down creatures and experiments on *them*. Most of the human experimentation these days is done by Helix's main rival company, Whyte Genetics."

"Creatures?"

Alex rubbed her eyes. It was so easy to forget everything was strange and new to outsiders. "Creatures. All those TV shows and books that have weird paranormal monsters in them? All those myths about extreme mutations? There's almost always a large helping of truth behind them. Look, I know you have a ton of questions—your mind is absolutely saturated with them—but let me explain things my way. Please?"

Jack nodded.

Alex didn't start talking again right away as she was distracted by the thoughts of the server bringing their food over. The girl—Jessica Stewart—was their age, and the prom queen type. She was wondering if she might catch the two of them making out in the back corner. Alex laughed. Girls around here had one-track minds.

Once Jessica left, disappointed she hadn't caught the two doing anything, but already planning to start some rumors anyway, Alex started talking again.

"Like I mentioned before, Helix Corp started back during the Cold War. There was a huge amount of paranoia in the country, and there were quite a few groups in the US worried about spies running around giving away secrets to our enemies. Many of these same groups were aware of the 'monsters' running around the world, and they instituted a program to hunt down these various monsters and try to merge some of their traits and DNA with humans. That way we could supposedly protect ourselves better.

"It may sound a little thin," Alex went on, "but from what I understand, people were in constant fear during the Cold War. Apparently they thought the world was literally about to end.

"The founders of Helix formed the company using weather and geological surveying as a cover. In reality they were searching—and still search—for anything paranormal they can scientifically exploit, usually at the request of the government."

Even if she hadn't been able to read Jack's thoughts, she could tell by his expression that her words had a sobering effect on him. She was serious, and he believed her.

"How were people at Helix in the old days able to find these... creatures?" he asked. "Or the people with gifts?"

"I don't have anything concrete there. The way the story goes, they were approached by a man who claimed to be able to sense abilities in people. I've always wondered how this man— I've only heard him referred to as 'the Recruiter'—knew to go to Helix in the first place. All the hard details are above my paygrade. Anyway, shortly after he joined the company, the experiments began. To protect Helix and the secrets it possessed, they sought out people who could read minds to work as internal security."

"Security?" Jack asked. Alex heard the question a moment before he spoke it. "Hold on. Do you work for security at Helix? Did you work with my dad?"

"Jack... your dad is my boss."

Jack took a moment to absorb this. "Did he know about...?"

"He knew about my ability, yes," she answered. "He knew about almost everything going on at Helix, I imagine. That's why I'm helping you, Jack. I think one of the reasons your dad was taken was because of his position at Helix. He knows things that could put our company, and our *country*, in extreme danger if they got out."

"Taken?"

"Yes."

"So I was right. And not by animals. He didn't vanish. He was *abducted*. But what could he know? I'm sorry, I'm just having a hard time believing the stuff he knows could do as much harm as you say."

"Jack, there's stuff *I* know that could harm the country. *I* know about experimental viruses, genetic experiments, locations of federally protected supernatural creatures, and a fistful of other crap. Your dad knows way more than I do. I imagine—as do the head honchos at Helix from what I've been told—he was taken for something much more sensitive than even the stuff I just mentioned."

Jack paused. "How can you not know everything he knows? You can read his mind."

"I can hear his thoughts. It's not quite the same thing. If he knows something, but doesn't think about it in my presence, I can't just go in and dig it out."

"Oh."

"Listen," Alex said. "I don't want you to think that I'm only trying to find your dad because of impersonal reasons. I like your dad. He was—*is*—a better dad to me than my own. His training is partly why I'm good at what I do. You should know better than anyone how patient and calm he is."

Jack nodded, and Alex experienced a rush of thoughts about the dozens of times his dad had shown those traits. Jack had no idea how lucky he was to have a dad that cared so much.

"Okay," Jack said, "so what really happened the night my dad was taken?"

"Something broke into Helix and freed an experiment. An old experiment."

"Some*thing*?" Jack prompted.

"We call them Hounds," Alex said more quietly. "Courtesy of Whyte Genetics. Short version is they're genetically manipulated humans mixed with werewolf DNA."

"Werewolf?" Jack's jaw dropped. "They're real?"

She nodded.

"As in half-man half-wolf and super strong and violent?"

"You have no idea," Alex said, popping a fry into her mouth. She finished chewing then continued. "They're all boney spikes and teeth. Their humanity all but gone. Anyway, one of them got into Helix's secure area, freed the experiment, and killed a bunch of people in the process. I called your dad that night—"

"That was you on the phone?" he interrupted.

"Yeah. I was in charge that night." Alex gave Jack a moment to verbalize his thoughts, but he never did. He was torn between shock and anger, and then... then it was like it didn't matter to him. His mind seemed to click into place, and the inevitable question formed.

"So the next morning, when Deputy Path brought me to the scene, he spoke on the phone to the 'acting head of internal security.' Was he—?"

"Talking to me? Yes, he was."

"You're in charge of Helix security right now? Then... then why don't you just go in there and make people do what you want? Why don't you just get the info we need to find my dad? Why am I digging around in random archives?"

Alex held up a hand to silence the barrage of questions. "The title doesn't mean anything, Jack. I don't have a higher-level clearance than before. I don't have access to nearly any of the same stuff as your dad. Most importantly, the CEO of Helix doesn't trust me enough to handle all this stuff. I'm there to make sure people don't steal secrets, not investigate the ones already hidden inside."

"Okay," Jack said slowly. He rubbed his eyes, not quite able to get rid of the shell-shock Alex saw in them. "That's nuts though. Seems like the CEO—what's his name? Gaines?— seems like he should use his people a little better. You must know him pretty well if you work that high up in Helix. Sounds like a moron."

"You have no idea," Alex said. Jack's thoughts stayed calm. Too calm. "I expected you to be angrier."

Jack shook his head. "Me too. I feel like I *should* want to jump across the table and strangle you for lying to me. But I just can't. It isn't your fault. My dad wouldn't blame you, I don't think. So why should I? I don't know. Maybe I'm just too tired to be angry right now."

Not at all what I expected, Alex thought. She noticed they'd barely touched their food. "When things get crazy—which hasn't really happened much—the first person I call is your dad. I respect him more than I do anyone else. In truth, he's one of the very few people I trust in the whole world. That's why I want to find him almost as badly as you do."

"Fair enough," Jack said, and then shook his head. "I have so many questions..."

Alex tapped the side of her head, "Oh, trust me, I know. Ask away."

"Okay. Well... my dad always talked about how he got all his knowledge from his dad—my grandfather, Wyatt Bishop, who worked for Helix too. And the guy who called me in the parking lot said he knew him, too. Did Wyatt know about all this... stuff?"

"Your grandfather was before my time," she answered, "but he's a legend among the people who *really* know what's up. Which, by the way, is a small group. Of the thousands who work for Helix, and that's just here in Calm Waters, only a tiny fraction have any real idea what Helix is really all about. Anyway, rumor is your grandfather could track anything. He could always lead Helix straight to the creature they were hunting. Without fail. You asked earlier about being born with gifts? Supposedly his were all-natural."

Jack shook his head. "My own grandfather..." Then he fell silent, and Alex felt his thoughts go in a thousand different directions. He suddenly wasn't as calm as he appeared.

"You know what? Maybe that's enough for tonight," she said. She checked her watch and saw it was almost 10:30 PM. "I know you have more questions, and I promise I'll answer them all. How about you write them down as they cross your mind."

"Yeah. That's... that's a good idea."

They got up, and Alex left her mostly untouched food cooling in its own grease. Jack made for the door, then ran back to the table and put his burger in a small, brown, to-go bag and brought it outside with him. As they neared the car, Jack spoke.

"Alex?"

She turned around to face Jack, knowing exactly what he was going to say. One thing she had learned a long time ago was sometimes thoughts weren't enough. Sometimes people needed to say things out loud anyway. "What's up?"

"Thanks."

"No problem," she replied. "And look, I'm sorry about holding stuff back from you earlier. I really was eventually going to tell you. It still bothers me that he told you before I could. Speaking of which, we still need to talk about our supposed 'Insider' soon. We need to figure out what he's all about."

"It's okay. Really. When do you want to get together again?"

Tomorrow would have been ideal, but she still had two days of paperwork to get done in one day. "How about Wednesday afternoon? We'll skip class. I need tomorrow to relax."

Jack's eyebrows rose at her words. "I'm kinda scared to ask what a security specialist who can read minds does to 'relax.'"

"I go to Helix's underground shooting range," she said. "What else would I do?"

CHAPTER 9

Jack

I walked through my front door around 11:00 PM. Aunt Martha was sitting on the couch reading an old paperback novel. The novel had a shirtless man holding a half-dressed woman on the cover, and of course both the figures had long hair flowing in a breeze. I never would have figured my Aunt Martha as the romance novel type.

She didn't say anything as I walked in, and I didn't say anything to her. I walked upstairs and threw myself on the bed. I was exhausted, and my head had begun to ache again. I was pretty sure I had a bottle of Tylenol—the kind with caffeine baked into it—buried under the disaster of papers and text-books on my desk. But that would mean getting up, and I really didn't want to do that right now.

Instead I unzipped my backpack and pulled out the papers covered in the symbols. They still looked like gibberish. Were these actually supposed to be understood, or were they just doodles? It all boiled down to whether or not I thought this "Insider" who had given them to me legitimately wanted to help. And I couldn't know that for sure.

I flipped through page after page. They each were written in that same shimmering, purplish ink, and each was covered from edge to edge with the symbols, but only on the one side. None of the pages were identical, but studying them, I could pick out that certain symbols were repeated more often than others.

But what did that mean? I didn't even have the needed context to even start figuring out where to *begin* translating.

The man on the phone—in my head I was coming to think of him as *the Insider*—said my grandfather made these pages. And after what Alex had told me, I believed it. But that meant these papers were even older than I was. Fingering the edges of the paper, I saw a little wear, but nothing like the yellowing and faded documents I scanned every day at Helix.

The symbols again swan in my vision, and I put the papers down to rub my eyes. Even with my eyes closed, the afterimage seemed burned on my eyelids. My headache moved from a dull ache to a throbbing pain. I sat up and pulled open the greasy bag of food from the diner. Maybe all I needed was a little protein. The smell of cold burgers assaulted my nose, and I closed the bag again. Maybe food wasn't such a good idea after all.

I finally broke down and rummaged through the mess on my desk to find that Tylenol. I wasn't going to last much longer without something to take the edge off the pain. The pills went down with the last bit of liquid from a mostly-empty water bottle.

Lying on my bed once more, I turned my thoughts back to my chat with Alex at the diner. I knew most people would have a healthy degree of mistrust for her, but I couldn't help but forgive any errors on her part. She wanted to find my dad, and for me that was good enough. Plus I had literally no one else to help me.

I had a hard time believing my dad knew about this crazy supernatural world hiding in plain sight underneath every-one's noses. And not just my dad, but my grandfather too. My dad had promised to explain something to me when he got back from investigating the "incident" at Helix, and now I wondered if he meant to talk to me about all this.

My grandfather worked for Helix, and then my dad. Both of them in security. Had I been expected to follow in their footsteps?

I hoped not. That world didn't feel like a good fit for me.

Through my open doorway I saw the closed door leading into my dad's room. I hadn't dared go in there since returning from the hospital. I rose, walked quickly to his door, and grasped the doorknob. Before I could change my mind, I turned the knob and slipped in.

It was exactly how Dad had left it.

My eyes were drawn to the small bookcase by the window. Most of the books had to do with the occult and paranormal. Strange how that collection had a completely different meaning to me now. I used to think that stuff was just a weird hobby for Dad, but now...

"Can you imagine if this stuff were real, Dad?" I had once

asked him. *"It would be insane. The world would go freaking crazy. Good thing it's all Hollywood crap, right?"*

"Yeah," he had said with a half-smile. *"Good thing."*

On the bottom shelf a group of binders caught my eye. Photo albums. I reached for the one the far right—the one I assumed would be the newest—then thought better of it and moved towards the opposite end of the row. Talking with Alex about my dad and grandfather today had me wondering about the old days, I guess.

I'd only flipped a few pages before finding pictures of my grandfather, Wyatt. He resembled an Old West cowboy, which was no surprise since his father had apparently named him after Wyatt Earp. Long mustaches framed a thin mouth. His eyes were clear and light in the black and white photo, so I assumed they were blue or green. There was a marked intensity in them, like he was staring straight at me from the picture.

In one picture he wore a holstered gun at his side, but I couldn't tell what kind. Not that I would have known the exact make and model had it been sitting in front of me. What little I knew of guns came from movies, but it looked like a revolver of some sort. It looked like it *belonged* there on his hip, a perfect extension of himself.

I wished I'd had the chance to know him. To talk to him.

My dad talked about him when asked, but he never brought up Wyatt on his own. But in one of life's crazy coincidences, while I was being born, my grandfather had been in an accident. Apparently he'd died just minutes before I made my grand entrance into the world.

Dad never really told me the details, just that it was some kind of accident at work.

At Helix.

No...

Was I becoming paranoid? What was the saying? *It isn't paranoia if it's true.* Something like that. Given everything I'd learned today, and given the culture of lies and cover-ups Helix Corporation seemed to be giving a big thumbs-up to, I had a hard time *not* believing his death had been more than a simple accident.

It seemed every time I turned around, my grasp on what I *thought* I knew got weaker and weaker, and I couldn't do anything about it right at this moment. I could sit here and stare at old family photos, but what good would they do me? I doubted any answers could be found here. Yet at the same time I knew my brain would be spinning like a hamster wheel all night.

And this brutal headache just wouldn't fade.

I closed the photo album carefully—reverently, even—and slid it back into its spot, then walked out, closing the door behind me and leaving the room the way it had been before I entered. Changing anything about Dad's room seemed... wrong.

I paused in the hallway and rubbed my hands over my face. I don't think I'd ever truly known exhaustion before that moment. The tiredness I experienced wasn't just physical—though I'll admit my body wasn't exactly doing great—but emotional and mental too. I knew I needed rest, but I also knew I'd wake up tomorrow and have all the same problems. All the same stresses. My dad would still be gone. It was overwhelming, and I spent every shred of willpower not sinking to the ground and crying my eyes out on my home's hardwood floors.

But I didn't have time to sit around trying to get over all of it. That, of course, assumed I actually *could* get over this feeling of helplessness. A depressing thought.

I hit the light as I shambled back into my room, then collapsed on my bed again and let my eyes close.

I was asleep instantly.

CHAPTER 10

Jack

Sleep didn't stick with me. I woke up every half hour with new questions. Between thinking of all of the amazing uses of mindreading, I had fantasies of my dad walking through the front door. Then the fantasies dissolved into nightmares about a cop showing up at the door again, this time telling me they'd found my dad's body.

Soon the clock read 7:00 AM, and I realized I had no chance of getting any more rest.

I took a long, hot shower and willed the water to ease some of the ache in my muscles. It seemed to do the trick, and even my head felt a little better. I decided to skip my classes again. I just didn't feel like dealing with it today. I had bigger things to focus on.

I walked quietly down the stairs, not wanting to wake my aunt. A pointless endeavor since she was already up, fully dressed, and reading the morning newspaper. I didn't even know we got an actual, physical newspaper. A bowl, spoon, and box of cereal awaited me on the counter. Did she ever sleep?

"Morning," I said.

She gave me a raised eyebrow in response.

I ate my cereal, then went back upstairs and closed my bedroom door. It was time for some research, but I didn't want my Aunt Martha walking in behind me wondering what I was doing with these borrowed—I *did* plan on returning them eventually—papers full of strange symbols.

A quick glance at my phone showed twenty texts. Geez. I checked for any from Alex, but every single one was from Barry.

DUDE! WHERE R U?

WE NEED 2 TALK ...

R U A IDIOT? CALL ME!

CALL ME!

The texts got worse and worse. Apart from being one of those guys who always texted in all caps, Barry was also one of those friends who could either be really great, or a complete idiot, which was why I'd stopped hanging out with him several times over the past few years. He'd say something dumb, and we'd shove each other until one of us would throw our hands up and walk away. We'd always brush it off later. But these texts pretty much made me want to punch him in the face.

I knew I needed to give him a call back, but I didn't want to get into it with him right now. Still, I didn't want to be a complete dirtbag, so I shot him a quick text without reading through the rest of his messages.

Things are a little crazy. I'll talk to you later.

I wasn't the type to abbreviate words in my texts. My brain just couldn't shorten the words like everyone else did. I tried, but I ended up spending more time trying to figure out the best way to shorten the word than I would have if I had just spelled it all out in the first place.

After tossing the phone aside I dropped into the chair in front of my desk and turned on my computer. I pulled up Google and started running general queries on symbology and codes. It proved to be the wrong thing to do as I quickly became overwhelmed and frustrated by the millions of entries popping up, half of which were porn. It made me want to quit for the day even though I'd just started.

Instead, I pulled out the sheets of symbol-covered papers again. No matter what I did or thought about, I always seemed to return to those papers. The answers were there, I just had to figure out the best way to approach them.

Rather than flipping quickly through the pages, I picked up the top page and set to studying it, taking my time. Like always, the symbols made my head pound, but instead of putting the paper down, I continued to stare. The symbols spun and pulsed before my eyes even more than normal, but I forced my focus to remain on them. I tried to see past them, pretending it was all an optical illusion.

And suddenly, I saw something.

A face.

I was so shocked that I blinked and lost all my focus. Shaking my head to clear it, I set the paper aside. I knew I wasn't imagining what I'd seen. And the face, though unclear, seemed familiar. Maybe that was the key to all of this? Instead of wondering what the symbols meant and how to read them, maybe I should be focusing on something hidden... *behind* them.

My head was absolutely murdering me now, and my stomach rolled with nausea, making me wish I hadn't eaten anything. I grabbed my phone again to check the time.

Noon.

Already?

My phone must be wrong. I moved the mouse around on my desk to get the screen saver off my computer screen, then checked the time in the corner.

Noon.

Holy crap. I'd been staring at that paper for *hours*.

I stood up to walk downstairs, and the next thing I knew I was lying on my bed staring at my doorway sideways.

What was going on with me?

I tried to push myself up, and a massive spike of pain shot

through my head. Again. This was getting old. I squeezed my eyes shut and reached blindly for my pillow. My hand closed on it, and I pulled it over my head.

Maybe all I needed was a little more rest. I lay there for an eternity before I drifted to sleep.

I stood in a clearing, redwoods surrounding me. It was nighttime, and through the branches of the trees I could see the crescent of the moon. I remembered the pain in my head and falling onto my bed, so this had to mean I was dreaming. But this dream already seemed more vivid than any other dream I'd ever had.

The air was cold, and goose bumps popped up on my arms. I tried rubbing my arms to restore a little warmth, but my body was unresponsive. I couldn't do anything other than look ahead into the woods.

I felt like I was waiting for something. Watching for something. It was an odd sensation, and one that didn't feel like it actually belonged to me. But if not to me, then to whom?

The colors of the forest were vibrant even though it was dark. In fact, the colors seemed a little *too* vibrant. I shouldn't have been able to see anything this clearly. Everything had a slight purple tint, the same shade as the ink on the papers the Insider had given me.

In the distance, something moved.

The form moved quickly and purposefully between the trees, seeming unaware of my presence. It stood out as a bright purple blob in the darkness, reminding me of the way people and animals showed up on the infrared goggles the military types wore in movies. Only I wasn't wearing any goggles.

My hands moved without my consent, and I found myself looking down at a revolver. The hands weren't mine. They were older and rougher, and they handled the pistol with ease and familiarity. They opened the cylinder and ran a thumb over the rounds chambered inside before professionally snapping it back into place.

What the heck was I doing with a gun? I'd never even held a gun, despite my dad's many offers to take me shooting.

I had a bad feeling about where this was all going.

With cautious steps, I followed the figure through the woods. It was a simple process, because not only could I almost always see the figure in the distance, but when I did lose sight for a brief moment I could still see its tracks.

They looked just like my dad's tracks had back in that clearing when all this crazy stuff first started. The tracks shimmered slightly on the ground, but this time I knew it wasn't because of the light, nor had my dad's tracks been tricks of the light. I wasn't just seeing the *tracks*, I was seeing a residue left by the figure I was following. The weirdest thing about all of this was that the bits of knowledge and clarity filtering into my mind didn't seem to belong to me. The understanding dripped into my consciousness from some other source. All the new information made sense to a certain degree... yet it *shouldn't* have made sense.

What the heck was going on?

My body—though I was pretty sure now I wasn't in *my* body—continued forward, trailing the figure ahead. My steps were cautious, as I didn't want the creature to notice me. Soon my steps took me parallel to a road. An old car sped past, its headlights briefly illuminating the forest ahead, as well as a sign that said "Welcome to Calm Waters!"

The sign looked different from the one I knew. I couldn't put my finger on it, but I knew there was something odd about it.

Ahead, the figure paused. It straightened, reminding me of an animal testing the scents in the air. Then it spun around and stared straight at me before sprinting in the opposite direction.

My hands lifted the revolver, and without hesitation I pulled the trigger.

My eyes snapped open. Sunlight flooded the room. I rubbed the sleep from my eyes and rolled out of bed. My head still ached dully, but it was a huge improvement over the pain I'd felt earlier.

I walked over to my desk and turned on my computer. The date in the bottom corner of the screen said it was Wednesday morning, 8:00 AM.

I'd been out for nearly a full day.

What was going on with me?

The smell of bacon reached my nose, making my stomach growl. I was starving. I walked down the stairs into the kitchen where my Aunt Martha was cooking up breakfast.

"Is it really Wednesday?" I asked.

"Yep."

"I've been asleep for a day?" I rubbed my temples. "Weren't you worried or something? Geez, I was in a freaking coma or something."

"Please," she said with a half laugh. "If there'd been anything to actually worry about, I'd have called a doctor. Eat your food."

Guess there wasn't much left I could ask. It was a bit weird, but then again, Martha had always been a little weird herself.

She handed me a plate heaped with bacon, eggs, and toast. It looked like enough to feed an entire family. Twice.

"This is a lot of food," I said.

"And?"

Good grief. "Uh, and it looks good."

I sat down and began shoveling food into my mouth. I was soon out of bacon, and another small plate appeared at my elbow with another half dozen pieces piled on it. It wasn't until I was staring at an empty plate that I realized I'd eaten every scrap of food my aunt had cooked for me.

I took my time getting ready for school. Staying home was likely the safe option, but I needed to talk to someone about the face I'd seen behind the symbols in the paper. I needed to talk to someone about the dream I'd just had, and the fact I'd been out for the count for a day.

I needed to meet up with Alex.

CHAPTER 11

Jack

The closer I got to CWJC, the less I actually wanted to arrive at my destination.

This is a terrible idea.

My head felt clouded and achy, and the thought of having to endure the stares of the teachers and other students again almost made me turn around and go back home. But I sucked it up. Sitting in my room wouldn't magically make everything better. Plus my dad always said he had new ideas and break-throughs when he changed his scenery. Time to test that theory. I willed myself to stand a little straighter and kept on walking.

The sky was clear, and the air outside was crisp enough to need a light jacket. I could barely see my breath as I exhaled. I didn't live very far from the junior college, so I walked on days when the weather permitted. I noticed an unnatural silence as I passed through the various residential areas leading to the school. No one walked their dog, and even the birds and other animals were quiet. In fact, the only movement was the stirring of the trees and the random bits of trash tumbling down the street carried by the wind. I imagined the apocalypse would be a lot like this.

The whole scene creeped me out.

I put my head down and picked up the pace.

Without warning, the hairs on the back of my neck stood on end, followed by the sensation of something watching me. It wasn't like when someone stared at me during class, or a stranger in the supermarket. This had an intense feeling behind it. Like hunger.

Or hate.

I've heard of people who have acute fears of heights or water or whatever. That level of fear never really made sense to me before. Now it did.

I came to a complete stop, and without wanting to, I had my arms wrapped around me as if I were freezing in the middle of a snowstorm.

I glanced to the right and didn't see anything. Same to the left. Ahead, nothing seemed out of the ordinary.

That only left behind.

The urge to spin around as quickly as possible overwhelmed me, but I couldn't do it. My body wouldn't respond like I wanted it to. *Needed* it to. Instead, I made a slow turn.

I saw nothing.

Letting out a slow breath, I laughed. A nervous laugh, mixed with relief and fear.

Back in high school, I used to hang out with a kid named Steve, and once he showed me a video he had taken while on vacation in Hawaii. He went on one of those shark encounter trips where they toss a cage out into the water and the sharks circle all the divers inside. Steve talked about how awesome the trip had been, and he showed us a video of him on the boat waiting his turn to get in the water. One of the crewmembers pulled out a long strip of dead fish and began slapping the water with it. Next thing you know, a shark has its ugly head all the way out of the water chomping on this piece of chum. The crewmember starts playing tug-of-war with the shark, and the predator has part of itself up on the back of the boat trying to get all of the food.

What I remember most was Steve's laughing. Nervous. A touch maniacal. It was the laughter of someone facing something truly terrifying. Of someone realizing he's about to step into a cage surrounded by dozens of monsters.

Laugh or go crazy, pissing yourself.

We all gave him a hard time about the laughter, but right then on the street I understood the emotion.

I turned back around, toward school, and only just managed to choke off the scream that tried to escape my throat.

Three houses up the road, the word "HELP" was scrawled across the garage door.

My right hand came up to cover my mouth to keep my terror inside. I looked frantically from side to side, then spun around in a quick circle. Was this some kind of sick joke? The letters on the garage door, shaky and uneven, felt as if they were calling specifically to me. I couldn't just *see* the letters, I could also *feel* them. Like someone had let out their most frightened, terrified scream, but did so in writing.

And then I realized the letters were the same purplish color as the tracks and the figure from my dream. The same color as my dad's tracks from the woods and the strange symbols from the papers I carried in my backpack.

The residue.

A residue from *what* I didn't know, but it was the only description that made sense to me.

And... I *knew* that house. A girl from school lived there. What was her name? Erin? Annie? No. Abby. That was it. Abby. Her last name was something generic. Smith or something.

I dug into my pocket and yanked out my phone. My shaking fingers began dialing, and I looked down to make sure I had hit the right buttons. Crap. 811. I deleted the numbers and punched them in again. But my thumb hovered over the "CALL" button. How was I going to explain this to the police? Would I say I saw something suspicious? Someone spooky sneaking around the house?

Spooky? Who even used that word anymore?

I shook my head and looked up to see if anything would give me an idea.

The word was gone.

"You have got to be kidding me." I wanted to hurl my phone at the garage door.

"Son? You all right?"

A scream got free that time as I spun to my left. An old guy in a robe stood on his porch holding his morning newspaper.

"Didn't mean to spook you," he said with a chuckle.

I guess some people did still use the word, or at least a variation of it.

"You look a little pale," he said. "You okay?"

"Great," I forced out. I peeked back at the house a few yards up the road. The word was still gone, like it had never been there at all. "Just headed to the college."

"Okay," he said with a smile. I didn't need Alex's mind-reading ability to tell the guy probably thought I was strung out on something. "Better get going then."

I pointed to the house. "That's the Smith place, right?"

"Yeah. What of it, son?"

"Nothing," I said as casually as possible. It sounded fake, even to my own ears. "Was just thinking of, uh, asking Abby out... or something. Wanted to... you know..."

Lying wasn't a skill I'd perfected.

"Ah." The old man smiled again, this time genuinely. He motioned me closer, and I reluctantly obeyed. An older dude in a bathrobe had "sicko" written all over him. "I see what's going on here. She does indeed live there. I keep an eye on my neighbors, you see. Purely for safety reasons," he added quickly before continuing. "Anyway, the girl gets home from school early. Her dad picks her up since she seems to not have a sixth period at the high school. At least that's what I think seems to be going on. She's a senior this year, but you're walking toward the JC. Ah, so you're gonna ask her to the Homecoming thing at the high school. Very nice. I can respect a man who follows tradition."

What. The. Heck.

I'd probably uncovered a stalker of some kind. Geez. Could this day get any more insane?

"Uh, thanks," I said, backing away. I felt a little gross being close to him. His dirty, loose bathrobe made me feel ill for some reason. "Thanks for your, uh, help. See you around."

I didn't quite run, but I probably set a new record for speed-walking.

As I passed Abby's house on the left, I glanced at it again. The words were nowhere to be seen.

For some reason that made me feel even worse.

English 101 was already half over when I walked in, and there was no real easy way to make it to my desk on the opposite side of the room from the door. Apparently they were taking a pop quiz, but every head swiveled to stare at me as I walked in. That included Alex's. Her eyes narrowed, and she shook her head slightly.

What was that about?

"Mr. Bishop, please come here," Mrs. Terrier said.

I normally enjoyed English, but I couldn't stand Mrs. Terrier. Her entire purpose as a teacher was not to make her students better. Instead she always spent the first half of class berating us for how poor our work was, following up in the second half of the class telling us how little she looked forward to grading our next assignments.

And she wondered why she was the lowest-rated teacher at the JC.

I approached her desk and said in a low voice, "Yes, Mrs. Terrier?"

"What time does my class start?"

"Eight a.m."

"What time is it now?"

I looked at the clock before answering. "Eight thirty-six a.m."

"So what you are saying is, you're late?"

"Yes, ma'am," I answered. Geez. What was her deal? "I had a migraine all night—"

"You act as if I care about your excuses, Mr. Bishop," she interrupted. "Let me clarify for you. I don't care. What I do care about is that you have interrupted class in the middle of a pop quiz."

"I'm sorry," I said hesitantly. "Things have been a little rough since my dad—"

"Ah, yes," she interrupted again. "Your father. He seems to have caused quite a few problems for a lot of people recently."

What was that supposed to mean? Her tone pissed me off. It was one thing to be upset about a student, but this was downright hostile.

"Look," I said as calmly as possible. "I've already apologized. I'd like to sit down now and take the quiz if that's all right. I can probably get through a good bit of it and get at least partial credit."

"No," she said, shaking her head. "I don't think so. You can sit down and quietly wait for class to end. I'm giving you zero credit on the quiz for being late. No make-ups."

"But—"

"I'm sorry, but did I not make myself clear?"

Unbelievable. I shook my head and walked to an open chair. Some kids were giving me glares as if I had personally ruined their day just by walking in. Alex caught my eye and gave me a look that said, *Leave it be.*

Whatever.

The last twenty minutes of class passed in agonizing slowness. The whole situation pissed me off. I didn't even need or want to be here today. I could have taken a few extra days off from school to deal with everything. But no, I was here, trying to be a decent college student, dealing with Mrs. Terrier's unexplained personal vendetta against me. Whatever. I just had to sit around for a few more minutes, then I could grab Alex and get out of here. So much for my dad's theory.

A buzz rang over the school's PA system, announcing the end of class. I was out the door before anyone else had even gotten out of their chair.

Alex was only a few steps behind me. "Jack, we need to talk."

"Can you believe her?" I pointing at the classroom. "Where does she get off treating me like that?"

"Jack, shut up and walk with me." The sharp edge in her voice killed the angry words in my throat.

We walked around behind the classrooms where the other kids typically went to get high between classes. I could smell the weed lingering in the air. Alex pulled out her phone and tapped the screen a few times before handing it to me.

"What's this?" I asked.

"This is what you missed while you were unconscious for the past day."

"Wait a minute, how did you—"

"Your Aunt Martha," she said before I could finish. "I called when you weren't answering my texts or calls."

"So you actually talked—"

"Yeah," she said before I could finish. This mindreading thing was getting on my nerves right now. "We had a nice long conversation about you. Now shut up and look at my phone."

The local news played on the tiny screen. I recognized the news anchor from the report the other night about the "disaster" at Helix.

"Alisha Morena here with breaking news," she said. *"Late Saturday evening, the Calm Waters, California location of Helix Corporation was struck by a tragic equipment malfunction that cost several employees their lives.*

"It has come to our attention, through a credible source within Helix, that the company has begun serious talks of shutting down their Calm Waters location, beginning with layoffs. An estimated twenty percent of their entire staff at this location lost their jobs just yesterday afternoon, and more layoffs are rumored to be coming as the company liquidates all its assets in Calm Waters.

"Rumors and speculation are running rampant through the community, and one can't help but wonder how the town of Calm Waters will even be able to exist without Helix.

"Additionally, further information has come to light about the tragic accident that occurred at Helix. An official report from Helix Corporation states the malfunction was a result of sabotage. It is being reported that the head of security for Helix Corporation's Calm Waters location, Daniel Bishop, left the building and equipment unsupervised the night of the accident, which allowed someone— who yet remains unidentified—to gain access to the equipment and cause the malfunction.

"It is not yet known if this accident is the root cause for the drastic reshuffling of Helix Corporation assets, but given that Daniel

Bishop went missing immediately after the accident occurred, it is hard not to connect the two together. We now go live to Washington, DC, where an official Helix representative is answering questions regarding this news."

The image cut to Mel Smart, in front of Helix's main building in Washington, DC.

"I'm afraid I cannot comment on the rumors surrounding Mr. Bishop's involvement in the tragedy at our Calm Waters branch. We can only hope he resurfaces at some point to clarify what has happened. Until then, his absence raises all sorts of undesirable questions."

"Are the layoffs a result of the accident?" someone asked, overriding all the other questions dozens of reporters were trying to get answers for. *"Is it Daniel Bishop's fault the company is shutting down that location?"*

Mel Smart raised his hands and made a placating gesture to the masses around him. There was a gleam in his eye, one that said he was relishing all of this attention.

"Please, please. It doesn't do anyone any good to speculate on these events, so I've been authorized to clarify the situation. Helix is shutting down its Calm Waters Branch. Not all at once, but slowly over the next year. It was determined after this breach of security— among other internal issues—that this branch was hurting the community rather than helping."

I shut off the phone and shoved it back into Alex's hands. "I don't believe this. They're pinning *everything* on my dad. No wonder everyone looks like they want to kill me right now. The way Helix and the news are spinning this, my dad is the cause of the layoffs for our whole town." My mind made the next horrifying jump in logic. "Alex," I said, "please tell me Mrs. Terrier's husband wasn't working that night."

"He was one of the casualties."

"Why is she even *here*?"

"The same reason *you* are." She took a step closer and lowered her voice. "Everyone deals in different ways."

"I've got to get over to Helix and have them fix this," I said, panicked. But Alex was already shaking her head. "What?"

"I called yesterday to tell you. Helix has revoked all your rights to work there. In fact, there's a standing order to remove you—by force if needed—from the property should you even set foot inside the building."

Without a word I turned away from Alex and began walking. To where, I didn't really know. Anywhere but on campus. My dad taught me that blowing up in anger rarely solved anything, and while I was pretty sure turning and walking away wasn't a whole lot better, I needed to walk away before I said something I'd later regret.

I could feel Alex walking close behind me. After a few more steps, she put a hand on my arm, and with a sigh I stopped.

"Look," I said, without turning. "I'm sorry. This is all just a little too much to take in. I feel like—"

"You're not going crazy, Jack," she said. "But maybe they *are* all out to get you. This feels... off. Oddly personal."

I stretched my neck from side to side and felt it pop. Nervous habit. "Do me a favor and stop interrupting me and finishing my thoughts." I turned around and recognized genuine concern in her eyes. Everything was so serious. So bleak. I forced a smile. "Guys like me like to hear themselves talk."

Alex shook her head and sighed before forcing her own smile. "I know what you're trying to do here." She tapped the side of her head. "I know what's going on up there." Her eyes suddenly narrowed. "Son of a—"

"Hey Jack, is this the reason you've been too busy to give me a freaking call?"

Barry Peters, along with a few other guys I recognized, walked up from our right. He'd probably been looking for me.

"Hey, Barry," I said with a nod of my head. "Sorry I didn't call. Things have been a tad stressful for me the last several days."

He nodded his head in an exaggerated fashion. What was going on here?

"Oh, I know. I watch the news. My mom came home from Helix yesterday without a job. Things have been a 'tad stressful' for me too. For everyone. Doesn't mean you don't call your friend. I've texted you a few dozen times, man. Friends call each other back."

The other guys behind him were nodding too.

This just kept getting worse. This was some high-school level idiocy on his part. I should have felt bad for Barry, but instead I was angry. This was typical Barry. We'd fought over less. Who needs enemies when I've got a friend like this?

"I'm sorry about your mom, Barry. I really am. But at least your parents aren't missing. So cut me a little slack for not calling you up to gossip like a twelve-year-old girl. I had more important things on my mind."

"More important..." he trailed off, then nodded his head again. He took a few steps closer until he was right in my face, looking up at me. "I see how it is. You had more important things to do... like your new girlfriend over there. Was she good? I thought you had a thing for redheads, but I guess everything is the same in the dark, right?"

The guys behind him were smiling cruelly now. The same guys he always went back to when he and I were pissed at each other. While some people tried to move on from high school, Barry wished he was still back there, living it up.

Alex edged closer. *Stay back*, I thought.

Barry planted his palms against my chest and pushed me a step backward. "You know, you're right," he continued. "I guess I *am* lucky my parents are both around. I'd hate to be in your spot, crying when we were kids about your mom taking off. Your dad gets a bunch of people killed, the rest of the town fired, and then he takes off too. You're right. I'm lucky my parents stick around. But who could blame yours for taking off?"

He shoved me again, and I lost my balance and fell flat on my back.

I was angry. More angry than I could recall ever being. I knew I'd treated Barry like crap these last couple of days, but that was no reason for getting this upset. Was he jealous I was spending time with Alex? That seemed a stretch. It all had to do with the news. With the story that everything in Calm Waters was my dad's fault. Helix had made me and my dad the target of everyone's anger to keep it away from *them*.

But I knew none of it was my dad's fault, and I was *sick* of people thinking otherwise.

Barry was shaking his head in disgust. His new friends were laughing. Alex looked like she might literally kill each and every one of them.

My head began pounding. Their laughter only made it hurt worse. I stood up and put a hand to my head.

"Aww," Barry said, closing the distance between us. "Did I *hurt* you?" He made to shove me again.

And then... something... happened.

Time slowed to a crawl. I could see a purple glow around him and around everyone else—an aura that pulsed and writhed. Something about the glow called to me. My blood boiled and my head throbbed. I glanced down at my hands like I had in my dream, only now lines of purple writhed around my fists. Lines of power.

Power begging to be let loose.

I stepped forward, put my hand against Barry's chest... and pushed.

The lines of power from my hands leapt out and slammed against Barry's purple aura. Like he'd been hit with a cattle prod, he flew backward into the group of his friends, the power cascading into them like arcing electricity, and they all collapsed in a heap.

And something else happened too. The moment our auras met, I understood every reason behind every emotion Barry had felt. I witnessed the moment when Barry's mom walked in the door tearfully holding her termination papers from Helix. I saw Barry staring at his phone, wondering why I wasn't calling. He actually *was* jealous at seeing me with Alex, and his emotions were starting to make him believe the news reports about my dad.

And now Barry's and his friends' auras called to me, begging to be *taken...*

A pulse of pain in my head made me squeeze my eyes shut,

and when I opened them everything was back to normal. Well, as normal as it could be with Barry and his three friends on the ground groaning in pain. Random students stood gaping at what had just happened.

I wasn't completely sure *what* had just gone down, but I felt completely drained. Whatever I had done, it had sapped nearly every bit of energy from me.

Alex grabbed my arm and leaned in to whisper in my ear. "We need to get out of here."

I let her pull me along toward the campus parking lot.

What the heck had just happened?

CHAPTER 12

Alex

Jack stared out the passenger-side window. He looked a little gray as he shielded his eyes against the glare of the late-morning sun. Alex pushed the button on her door controls to crack his window.

He took a deep shuddering breath of the cool air, and his skin seemed to regain a little of its color. He hadn't said a word since the incident with Barry and his group of idiots—not that he needed to say anything out loud.

The few students who had witnessed the "fight" were likely already spreading rumors of what they thought they saw. Barry and his goons would be lucky if they remembered a minute of it, and if they did, they would be embarrassed to admit how Jack had handled all of them with no visible effort. The truth was that no one present had any clue what had happened.

But Alex knew.

She'd seen this type of thing before in old footage of Jack's grandfather, Wyatt. When she'd been given the assignment to be part of Helix's security, Jack's father sat her down and made her watch ten straight hours of video covering Wyatt and what he could do.

We don't even know half of his skills, he had said at the time. *He kept most of them close to the chest. But you need to understand what you can—and keep an eye out for others with similar abilities.*

Alex watched the whole series of videos, mesmerized and nearly unblinking. Wyatt could track animals and people while blindfolded, or when there was no actual visible sign of their passing. In one video he had fended off a group of attackers with a simple shove—like Jack had just now done with Barry.

She'd had her ideas as to what was going on with Jack. Maybe that had been Daniel's whole goal to begin with: to prepare her to understand what Jack would eventually be able to do. The headaches—growing pains for the brain, some said —and the things he was supposedly seeing. Her suspicions had been confirmed by rummaging around in his head, filling in the gaps with what he hadn't yet verbally told her.

Wyatt had described it on one video as "awakening." Not that the term actually mattered.

Wyatt had a strong form of ESP, and Jack was growing into that power as well.

She turned down Vine Street, not entirely sure where to go. She tuned in to Jack's thoughts.

What the heck did I do? What was that aura around them? What was that stuff around my hands? Where's my dad? Where's my dad? Where's my dad?

It had been the same the whole drive. At some point she'd

have to cut through the silence and explain to him what was going on.

She'd caught brief hints of other things from his thoughts, too. Something about a dream, the papers he had apparently taken from Helix, and some weird and disjointed thought about a house with disappearing purple graffiti.

Ahead a house was blocked off by a half-dozen police cruisers. She wasn't close enough to pick out thoughts yet.

"Pull over," Jack said.

"Huh?"

She glanced at him, seeing his gaze fixed on the house ahead. She'd been distracted.

"Pull over. Now."

Jack

It was Abby Smith's home—the house where the word "HELP" had first appeared. The driveway was now blocked off by a half-dozen cop cars, and uniformed officers were putting up a perimeter of yellow police tape.

But that wasn't what grabbed my attention.

Purple graffiti covered every surface of the house. The words "HELP" and "KILLER" were plastered all over the outer walls and roof. The garage door, where the first word had appeared, now had what looked like a screaming face tagged on it. I didn't know Abby very well, but the drawing resembled her face screaming in pain and terror. Lines of tears were etched into the image. Agony and fear rolled like waves off of... everything.

The words repeated themselves over and over, overlapping in an extremely dense pattern surrounding the face. Away from the garage door the word density lessened, and they seemed to fade away into nothing, like they had been airbrushed by a pro.

I had the door to the car open and was walking toward the police officers before Alex even had time to put the car in park. My dad would have been furious about me even getting close to a crime scene like this, but I needed to see. I was inexplicably drawn toward the graffiti covering the home.

"Why are we stopping at this house?" Alex asked when she finally caught up. "Whose home is it?"

"Abby Smith and her family live here."

"The weird theatre girl? She's a year younger than us, right?"

"Yeah."

"You know her?"

"Alex, you can read my mind. You already know that I didn't know her well."

She put her hands up defensively. "Hey, you didn't want me completing your thoughts or whatever. What's got you all wound tight? Your thoughts are all over the place."

With a hand I waved to the image and words covering the garage door. "That. How can you *not* be freaked out by that?"

"By what?" She squinted her eyes a bit. I figured the "squinty-eyed-look" told me she was trying hard to get a grasp on my thoughts. Her expression changed from concentration to confusion as her gaze switched between me and the garage door. "I must be reading you wrong."

"Are you seriously going to say you don't see that?" I said.

I looked at the officers walking back and forth between the interior of the house and their vehicles. None of them even gave the graffiti a second glance.

I shook my head. "Oh, you've got to be kidding me." I closed my eyes and rubbed at them with the palms of my hands. When I opened my eyes again, Abby's face still pleaded at me for help from the garage door, screaming and crying silently.

"Your thoughts are completely jumbled, Jack. I need you to try and organize them."

"Of *course* my thoughts are a mess," I said. "You really aren't seeing what I'm seeing?"

I could hear the pleading in my own voice and was embarrassed. If she couldn't see the purplish graffiti, how did I know it wasn't all in my head? How did I know I wasn't just seeing things due to stress?

"I can't see it," she said quietly. By now the officers were giving us strange looks. It was only a matter of time before one of them told us to get lost. "Look, I can hear your thoughts and try to help you figure them out, but it's way harder for me if you aren't thinking straight. It's like taking the contents of a filing cabinet, throwing them all up in the air, and hoping I can snag the right file when they're all drifting down. Focus, Jack. Explain it to me."

"Okay. On the garage door is a weird painting... or something... of Abby Smith's face. She's screaming in terror and pain." I shivered, and not just because of the chill in the air. "Two words are repeated over and over: 'HELP' and 'KILLER.'

They're crazy saturated around the face and thin out the farther away they get from the door. They're all done in a purplish color. It's the same color as... well, never mind. I'll have to talk to you about that later."

One of the officers broke off from the group setting up the perimeter and walked over to us. He looked tired and more than a little haunted. I looked past him to the other officers and noticed they all wore the same expression. What had happened inside that house? Obviously something bad that they could actually see.

"What are you two doing out here?" he asked. His nametag read "A. Younger." "You can't be around here."

"This is Abby's house," Alex said. She was actually sniffling, and I could see tears at the corners of her eyes. "Is she... Is she...?"

I put my arm around her shoulders to reinforce the charade, ashamed at our behavior. We didn't care about Abby's well-being. Not really. We just wanted to know the situation. And I wanted to know what was going on with *me*.

Alex leaned into me and quietly—and falsely—sobbed. I didn't say anything. It's hard enough to know what to say to a person who's actually grieving, much less to a person who's faking.

The act worked. Officer Younger was a young guy, probably fresh out of training or something. Pretty girls crying make it easy for a guy to give away too much information. "I'm sorry, Miss, I'm afraid things are no good in there. Not for your friend, Abby, or her parents. Now I need the two of you to get out of here. Please."

He waited until we were all the way back in Alex's Civic,

then lowered his head and trudged back into the home. The way he tensed as he stepped through the door made me think it must be pretty bad inside.

Alex started the car and drove past the house. She let out a long breath. "What's going on here? I've got a bad feeling this is going to come back to what got loose from Helix. You should have heard that guy's thoughts. He wasn't taking it too well. I think it was the first time he'd seen a dead body."

"Oh?"

"The first one is always the worst," she said.

"If you say so. Let's go to my place and talk," I suggested, changing the subject. "I have a ton I need to tell you, and I'm thinking you can fill in some of the gaps."

"You have no idea."

"That's my point exactly," I said, shaking my head helplessly. "I don't have a *clue* what's going on. About anything. I keep thinking if I could just have a few minutes to talk with my dad he could clarify this for me. Help me understand. But he isn't here."

"I am."

She was staring straight ahead, refusing to meet my eyes. I had the feeling she knew way more than she had told me so far.

She reached up and tucked a rogue strand of blonde hair behind her ear. Beautiful. I didn't make any effort to hide the thought. What was the point? She could hear it if she wanted, and probably had dealt with it since boys her age stopped thinking girls had cooties. But the thing was, it wasn't just her looks that I thought were attractive. I mean, Alex was definitely hot, but it was the other stuff. How she was always in control. Her intelligence. And how she actually seemed to care about me. Her emotions felt sincere to me. That was the biggest thing right there. She was genuine.

And she believed me. Believed *in* me.

Maybe it was my imagination, but I thought I saw her blush a bit.

I reached over and gave her right arm a squeeze. "Thanks."

She nodded in return.

"There's no way that thing back at Abby's place was normal," I said. "I wonder what happened."

"That cop's mind was as jumbled as yours. I skimmed some of the details off his thoughts, but I'll find out the full story tonight."

"Not that I doubt your awesome mind-reading skills or whatever," I said, "but how are you going to go about that?"

Alex lifted one eyebrow and glanced at me from the corner of her eye. "Helix has people in the Calm Waters police department. They get us whatever we need, whenever we need it."

"Of course," I said, rolling my eyes. "What was I thinking?"

"There's a saying in one of my favorite old TV shows, Jack, and you'd do well to remember it."

"What saying is that?"

"Trust no one."

As I opened the front door to my place, I was greeted by the aroma of fresh-baked bread. Martha poked her head out of the kitchen and gave us a nod.

"Hey, Martha," Alex called. "Bread smells awesome."

"Thanks," came the reply. "I'll bring some up."

She didn't seem to care that I'd brought a girl home with me. In fact, she'd basically just told me to take Alex up to my room.

My Aunt Martha was either the best aunt ever, or the worst. I still hadn't decided.

As we walked up the stairs I began to worry about the condition and cleanliness of my room. What had it looked like when I left? I couldn't remember. But when I pushed open my door, I found the room in impeccable condition. Martha had cleaned, and cleaned well.

Alex raised an eyebrow. "Bit of a neat freak, are we? Oh, never mind. You're just as surprised as I am." She set her bag down and took a seat in my computer chair. "So—let's get talking."

"Okay," I said, "go for it. Tell me what's going on with me. Am I going nuts? Am I seeing things that aren't there?"

She shook her head. "No, you're definitely not going crazy. I think you inherited some stuff from your grandfather, Wyatt."

"Like what?"

"Have you heard of ESP?"

"Like, moving stuff around with my mind, or setting things on fire with a thought? I've read King, and I've seen *X-Files*."

"Not exactly," she replied. "You're thinking of telekinesis and pyrokinesis. ESP, in a more general way, is when the body receives information without the use of the normal senses. Tons of detectives throughout time have had a *very* minor form of ESP—they call it 'hunches.' For many people, though, the mind isn't good at receiving this data from a 'sixth sense.'" She used air quotes around the term and paused briefly to give me time to interject with a question.

I kept my mouth shut.

"For people like that—like you, it seems—the data is filtered through the brain and fed into one of the other senses," she went on. "In your case, it seems your eyes are the main area that has been... enhanced. You start seeing things no one else can. Technically, you aren't even really *seeing* them as much as *feeling their presence* in your mind."

"How do you know all this crap?" I asked.

Alex shrugged and leaned back in my desk chair. "I'm just parroting what I've been required to study. There are some old videos of Wyatt Bishop I was shown as an orientation of sorts. Wyatt himself explains a lot. He explained it as a 'psychic residue left behind.' There were all kinds of other incredible things he hinted at being able to do, but the residue was how he tracked things down."

"I have ESP," I said, shaking my head in wonder. "I'm sorry, this... this will take a bit for me to wrap my brain around. We need to test this. I need to know if this is legit. I mean, it seems like I have no choice to believe, especially after what I've seen. But... I don't know, Alex. I need more. Maybe this sounds dumb, but it needs to be repeatable."

Her face went blank. "Seriously? You want to test it? Wait. I have an idea." Her voice couldn't possibly have been filled with more sarcasm. "Let's go find another batch of your classmates and nearly kill them! Yeah, and then you'll have a better idea of what's going on."

"What do you mean?"

Alex frowned. "I'm not stupid, Jack. I saw what you did to Barry and his friends."

I was too shocked to even respond.

"That's right," she said quietly. "You almost killed them. Do you even know what you did?"

"It was crazy." My voice was low, barely above a whisper. I felt ashamed. Ashamed of my actions and ashamed to be feeling a little excited about this supposed power I had. If I had a power, maybe... maybe I actually *could* get my dad back.

"You don't want to go there, Jack," Alex said. "Thinking that way will lead you down a dark path."

"Are you going all Yoda on me?"

"No," she said with complete seriousness. "I'm warning you. If you let yourself get seduced by the amount of power you might actually now hold—which isn't even a fraction of what it will grow into—you'll be hunted down by Helix and slaughtered like a rabid dog."

Dead silence engulfed the room, and neither of us seemed willing to break it.

Finally I said, "How dangerous is ESP? Am I a danger to everyone around me?"

"How dangerous is a loaded gun?"

"I guess that depends on who's holding it."

"Exactly. But I understand your need to understand the ability. You just need to be careful, and I'm not going to be much help in training you how to use it. I don't actually know how it works." Alex sighed and held out her hand. "Let me see the papers you took from Helix."

The change in subject was like a breath of fresh air. I dug into my backpack and pulled them out, then handed her the top one. "I don't get it. I've stared at them for hours trying to notice a pattern or, well, anything. I feel like I should know what the symbols mean, but all I get is a headache."

She let out a disbelieving laugh and held up the papers to the light. "Well that explains a few things. Hold this up to the light and tell me what you see."

I took the symbol-covered paper from her and held it up for myself. The letters "WB" were watermarked on the page. Setting that paper aside I grabbed a dozen more and held each one up. All the papers had the same watermark.

"Why didn't I notice this before?"

"I don't know. Maybe you were too busy looking at the symbols." She pointed at the pile of papers next to me. "Those papers are from Wyatt Bishop's private collection of documents. They were stolen about five years ago."

"What do the symbols mean?"

She smiled innocently. "What symbols?"

"Tell me you're kidding."

"Afraid not."

"So only *I* can see the symbols," I said. Frustration boiled in me. How could I hope to do anything if no one else could see what I could? "Awesome. This is great. I mean, this is *totally* helping me find my dad. Help? Who needs it, right? *I* don't need help because *I* can see crap that no one else can. But only sometimes. It's a good thing it's all so *easy* to understand."

I was on the verge of shouting. My dad once told me frustration and a sense of helplessness often go hand in hand, and right now that was exactly how I felt.

"I'm sorry," Alex said. "My attitude was poorly timed. I don't know much about the symbols on the pages, just what I read in passing in an old journal of Wyatt's. They serve as a catalyst."

"What kind of catalyst?"

"No idea. I didn't get to read very much, and honestly, I never saw the need to study your grandfather's journals. I've been too busy trying to make my own ability better. And learning more about applied violence."

"Applied violence? Right. I'll regret asking this, but what does that mean? What kind of violence?"

Her expression gave me the impression I'd asked the world's stupidest question. "All of it."

Shaking my head—I had no good response for her—I rested my elbows on my knees and buried my face in my hands. Turning the subject back to the papers, I said, "I thought I saw a face in the symbols earlier. Completely freaked me out."

"It was probably just the strain on your eyes messing with you," she said dismissively.

I wasn't convinced. The face had been real.

"Was my dream just a hallucination?" I asked after a few minutes. "Or was it part of this whole ESP thing?"

"How vivid a dream was it?"

"Too real. I can remember all of it with perfect clarity, like it was a Hollywood production just for me."

Alex shrugged. "It's hard to say. I know a lot about ESP compared to you, but I'm not even close to being an expert on the topic. Everything I know about ESP is from the videos Wyatt made, and from secondhand reports." Her eyes took on a faraway look. "There were a few mentions of dreams in some of the stuff I read. Something about them being a side effect of the 'sixth sense.' Like I said though, I'm no expert. I usually stick with monsters I can see and shoot in the head."

Hearing Alex so matter-of-factly talking about shooting something's brains out should have been shocking to me, but now... it seemed like the rule was to expect the unexpected from just about everyone.

My grandfather had been just like me. Had he gone through the same stuff I was experiencing right now? Now, more than ever, I wished he had lived to be a part of my life. "Is there any way I can see those journals and videos of my grandfather?"

"Not a chance in hell."

"Really?" I asked. "You're in charge of internal security. Why can't you just walk in and grab them?"

"First, like I told you before, I'm head of security in name only. I'm responsible for all the problems without being given the tools to actually do my job. Second, I'm not allowed in that room. No one is, not without permission from the CEO of Helix, and he doesn't give permission. To anyone. Ever. He might just be the worst person on the planet." She counted off a third finger. "And third, if I did ask for permission, I'd have to explain why. That's a question I don't want to answer, because I don't want you to get pulled into this."

"If they ask, just lie. Tell them you're curious."

"Do you honestly think I'm the only person Helix employs who can read minds?" she asked. "The last thing I want is to be interrogated."

"Well how am I supposed to learn about my supposed ability if I don't have any resources?" I asked. "My best shot at understanding the realities of ESP is with those old videos.

Look, no offense, but you said yourself you don't know enough to help me beyond the basics... and even then it's a stretch."

"I agree with you, Jack," she said. "But it isn't like I can go in and grab them. Even if I decided to give Helix a big middle finger and run in there to grab them, I'd get caught within minutes. And even if I get to the room, it's locked and environmentally sealed. As far as I know, without permission, only the CEO of Helix and your dad have access to it. It's all classified."

"That all seems a bit much. Kinda *Mission: Impossible*," I said. "But don't worry, I'll just spend my nights looking up ESP on the internet. I mean, Wikipedia has everything, right? The internet is totally reliable."

My sarcasm got a short laugh out of her. She looked at her watch. "Geez, it's already one-thirty. I need to go."

"Back to school?"

"Seriously? Why would I do that?"

"I thought you liked school," I said. "You were valedictorian of our graduating class."

She laughed again, shaking her head as if the thought was absurd. "Jack, I cheat. Every single day. I don't study math or English or anything. Well, history I do actually study. It's useful. But everything else? No way."

"Wait a minute." Suddenly a few things clicked into place. "When you say you cheat, you don't mean..." I tapped the side of my head.

"Of course that's what I mean." She gave me a look like *I* was the one saying something crazy here. "I was brought up being told my ability was an advantage I should exploit. I use it in class to make sure I pass everything with flying colors. You'd be amazed how easy it is to get a perfect score on everything by poking around in people's heads during a test. I should probably thank you. You singlehandedly got me through English."

"You cheat!"

"And? Let's see, I can waste time studying for calculus and some computer science class, or I can pass the tests anyway with zero effort and spend my time at the shooting range and learning how to kill monsters." She held her hands out, making a scale. "Hmm. Studying or guns. Hmm. Yeah, guns always win."

"But it's... it's..."

"Dishonest? That's a matter of opinion. It's about priorities, Jack. Honestly, even if I wanted to sit down and study—which I don't—I couldn't. You have no idea the pressure that's put on me to succeed." She stood. "I'm going to head over to Helix and see if I can't find some information on what happened at the Smith house."

I stood too, and tried not to sound too eager. "What can I do?"

She stepped in real close. I could smell the light scent of soap on her. She put her hand on my chest, and my mouth was suddenly very dry.

"You're going to stay here and get some rest," she said, then pushed me down on the bed. She laughed and walked out the door. "And don't you even think about going to any classes this week," she called. "I don't want you to do anything stupid by accident. I'll call you later."

I listened as Alex walked down the stairs and out the door.

She was awesome.

CHAPTER 13

Jack

My brain hurt.

After Alex left I jumped right on my computer and started researching ESP. Putting aside my earlier sarcasm, I started with Wikipedia. Thankfully Alex wasn't here to witness my hypocrisy.

After Wiki, I did a general search on Google. It brought back over a half-million results. I clicked on hundreds of them.

In the end, it was a complete waste of time. Half the sites were bogus "scientists" offering ways to develop ESP. All I had to do was enter a valid credit card number to confirm a charge of three hundred dollars, and I was *guaranteed* to develop ESP within a week to two years. A majority of the remaining sites all talked about ESP as a "sixth sense," which wasn't anything new. A few sites compared it to devil worship—sites that were very 1980s "satanic panic."

What none of the sites actually did was give any specifics matching what I was going through. That either meant Alex, my dad, my grandfather, and my own experiences were bogus, or everyone else was just throwing stuff out there without actually knowing anything.

Since I was becoming convinced I wasn't crazy—meeting a girl who is a veritable mind-reader will change a guy's way of thinking pretty quick—I determined doing searches on the internet wasn't the most effective use of my time.

I considered following Alex's advice and going to bed early when my phone buzzed.

The caller ID was blank.

The Insider.

I hit the green answer button. "Hello?"

"*Mr. Bishop,*" the Insider responded. "*So good to hear from you again. I was a little worried you weren't going to recover from that sleep-inducing headache yesterday. Tell me, how are you feeling?*"

"Tired of splitting headaches. That's how I'm feeling."

"*Ah yes.*" He laughed as if I were a professional comedian. "*Well, at the very least I am certainly glad to know you and Alex are being completely truthful with each other. Honesty is the foundation of every solid relationship. She is right, you know. You really should stay away from school for a few days. What were you thinking going back there?*"

My body went numb like I'd just been dunked in a bathtub full of ice. How did he know? No, I knew how he was getting his information.

"You had me bugged," I said. I didn't bother keeping the

accusation from my voice. The man spoke of honesty, yet he was *spying* on my conversations and my actions?

"*Don't be a* child, *Mr. Bishop,*" he chided. "*Of course I have you bugged. You're practically my most valuable asset—well, top five at least. I'd be a fool not to keep track of you. You have a lot to learn about ESP, and you aren't going to learn it by clicking on two hundred and three internet pages.*"

My phone was bugged. Likely my room as well. Now he was telling me my computer was being tracked. So this was what all those nutjobs talking about "Big Brother" felt like. I guess it isn't paranoia if they really *are* watching everything you're doing.

"Then where am I going to get better information?" I asked. "From you? Sorry, but so far all you've done is call me up and be all cryptic."

"*Mr. Bishop, that is a very good point. I want you to look out your bedroom window.*"

I went to the window and lifted up one of the slats to see outside. There was a car parked on the street in front of my place. It was just a normal sedan, a Toyota Camry by the looks of it. Dark colored, nothing flashy added.

"You in that car?" I asked.

"*Don't be ridiculous. The only thing in that car is a set of car keys, an access card, and an earpiece for your phone. Go out your front door and get in the car. Now.*"

"What about my Aunt Martha?"

The Insider sighed audibly. "*She went to the store while you were focused on your research. You really need to pay better attention. I need you to listen very carefully to me, Mr. Bishop. We have a very small window to accomplish something tonight. You can continue questioning me, and then you'll never get anywhere. You decide. Preferably quickly."*

"Give me one reason to go along with what you have planned."

"Very well. Wyatt's research notes."

My breath caught. To me, this was like being offered the Holy Grail, and the Insider knew it.

I ran down the steps and out the door, pausing only to lock up behind me. The driver's side door of the Toyota was unlocked, and on the passenger seat lay a small envelope. I opened it and dumped the contents into my lap.

"Good," the Insider said. *"The earpiece will link to your phone just by turning it on. This will make it easier to do what needs to be done tonight. Plus you'll drive safer with both hands on the wheel. Ten and two."*

I slipped on the earpiece and turned it on, then put my phone in my pocket. "Can you hear me?"

"Perfectly clear, Mr. Bishop. Now, that access card will get you into Helix without any issues, but it will only work tonight. They were stupid and didn't bother revoking your father's access codes yet. Though I may have encouraged that stupidity."

I could swear he was gloating.

Squinting at the card, I could see my dad's name. The Insider wanted me to break into Helix. "How did you get this? You shouldn't have it."

"No, I shouldn't. But really, who cares? I walked right in and took it. I'm a hard man to recognize."

"If this goes wrong I'll be in huge trouble."

"If this goes wrong, Mr. Bishop, you'll likely be dead."

Could I do this? Was this necessary?

"Don't get cold feet now, Mr. Bishop. This is your best shot to give you a way to retrieve your father, and more importantly, to understand yourself and your newfound abilities. Take the car keys and start the engine. Head to Helix, but keep your speed at no more than thirty-five miles per hour."

There was no going back. Maybe he was manipulating me, but at this point I didn't care. I wanted to find my dad. If this would help me accomplish that, then what choice did I really have?

I started the car and began driving to Helix. "Why do you want me to find my dad?"

"At the risk of sounding melodramatic, let's just say that I'd rather not face an apocalypse any time soon."

I had fifteen minutes to kill at this speed. I figured I may as well get some answers. "What's with the papers of symbols you gave me?"

"Alexandra already explained part of that to you. They are a catalyst. Basically, they are nothing but supernatural doodles drawn psychically by Wyatt Bishop. They mean nothing. It's what they do that's important."

"Which is?"

"They rewrite the pathways of the brain to facilitate transmission of data. That's the reason for the headaches. Your brain is literally relearning how to think. Much like a stroke victim has to have their neural pathways remade. Same concept, but this is proactive rather than reactive. Though, I will say Alex was wrong about the face you saw. It is legitimate. There are differing opinions on that among the experts. It could be that you saw your own face or that of the writer—in this case, Wyatt. Once you see the face, things, as the kids these days say, 'get real.' But you don't need to worry about

those papers anymore. They've done their job—quicker than I had hoped, honestly—and I have someone retrieving them as we speak."

Someone was going through my room. I wasn't surprised, but I still felt a little violated.

"That just isn't right, going through my room like that. Haven't you heard of that thing called *privacy*?"

"*Privacy is a myth,*" the Insider said dismissively. "*The sooner you come to terms with that, the longer you'll live. Think big picture, Jack. Once you know your privacy is constantly violated, you know how to twist it all to your advantage.*"

Geez. This guy was more paranoid than I was.

"So," I said, trying to restart the conversation, "does any of this have anything to do with all the secrets my dad knows? Alex was saying the people who took him might be trying to pump info from him."

"*That's one way of putting it,*" he responded. "*But it isn't just what he knows, but who he knows.*"

"Who?"

"*Is there an owl in the car with you?*" He laughed at his own joke. Did the guy have a screw loose upstairs? "*Forgive me. Sometimes I let my humor get the better of me. Your father knows the majority of Helix's secrets, but more importantly he knows of one specific project. You'll see it referred to in Wyatt's notes as* Project Sentinel. *It's who Project Sentinel potentially is that people want from him. Helix's rival companies—though one in particular is at the head of the class at the moment—will do anything to get the information from him.*"

"Why?"

I could almost hear him nodding on the other end of the connection. "*Asking the right questions for once. Good. In the old days with the Romans and the Greeks and all that, it was the army who invented the best weapons that usually won the war. It's no different now. The smarter our technology, the more success we have. Only now it isn't so much about a country versus another country or organization—though we still do deal with that. Nowadays corporations are actually far more important than a simple line on a map. Corporations determine everything, whether people realize it or not."*

"So the corporation with the best weapon wins the war," I said. I had a sinking feeling in my gut, but I knew I had to ask the question anyway. "So... *who* is Project Sentinel?"

"I can tell you already know that answer," the Insider replied. *"Mr. Bishop, you are Project Sentinel. Well, at least that seems to be the way the cards are currently falling. To be honest with you, this project has been on the books for quite some time now. You're the latest in a long line of experiments and observations.*

"But yes, Mr. Bishop. You are what the corporations are fighting for, only they don't all know it yet. Your father didn't even know everything, but he knew you had potential for the Project. It's in your genes."

My palms were sweaty and my stomach churned with fear at hearing his words. I couldn't even conjure up enough spit in my mouth to swallow. A week ago I'd been a normal kid with normal friends at a normal school. I had a normal and boring job. Now I supposedly had ESP, was going on some cloak-and-dagger mission for a guy I had never met, and had the potential to become a weapon that people were fighting for.

Worse, *I* was the reason my dad had been abducted.

"Steady, Mr. Bishop," the Insider said calmly. *"You are two minutes from the Helix parking lot. I know you are feeling over-*

whelmed, but I promise things will get easier to swallow once you've read through Wyatt's material. You'll never think about him—or yourself for that matter—quite the same again. And I mean that in a good way. Just focus on one thing at a time, and do exactly what I say, when I say it. I've had this plan set in motion for months."

"Why are you helping me?" I managed. "Why should I trust you?"

"Ah, yes. I wondered when you would ask that." He paused, then said, *"Are my motives completely altruistic? Heavens, no. I'm a businessman. A very successful businessman. I'm inherently selfish, and I* hate *not knowing everything. Could I walk in and take all of Wyatt's materials myself? Of course I could. I took those pages of symbols five years ago.*

"But, Jack," he continued. *"This isn't about what* I *can do. This is about what* you *can do."*

"This is a test? Are you kidding me?"

"No, I am not, in fact, kidding. And you would do well to pass my test. If you can't get through this, you may not survive what comes next. I am helping you, Jack. Aside from Alex—who most definitely cannot help you with this—I am the only help you have."

Nodding, I took a deep breath, then another. *Suck it up Jack,* I said to myself. *This guy is the only person who can get you the answers you need.* The sick feeling slowly faded, leaving me calmer than before.

"Is this going to help me find my dad?" I asked.

"Mr. Bishop," the Insider said with resignation, *"I know you want to find your father. I understand, believe me. But you simply are not equipped for it yet. What if you were to find your father's location right this minute? What would you do about it? What could you do? If your answer is 'nothing,' then you win the prize.*

"*But if you learn about yourself, and your abilities,*" he continued, "*then you could very well walk into any installation in the world and rescue him. You'd have the ability. Make sense?*"

"Yeah."

"*Good. You worry about yourself. Let me worry about your father. Now, you're almost to the main Helix building. Drive to the back where the dumpsters are. You know the place. There is an entrance there used by the janitorial staff. Park in the space next to the walled-in dumpster.*"

I did exactly as he said, barely breathing. The Helix building sat dark tonight, like a majority of the night staff was gone. "Where is everyone?" I asked. "Usually the place is lit up like Christmas with the late shifts."

"*Mass carpet cleaning,*" he said, chuckling. "*Though the layoffs actually helped quite a bit too. The only people inside right now are the janitors and a skeleton crew of security. The noise from the cleaning machines will help mask the sound of your movements, and there isn't really anybody there to see you. Take your father's access card and punch five-three-three-seven-nine-one-zero-five on the pad. Oh, and take the empty duffel bag from the back seat. I imagine you'll need it.*"

I reached back and grabbed the bag, then got out of the car and walked up to the building. After I swiped my dad's access card I punched in the eight-digit code. The light on the door's electronic lock went from red to green, and just like that I was inside Helix.

"*Walk straight ahead until you have passed seven doors on your left, then turn right down the next hallway. Don't run. Walk at a steady, but not overly fast, pace.*"

I started forward, walking like I would from building to building at CWJC.

"Perfect," he said. *"Before you ask, yes, I am watching all of this through the security feed. I have access to everything through a back-door program. Don't say anything. The cleaning machines may mask some of your noise, but people will notice if it looks like you are talking to yourself, or on an earpiece."*

Counting off the doors, I reached seven then came to a hallway just like the Insider had promised. I turned right and continued down the hallway. The walls here were sterile white and polished like glass. No windows marked any of the rooms, just unlabeled, identical doors. I heard nothing from my earpiece, and a flutter of nervousness tickled my gut. Had my phone, or his, dropped the call?

I reached up and tapped the earpiece.

"Stop that," the Insider chided. *"You will draw attention to yourself. This is one of those times where you want to be as anonymous as possible. Remember, I will* not *help you get out of this mess if things go badly. You are not my only option, Mr. Bishop. My best option? Yes. But not my only one. There's a lovely girl in Sacramento who could do the job just as well."*

How comforting.

I kept my pace even as I walked down the hallway. It seemed unnaturally long, and the rational part of my brain figured I should have already run out of space. But hey, if ESP was real then maybe so were weird, elaborate, magical, seemingly endless hallways.

Still, the walk had my nerves rubbed raw, and the Insider's lack of communication wasn't making it better.

"You look edgy, Mr. Bishop," he said. *"Stop worrying so much.*

The walkway beneath you has subtly moved you below ground, which is why the hallway seems to go on far longer than it should. Now clear your mind and try to act norm— enter the door coming up on your right immediately."

His voice came through the earpiece tense and commanding, with no room for argument. I obeyed instantly and closed the door swiftly behind me, forcing myself to control my breathing. Slow breath in, slow breath out.

"Stay in here for a moment. Don't make a sound. A security patrol is walking down the hallway. I apologize, Mr. Bishop. They were ten and a half minutes early on their rounds. Don't touch anything in the room."

There was only one thing to touch: a sphere of smooth, polished metal the size of a large beach ball sat on the floor in the middle of the room. Nothing visible held it in place, but my senses started tingling. Something weird was going on in this room., and I took a step closer to the sphere, feeling drawn to it. Connected to it.

"Exit the room now," the Insider said into my ear. His voice snapped me back to reality. *"Quickly—you don't have all night. The timetable on this heist just became much narrower."*

I pulled open the door and turned right, heading the direction I was initially told to go. But the vision and feeling of that sphere stuck with me as I walked. It was dangerous, that much was obvious. Immensely powerful. But what *was* it?

"Open the next door on your left."

I was through it a moment later and feeling much calmer. This wasn't so bad. I even felt a rush of adrenaline.

Through the door, I found myself in another hallway, only

this one felt older. The white walls lacked the earlier polish and were a little closer to gray than pure white.

No. Not gray. Dull, faded *purple.*

Every surface—walls, ceiling, floor—was covered in an extremely light layer of psychic residue. An old residue. Older even than me.

A door on the right, a few dozen feet ahead, glowed a little brighter to my eyes—or to my *mind*, if Alex was right. But that wasn't the point. I knew instinctively my grandfather's belongings lay behind the door, and I walked straight toward it.

"On your right, a few feet ahead is a door..." The Insider trailed off as I reached the door and pushed it open. Then I heard him slow-clapping on the other end of the line. *"Apparently you know which door we want already. That is what I call progress. Now, you have only ten minutes to look at the room before we need to pack things up. There are no cameras in there, so don't die or anything. I won't have any contact with you once you go inside. Grab what you can and get out—"*

His voice cut off as I went through the door, and the lights flicking on instantly, apparently activated by motion sensors.

Inside the room another smaller room made of glass, sealed off by a single door. A hose protruded from one side, connected to the side of the glass room, which I figured was some sort of air circulation system. Inside the glass room stood shelves lined with movie reels and old books, as well as old artifacts that looked like they belonged in an Indiana Jones prop shop.

This was easily the most amazing thing I had ever seen.

No keypad kept the door to the glass room locked. The people here must have figured these rooms were so safe and secure that they didn't need extra security. I pulled the handle on the door, and it opened easily on soundless hinges. I stepped through, dropped the duffel bag on the ground, and turned in a slow circle in the small enclosure. What the room lacked in actual size, it made up for in content.

Even with the air constantly purified and recycled, I could smell the age of the materials. The musty scent of used bookstore mixed with metal from film canisters. The question I had to ask myself was: What should I take? There was far too much here for me to carry away in my bag, and I had no illusions of a second trip.

The film reels were organized in nice rows, each labeled in faded black marker. I grabbed one called "Field Tests" and another with the label "Discoveries." There was an old gun belt —Old West–style—on one of the shelves. It looked just like the one I had seen in the old photo of my grandfather. In the holster was an antique-looking revolver. I left it where it was. As awesome as the belt was, when would I possibly need a gun?

I didn't know what was important here. Well, I assumed *everything* was important, but that didn't exactly help the situation. Out of the corner of my eye I caught a glimmer of purple. A bit of residue a bit fresher than the rest. No, not fresher. More... saturated? Denser? The residue covered four thick books. They didn't have any markings on them, but I felt an instant connection to those books.

I put them in the bag, too.

I'd gotten what I came for. I couldn't say how I knew, but I did. Even the film reels, I realized, were mere icing on the cake. The real score here was the four-volume set of books I had just liberated. I could weigh myself down with more books and metal film canisters, but that would make it more obvious to the casual glance in here that something was missing.

The bag wasn't too heavy—college textbooks were way worse than this—as I pushed through the glass door and prepared to exit back into the hallway. I had no contact with the Insider the whole time I'd been inside, so he had no way to warn me if the coast was clear on the other side of the door.

Whatever. No guts, no glory.

I pulled the door open and stepped into the hallway. No monsters or security guards, or worse—Alex—were there waiting for me. How would I explain all of this to her? It's not like I could lie. Truth, then.

"That took less time than I expected," the Insider said in my earpiece. *"I trust you got what you needed?"*

I nodded.

"Good. Now, getting out is going to be a little tough. After that Hound came tearing through the place, Helix had to block off some areas for repair. They also had to destroy some other unrelated, less secretive areas of the building to act as a cover for reporters and employees. One predictable lie after another. All to cover up what got loose. Ah well. Oh, go through the door at the end of the hall and turn left."

Left? That way went even deeper into the building. How was I going to get back to the car? But I did what he said. He'd gotten me this far.

"Mr. Bishop, I need you to pick up the pace a bit."

Did I hear nervousness in his voice? Oh, man. Next he'd be telling me pleasantly to run like my life depended on it.

"In fact, I'm going to suggest you make use of those young legs of yours and run. The security rounds have been changed from what I

was expecting. I estimate you have thirty seconds to get to the hallway sixty yards ahead of you."

Crap.

I hitched up the bag and broke into an all-out sprint. As it was, I almost missed the narrow hallway. The white of the walls made everything blend together. I slid to a stop, wanting to gasp for breath but worried the sound would attract guards.

"Huh. Twenty seconds. Not bad considering you were carrying that bag. Give me a moment while I look for an alternate route."

I wanted to scream in frustration, but I figured that would be bad for my current situation.

"Ah, here we go," he said. *"Yes, this will do nicely. Are you claustrophobic?"*

I shook my head.

"Excellent! There's an emergency exit leading out to the woods beyond the perimeter fencing of this building. You'll have to climb a bit, but the good news is no security is coming your way. Just walk straight ahead, then take the fifteenth door on the left."

The fifteenth door led to a series of metal rungs embedded in a wall. The climb was long, and at the top I had to balance myself to swipe the security card along a strip at an overhead hatch.

No lights marked the outside of the hatch when I climbed out. Behind me I saw the bright glow of exterior lights and the fence surrounding the Helix building.

"How am I supposed to get back to the car from here?"

"Wonderful question, Mr. Bishop. You don't," the Insider replied. *"That car was stolen from a tourist at a campground fifty miles away. Don't worry, no one will find any of your fingerprints on it. Trust me.*

Walk south, away from the Helix building behind you, and you will come to the highway. There is a rest stop at the edge of town, and another car is waiting for you that you can use to drive home."

"Is that one stolen too?"

The Insider sighed on his end of the call. *"Considering you just stole some obscenely valuable items from a room the US military's generals don't even have clearance to see, I hardly think you should have any issues with two car thefts. Get the car, drive home, and get some rest. Trust me when I say you won't be getting much sleep over the next few days. I'll call you later to check on your progress."*

With that, he was gone. I took off the earpiece and shoved it in my pocket.

The forest around me obscured the moonlight, making it hard to see more than a few feet in front of me even after my eyes adjusted to the low light. The only thing I had guiding me was the dwindling light at my back from Helix. Soon even that faded away.

Aside from the small twigs snapping under my steps, all I heard was the occasional sound of a car driving by. One of the things about living in the redwoods is that tourist season is never really over. Oh, sure, the main attractions close down for parts of the year, but some people just like driving the Redwood Highway. There's something about the look and smell of the redwoods that people love, no matter the time of year.

The woods opened up ahead of me onto a rest stop. A dozen cars dotted the various parking spots, and I knew all of them but one would contain someone trying to catch a few hours of sleep before continuing on to wherever the heck they were going.

I made my way as stealthily as possible past each car, glancing in to see if it was full or empty. The sixth car I checked —an older-model Ford Focus—sat empty. I tried the handle and it popped open, and I found the keys lying on the seat. After carefully placing my bag of stolen goods in the passenger seat, I sat down and pulled the driver's seat forward. Whoever had stolen the car—the Insider?—must have had long legs. Or maybe that was just to mess with me.

No one from any of the other cars seemed to have noticed my arrival from the woods. I thought about waiting just to be sure. Yeah, that would be the safe thing. The cautious thing.

Instead I shoved the key in the ignition, started the car, and floored the accelerator. I left a cloud of smoke and a trail of burned rubber behind me.

CHAPTER 14

Alex

"We've had a break-in."

Alex fought off the urge to throw her phone against the nearest wall of her bedroom. She hated talking on the phone to anyone, because she couldn't get a proper read on their thoughts. And if she couldn't get a proper read on a person's thoughts, then she lost her advantage.

When Alex lost her advantage, she became cranky.

"When did this happen?" She kept her voice as smooth and flat as possible, and pulled a notepad in front of her so she could take notes in case this was actually important.

"An hour ago."

And? So? She wanted to scream at the guy on the other side of the connection. Was he purposely holding back on details to piss her off? Was this some sort of power trip because of her gender? Was he just a *complete moron*? She couldn't take it anymore.

"Details! Stop screwing around and give me details before I have you shipped off to our installation at the northern tip of Alaska."

"*S-sorry, ma'am,*" he stammered. Was that fear in his voice, or laughter? The phone creaked in her hand as her grip tightened. This wouldn't have been a problem if her title as Acting Chief of Security had any real power behind it. Instead, her job title was as hollow as this person's brain. "*Th-the break-in wasn't reported until f-five minutes ago.*"

Weird.

"Any idea why?"

Something in her tone must have calmed him down. His words began coming out more clearly. She had half a mind to get in her car and drive to Helix just so she could read everyone with accuracy.

"*Someone hacked into our security feeds,*" he said. "*No one even realized what had happened until one of the security guards went into the surveillance room and saw himself still on patrol.*"

"Unbelievable." Alex rubbed her face with her free hand. "What's your name?"

"*Harrison Raynes.*"

Ah, she thought, *the new kid.* "How did this happen, Raynes?"

"*The tech guys are trying to figure that out right now, ma'am. I'm in the security room, and the only thing they can agree on is there is no way this should have happened. They're saying something about there not being any record of the intrusion, and the hacker must have had direct and official access to the system.*"

"What was taken?"

"That's the thing, ma'am," Raynes said. *"We have no clue. We've searched in all the main areas and don't see anything."*

"Then stop looking in the main areas and look in the places no one is supposed to ever reach."

"But ma'am, no one can possibly get into those places."

"Just like no one could have gotten access to our security feeds, am I right?"

Her pen tore through the notepad, then a soft *click*, and the fine tip of the pen snapped. *I should murder them all in their sleep.* She threw both the pen and notepad across her room.

In the history of the Helix's Calm Waters location, there had now only been three break-ins: one five years ago, and now two others within the last two weeks. No matter how good the security team, they were bound to get lazy when they were never tested. Jack's father had brought up that point more than a few times.

But still, patience only went so far.

"Call me when you find anything useful," Alex snarled, and hung up before he could respond.

Anger drained from her as exhaustion from the last week took over. She sat heavily on her bed and looked around her bedroom. It had no personality, she realized. Not like Jack's. The walls were a light tan that matched the slightly darker-colored carpet. She had a bed, a desk, and a computer chair. No posters lined her walls. No popular books were stacked on her desk—her laptop and a simple desk light were the only items perched there. She had tried numerous times to decorate to her tastes, but she always came upon the same realization: she didn't know *what* she liked. She was starting to think she didn't have any personal tastes.

Every time she thought she was interested in some movie, CD, or random bit of decoration she would remember one of the students at school thinking about it. Was the sudden interest actually her own, or had it just been pilfered from someone else's mind?

So she'd never bought anything to brighten the place up. What was the point?

Her watch beeped, announcing 1:00 AM. Tomorrow would be brutal. Since the incident at Helix—the *first* incident—sleep rarely came to her before two in the morning. Her mind just couldn't wind down.

Alex's phone rang again. The caller ID displayed Helix.

"What have you got?" she asked.

"A security team found a door that hadn't closed all the way," Raynes said. *"It was down in the storage area underneath the complex. Looks like the intruder came in using an access code belonging to Daniel Bishop, and then escaped through an old emergency tunnel. None of the cameras caught anything, but all the doors logged the times they were used."*

"What was in the storage room that was opened?"

"Some old film reels and books belonging to a bunch of the old-timers."

Old-timers? A sudden thought struck her. *No, it couldn't be.* "Did anything in there belong to Wyatt Bishop?"

"Uh, let me see." The sound of typing for a few moments then, *"Huh. Yeah, this unit had mostly his stuff in it. Wow, the system says there are some pretty heavy restrictions on this room. How do you think someone got in?"*

"When I know, I'll be sure to *not tell you*," Alex said.

"*Oh. Right. I'll take a catalog list down there and see what was taken. You want me to give you another call when that's done?*"

"What do you think?"

"*On it.*"

Alex shook her head as the line went dead. Those who knew the real hierarchy at Helix knew Alex had been Mr. Bishop's second-in-command. Now with Mr. Bishop missing, she had been flooded with calls regarding mundane inquiries. Thankfully she only got them from the real security team that handled the sensitive matters at Helix. The other security team—the one kept for the normal masses to see—assumed Alex was a mere intern of sorts. Just the thought of being bothered with the trivial details they would bring up made her head hurt.

Her phone rang. Again.

She answered it without looking. Her patience was gone. "Seriously?" she exploded. "Do I need to come down there and hold your hand? How did you even *get* a job in security?"

"*Having a bad night, are we, Miss Courtney?*" The overly friendly, answering voice wasn't Haynes's. "*I imagine you are supremely busy dealing with the little break-in that happened an hour ago. How goes the progress?*"

Alex yanked the phone from her ear and stared at the display. It was blank, like no one was calling at all. But Alex knew exactly who she was talking to.

The Insider.

She put the phone back to her ear, but the man on the other side began talking again before she could say anything.

"*Miss Courtney,*" he said, "*we don't have a lot of time, and there are a huge number of things we need to discuss. The first of which is our mutual friend, Jack Bishop.*"

"What about him?" Alex asked. "And why should I talk to you about anything? You told him *about* me without my consent."

The Insider laughed lightly. "*Of course I did. Events were already moving faster than intended, and we risked falling completely behind. And now things are going* perfectly. *But enough of that. Tomorrow afternoon you will want to pay Jack a visit. I am positive he will want to talk with you about some... items he procured tonight.*"

"That was *him*?" she hissed. "How am I supposed to cover up that he was involved in the break-in at Helix? How did he even get in to begin with?"

"*Don't worry yourself over how to cover up his involvement. It's taken care of. He had a little help from me.*" The Insider chuckled again. "*How else was he supposed to get those materials? You told him you couldn't just go in and grab the things he needed.*"

"How did you—"

"*You, of all people, Miss Courtney, should know that someone is always listening. I hear* everything."

"You son of a—"

"*Easy there, Miss Courtney. What would your father say if he heard you uttering such language? Then again, how many people even know who your father really is?*" The question hung between them in silence for a few moments before he spoke again. "*But I am off-topic. Where was I? Oh yes. Jack Bishop. Let's have a discussion, shall we? I have some projects you need to get more involved in at Helix. I'll have to talk fast, so it would be best if you remained silent. Agreed?*"

He knows everything about me, Alex thought.

She could count on one hand the number of times she'd been frightened and intimidated over the past few years. But never had she felt so outmatched. This Insider was, perhaps, the most terrifying man she'd ever met.

"Agreed."

CHAPTER 15

Jack

Incredible.

My clock showed two in the morning, but I was far too wired to even consider going to bed. One quick glance inside one of the books I had stolen had tantalized me enough to shed any exhaustion I previously felt. I opened to page one of the thickest of the bound volumes. The book held no table of contents, nothing to tell me anything about the volume's subjects, and for some reason that made it even more exciting.

This was pure discovery. I felt like one of those treasure hunter guys on the Discovery Channel.

The first words made me shake my head in awe.

What happens when the paranormal crosses with science? Most people who haven't seen what I've seen would say science itself makes the paranormal impossible. I happen to think the paranormal involves the things science isn't advanced enough to explain yet. I'm a perfect example of this.

These books were a veritable gold mine.

Should I continue reading straight through, I thought, *or should I skip around?* Screw it.

I didn't know how long I had with these books. The Insider might come and take them like he had taken the papers covered in symbols. So I skimmed, going in order but turning the pages quickly, hoping something would jump out at me.

There were mentions of monsters from every kid's nightmares: vampires, werewolves, spirits, the undead. They all existed, according to my grandfather's notes. I thought back to what Alex had said about the Hounds being modeled after werewolves. It was one of those things where you just nod your head and smile so as not to offend. No one in their right mind would truly believe it. But then to read that one of your relatives believed in *all* of it... well, it suddenly gave everything a bit more traction in my head.

I'd *wanted* to believe these crazy, paranormal things were possible, but hearing it from someone I barely knew, like Alex, hadn't helped my brain reconcile the familiar with the strange and new. Hearing it from my grandfather, in his own words... that was different. It clicked for me now, like the last piece of a puzzle completing the picture.

And if there *were* a bunch of monsters running around, and other people that could do stuff like me, then maybe the world wasn't crazy. Maybe *I* wasn't crazy.

For every paranormal creature or ability Wyatt mentioned in the journal, he would then mention what science had done to mimic those things. To him they went hand in hand.

He wrote of experiments to try and replicate the genetic oddities that made these creatures. Experiments and medical trials to try and suppress or enhance those abnormalities in normal individuals. For every natural monster in the world, there were two created by man.

One phrase caught my attention in these sections.

Here's the thing. The world can be a terrifying place with creatures that strike fear in us. But they aren't the things that go bump in the night. No sir. That special privilege is man's domain. For everything bad a creature does, a normal man is capable of so many more worse things. That's what we try to prevent here at Helix, or so they tell me. We try to keep ourselves and other people under control.

The implications made my head spin. I flipped another few pages, then stopped dead. I rubbed at my eyes to make sure I wasn't imagining it.

I'm tired of people reading my mind. My thoughts are my own, and it ain't right that a person can read them like an open book. I've decided to figure out a way to use my abilities to put a wall up inside my head. I don't know if it will work or not, but I reckon I should do my best to find out.

If Helix can have a guy that can read minds, so can the competi-

tion. The last thing I need is one of those Commie fools reaching in my head and plucking out national secrets. The only thing worse than the Commies ripping out my thoughts would be those idiots that broke away from Helix and formed their own company. They just wouldn't be able to help themselves.

I blazed through the next few pages, hoping to find a how-to guide for preventing my mind from being read, but mostly it was all a bunch of random tangents about how the line between helping and hurting had blurred at Helix. It wasn't until I had thumbed through a majority of the volume that the subject came up again.

Every now and again I surprise myself. I figured it out, much to the consternation of Gaines. He kept shouting at me over and over again, "How are you doing it? You shouldn't be able to do that!" All I could do was laugh. I guess those mind-reading folks hate not knowing what a person is thinking. They're all about control.

I thought about Alex and nodded in agreement. She liked being in the driver's seat. If her ability to read everything around her was taken away, I imagined she would go nuts.

And this Gaines my grandfather mentioned... he was the CEO at Helix. Assuming it was the same Gaines, which I felt certain it was. Interesting.

I checked the time on my phone and was shocked to see it was four in the morning. Good thing I wasn't planning on going to school. My mind raced with the information I'd read, so there wouldn't be any chance of sleep tonight.

My eyes were drawn back to the text in front of me.

The key for me was imagining my mind like a room. Rooms have all sorts of entrances and exits. Doors, windows, vents, even cracks in the floor. Once I pictured it all that way, I could close them all off, keeping Gaines from getting into my head. The first few times he thought it was a sort of game, but when I was able to fully shut him out, he lost it. He wasn't just screaming at me verbally. I could see the emotional residue coming off of him in waves, coating everyone and everything around him.

That made me laugh even more.

Un-freaking-real. I couldn't see Alex going *that* crazy, but my grandfather brought up more questions than he managed to answer. The way he described the residue sounded a lot like what I saw left behind by people. What would Alex do if she couldn't read me? Maybe I was over thinking it. Maybe I was wrong about her. Maybe, if I managed to shut her out, maybe she would actually be glad to not hear someone's every thought for a change.

Or maybe she would just punch me.

Or shoot me.

I determined the best time to practice this was when she didn't have a gun. She seemed to like shooting far more than was healthy.

I hadn't even scratched the surface of what was in this

book. It had taught me more in a few hours than the Insider or Alex had managed to teach me put together.

My gaze fell on the open duffel bag containing three more volumes and some film reels, and for the first time in my life, I wanted nothing more than to study.

My body was telling me a different story, however. The stress of the day was catching up with me. As wired as I had been only a few minutes ago, I began crashing from the adrenaline and discovery-high.

But I didn't want to go to sleep. That irrational fear and paranoia lingered at the back of my mind. If I went to sleep, would the books still be there when I got up?

I looked around my room. I needed a good hiding spot. Under the mattress... well, that was far too obvious. The closet? No. Geez, I was complete garbage at hiding stuff. I finally decided on the air vent, though it seemed equally obvious. It was the only place big enough for the duffel bag. There was no getting around it. No better idea.

I grabbed a screwdriver lying on my desk and undid the vent. The bag went in, and the vent cover went back on. I turned the metal covering so the vent slats faced upward, making it harder to see in.

Finally, I changed into some shorts and flipped off my light.

Some more heavy reading was on the agenda for tomorrow, and I couldn't have been more excited.

I was in the dream again.

Everything was the same as before, from the scent of the woods to the temperature of the air around me. The absence of control was there as well.

Ahead of me I could see the purplish form of the thing—person?—I followed through the redwoods. My eyes dropped of their own accord and once again I stared at the antique revolver in my hands. A revolver I now recognized.

It was the same gun I had noticed in the room underneath Helix. My grandfather's revolver.

What was going on?

Was this actually a dream, or something else entirely?

I followed after the figure ahead just like before, seeing the sign going into Calm Waters, and again witnessed the figure in the distance catch wind of me and dart away. My hands brought up the revolver and pulled the trigger with no hesitation. The gun bucked in my hand, once, twice, then a third time in a continuous roar. A light haze of smoke clouded the air ahead of me, but it didn't deter my line of sight on the figure.

The figure stumbled away from me now, slower and more erratic than before but still loping at a quick pace.

My hands lowered the gun and I immediately sprinted after the figure. Branches whipped at my face and arms as I ran. But no matter how fast my body moved, I couldn't seem to catch the fleeing figure in the distance.

Out of the corner of my eye, a bright splotch appeared on a leaf up ahead, and I slowed down to a halt to take a look. Up close I could see that it was blood, but it glowed brightly, and my mind seemed to accept this as normal. My left hand reached out and touched the substance, then rubbed it between my index finger and thumb. The blood had the psychic residue in it.

Ahead I spotted more droplets of blood staining other bits of foliage.

I followed the path without breaking back into a run. A sense of overwhelming caution washed over me. The emotions felt like they were mine, but at the same time I knew they didn't truly belong to me.

The trail of blood ended a few yards ahead.

A twig snapped to my right, and I spun, bringing the revolver up. My response wasn't fast enough, though, as something barreled into me. My back slammed into a tree, and my head hit the trunk hard. The gun slipped from my grip.

Hands tightened around my throat. My vision cleared enough to get a look at the person assaulting me.

Except it wasn't a *person*.

It was short and thin in a way that reminded me of a normal teenager, but stronger than a person of its size should have been. It bared its teeth, all of them pointed like a shark's rather than a human's. But what drew my attention was the *glow*. It was just like when Barry had tried picking a fight with me. It had that same aura, and it called to me.

Or it called to the body of the person I inhabited in this dream. The melting pot of emotions and impressions were hard to untangle.

Except... was this actually a dream? It felt closer to... well, a memory, I suppose.

Was this a memory of my grandfather's? It should have seemed impossible, but the word "impossible" didn't mean as much as it used to.

My hand came up, glowing with purple light, brighter in some places than when I had experienced it for myself before, and yet also darker in others, almost black. It was *stronger*, that much was certain. My hand didn't clench into a fist, but rather reached out and grabbed the aura around the creature's head.

Then my hand squeezed.

The creature squealed in pain and slammed my head against the tree again before running off into the forest.

I slid down to the ground, gasping for air. And as the creature limped away, I could see the wound in it's leg where one of my bullets had struck. I coughed and grabbed the gun in a shaking hand.

My eyes opened to the sight of the ceiling above me in my room. I brought my hands up and stared at them. Young and free of the wear and age I had seen in my dream.

Had that really been my grandfather's body I'd inhabited in the dream? The gun had been his, and that, together with the purple and black glow helped my mind connect the dots. If this was indeed a memory, why was I experiencing it in the first place? How was this even possible?

Maybe it was a stupid question. How was anything I had experienced in the last week "possible"?

I rolled out of bed and unscrewed the vent, finding the duffel bag full of the stolen books and film-reels exactly where I had left it. Should I read the same volume? One of the others? I also had another question. How was I going to watch a film reel?

My mouth tasted like I'd licked a dirty sink. I rubbed at my eyes and pushed my way to the bathroom down the hall. The scent of bacon and eggs filled the air. I swear, my aunt must have thought I was starved within an inch of my life before she arrived.

There really isn't anything like a hot shower. I only function at about ten percent efficiency in the mornings as is, even with a shower, but without one? I'm at negative eighty.

This morning was different, though. I had stuff to learn about. That stuff being... me. My power. My family.

My future.

I went through the motions as quickly as possible and was out of the water and dressed in ten minutes.

The books peeked out at me from the black, half-unzipped duffel bag. Tempting me.

And then my phone rang, killing the mood.

I picked it up and saw Alex's name on the display. It occurred to me I should get a picture of her... for when she called, of course.

"What's up, Alex?" I asked as I answered.

There was nothing on the line for a few seconds. I checked the screen to see if the call had dropped. Nope. Still there.

"Hello? You there, Alex?"

I heard a deep breath. *"You* idiot! *'What's up?' I'll tell you what's up, you moron."* She was kinda cute when she got angry. The yelling didn't bother me at all. *"I had to find out from the Insider that he helped you break into* Helix. *Are you completely stupid?"*

"I was going—"

"*Did I say I was done?*" The speaker on the phone crackled as she screamed from her end of the call. "*Do you have any idea how bad things could have gone for you? Do you? Why would you even trust the Insider?*"

"You couldn't help me get the things I needed, Alex." The words came out before I could stop them. The good news was I didn't yell them or anything. They came out quiet.

She sighed. "*I know.*"

I ran a hand through my hair, still damp from the shower. "Look," I said. I felt like a complete jerk. "Why don't you come over and at least let me tell you things from my side of the fence?"

"*I'm already here,*" she said quietly. "*I'm at your front door.*"

Right on cue, a knock sounded from downstairs.

"I got it, Martha!" I yelled as I ran down the stairs. As I did, I pulled up the camera on my phone.

I looked though the peephole in the door and saw a calm, but still slightly angry, Alex with her phone pressed to her ear. Her eyes widened as she heard what I was thinking, but it was too late. I flung open the door and took a picture of her with my phone.

She looked like she wanted to murder me.

"What?" I asked. "Too soon?"

CHAPTER 16

Alex

Jack held the phone up with an innocent grin plastered across his face. The first thought to cross Alex's mind was a quick calculation of how many rounds she could pump into him before anyone would notice. Then she realized she'd left her gun in the car with the suppressor that would have made killing him much quieter.

Bare hands would have to suffice.

"What?" he asked. "Too soon?"

She observed in his mind the odd combination of satisfaction at the picture, and guilt over not telling her about the previous night's activities. Underneath all the emotions roiling around lay an overwhelming excitement.

He's in a really good mood.

She found his mood contagious. It bled into her and washed away the anger. The annoyance stayed, but she no longer wanted to unload sixteen rounds—minimum—into his chest.

Progress.

"Alex, I'm sorry I didn't tell you about last night," he said. *But I'm totally not even close to sorry for taking a picture*, he thought. *Perfect timing!* "I literally had no time to make the decision to go, and I was on the phone for almost the entire time."

"And the rest of the time? When you *weren't* on the phone?"

His eyes widened in excitement. "I'll show you."

He turned and sprinted—actually sprinted—up the stairs towards his room, his head a jumble of thoughts ranging from how good bacon smelled to paranormal creatures to wondering if he should make the picture he just took his desktop wallpaper.

Alex closed the door behind her and calmly took the stairs. She could barely process that Jack, with the help of the Insider, had been able to so easily infiltrate Helix and take whatever he wanted.

The Insider hadn't told her exactly what had been taken, but among the topics they discussed over thirty minutes was something called "Project Sentinel." She didn't have any real details, but she'd heard the name in the minds of a few of the company officers when they visited the Calm Waters facility. She'd also heard it in the mind of Jack's father.

"*Do yourself a favor*," the Insider said. "*See what you can find out about a Helix program by the name of Project Sentinel. It may just make a few of your job responsibilities make a lot more sense. Ever wonder why it was important for you to always be in Jack's classes? Ask about the program. Say you want a bigger role. Get on board. Make yourself useful."*

There hadn't been time to go down that particular rabbit hole just yet. When the call with the Insider had finally ended she had been exhausted. And now she was here with dozens of questions, and only Jack's mind to pick clean of any potential information.

She entered his room to find him sitting on his bed. He smiled hesitantly and patted the mattress next to him.

Awkward...

Then she noticed the black duffel bag behind him. To his right lay a thick book that reminded her of the old books she had read upon entering Helix's security division.

She picked through his mind. *Ah. Of course.*

Of everything he could have stolen from that room, Jack had chosen to take his grandfather's journals. The originals. No wonder he appeared so excited. They would be like textbooks for him.

Admittedly, Alex shared a smaller dose of the same excitement Jack felt. This was huge. She'd only ever leafed through these books, once, and under strict supervision. But she had to wonder: how had Jack known which books to take? Had the Insider known that much?

Jack was right. She couldn't have helped him get these. There had been a room full of items, but somehow he'd taken the items that would be able to help them the most.

Last night it had all seemed so foolish. So utterly stupid of Jack to sneak into Helix. But now she understood. A room full of items belonging to his grandfather? A grandfather with the same abilities Jack now possessed? Of *course* he had jumped at the chance, throwing all sense of safety and logic to the wind.

"Wyatt's journals," she said finally.

He nodded his head and pointed at her. "Now you see why I risked it."

"I've seen that room, Jack." She walked across the room and sat next to him. "It contains dozens and dozens of books. And more. You took film reels, too? Really? Did you just grab what you could? How did you know which were your grandfather's journals?"

Jack shook his head, and she heard Jack's thoughts a moment before he spoke them. "They had the residue on them. It was thick, even though it was old, as if he'd marked them so someone like me—someone like *him*—would recognize them even if they were mixed in with a million other books. These books are incredible, Alex..." He looked bewildered. "I've never felt so completely weirded out by something, yet so completely connected to someone before. I was up all night, and still only had time to read one of them..." He waved at the books as he trailed off.

She nodded, her mind automatically filtering out the random junk floating through his head. "I should punch you in the throat for the risk, but I can't. This was too good to pass up. You were right."

"Wait, you mean you aren't pissed that I broke into Helix?"

"Of course I am," she snapped. "I'm just exhausted. Do you have any idea how many phone calls I received last night, or how many reports I'll have to fill out?"

She didn't really have any reports to complete; that's what

the other security guards were for. But still. *I could have had a lot of reports.*

Jack had the good sense to look a little sheepish. "So they found out pretty quickly then?"

"Yeah, and they kept *me* up all night with updates." She hesitated, but decided not to mention the conversation with the Insider just yet. "What did you learn?"

He put three books aside and opened the fourth on his lap. "Honestly, it's all nuts. If I weren't seeing psychic residue, and having dreams, not to mention I almost killed a friend of mine, I'd think my grandfather was a mental patient. But now... this all makes an odd amount of *sense*. Well, as much sense as anything does. I'm still processing my new abilities, the cover-up at Helix, my missing dad. Even you being able to read minds."

His eyes narrowed, and he began to think of a... room? A room in his mind? "I wanna try something," he said. "Don't freak out or anything."

"Why would I—"

Jack's thoughts dimmed.

They faded in and out, like the volume of a stereo being continually adjusted up and down. Sometimes normal, and other times it dropped to almost a whisper. Sweat beaded his forehead as he tried to focus. His only thought was of a room— his own room judging from his mind—and closing off all the entrances. But he was, somehow, blocking her ability to read his mind. To a minimal degree, anyway.

He let out a breath, and everything came flooding back.

She didn't know if she should be impressed or furious. "How... how did you do that?" Alex asked.

"It worked?" Jack asked, exhausted. "I shut you out?" He flopped back onto the bed and covered his eyes with his hands. "All that concentrating is exhausting... and yeah, I know how that sounds."

"You didn't shut me out completely," Alex said, ignoring the joke, "but it kept going in and out, like listening to a radio station while going through a canyon. Kept going in and out. How did you do that? Why you were thinking of a room?"

"Go to page 353 in the journal. I stumbled on it last night."

Alex took the book and flipped the pages until she reached the correct page. She shook her head as she read the steps described by Wyatt, then stopped reading when she spotted the name *Gaines*.

Why am I not surprised?

"You okay?" Jack asked.

She flinched and looked up at him. He leaned on his elbows, a concerned expression on his face.

"Yeah. Why?"

"You've been staring at that page for, like, five minutes."

She handed him the book. "Sorry, the passage caught me off guard. I must have gotten lost in my thoughts." *Something that never happens to me. Ever.*

"What was buggin' you?"

She shrugged. "The name mentioned there. Gaines. The name doesn't ring any bells for you?"

"Yeah, you said a guy with that same name is the CEO of Helix. Did my grandfather know the same guy, or was that his father or something?"

"Same guy. He's been around forever."

Jack shrugged and sat up the rest of the way. "Okay. Some

guy that can read minds like you? You said yourself there are other people at Helix that can do what you do. Never mind he's the president of a company covering up my father's abduction. I just don't care about him. Why should I? What good has he ever done for me or my family?"

Alex nodded. *All good points.* "Makes sense. I guess he's been kinda absent for everyone, huh?"

"Uh, sure." Jack's eyes narrowed first in confusion, then suspicion. Alex tracked his thoughts until he arrived at the answer. "No. Wait. Is he...?"

"Yup. My father."

"Oh man, that—"

"Sucks," Alex finished. "You said it. Well, thought it."

Jack fell silent for a few moments before speaking again. "I feel like I should apologize to you. But let's be honest, I can't feel different about him because he's your dad. Right now Helix is tanking my life. Why don't you two have the same last name?"

It was Alex's turn to shrug. "He didn't want me getting any special treatment. I think, in his own way, he also wanted to protect me from the people that would naturally go after him. Hardly anyone knows we're related. But that imposed distance also put a wall between us, for better or worse. We don't talk much. It's why..."

"Why what?"

"It's why I like your dad so much," she said. "He didn't even have to try to be like a dad to me, he just was. He knew what I could do and rolled with it. He always brought me an éclair with a candle stuck in it for my birthday. He knew it was my favorite dessert. At least, I think it's my favorite dessert. Your dad was—*is*—a good man, you know?"

Alex turned her head and noticed Jack staring at the floor. He had a sad smile on his face, and his thoughts were easy to read: *I miss him.*

"I miss him," he said aloud.

"Me too."

"I need to get him back," Jack said quietly. "I'm not really sure how much longer I can deal with this."

Alex saw past the jokes, smiles, and moments of immaturity Jack constantly put up as a wall around him. He was just a guy with no parents around and with powers blooming within him that frightened him as much as they thrilled him.

"We'll go over these books later," she said. "For now we have some stuff to do."

"What kind of stuff?"

She gave him a smile full of confidence. "We're going to check out that house where the murders happened. Where you saw that image of Abby Smith."

Jack blinked in disbelief. "If this is your idea of lightening the mood, you need to work on your people skills. Seriously?"

"Seriously."

"How do we have access to the place?" he asked. "Won't the cops be all over?"

"Nope." She slapped him on the back and stood up. "While there are some absurd drawbacks to being in charge of Helix's secret security—the number of phone calls by itself is enough to drive a girl crazy—there are some perks too."

"Like?"

"Like having the cops in Helix's back pocket. Remember?"

"Oh." A moment later in a stronger voice, "Well all right then. Let's get going. What are we looking for?"

Alex grinned again. *Get the mood away from his borderline depression.* "*I'm* going to look for physical clues." She reached out her hand and pulled Jack up. "*You* are going to use your psychic superpower and see if we can't figure out what *really* happened there."

"Alright, then. Let's do it," Jack said.

CHAPTER 17

Jack

Yellow police tape stirred lazily in the mid-morning breeze. The Smith home had a vacant air. Maybe it was just my imagination, but the home itself seemed dead, like its former occupants.

The psychic residue on the front of the house was gone. I considered this a good thing. After a morning full of discovery, the excitement of going to a crime scene had worn off by the time we arrived. I think had the residue lingered, I would have lost all my motivation. I wasn't sure what Alex hoped we might find, but she was the boss.

It was early enough most people were still inside their own homes, but late enough all the local kids were already at school. There was no one out and about, and no one to wonder why two college kids were walking up to a house where a bunch of murders had just been committed. I could only imagine the conclusions people would have jumped to.

I got out of the car and closed the door as quietly as I could. Just because no one appeared to be watching didn't mean I wanted to draw their attention. What if the creepy dude in the robe watched through his peephole?

"See anything?" Alex asked. She likely already knew the answer, but it was nice that she verbalized her questions. Maybe it was habit.

"Nada."

"Let's go in."

She pulled a small bag from her back right pocket, a clear baggie containing a single house key. I noticed for the first time she wore tight latex gloves.

"Gloves?"

"I don't like leaving prints." She reached into her left back pocket and pulled out another pair, which she handed to me. "Put these on. I don't want you leaving prints either."

"I thought the police were in Helix's back pocket."

"Oh they are," she said, while walking to the front door. "But we don't want to disturb a scene any more than necessary. Wouldn't want to screw up some potential evidence, would we? Plus, we aren't officially supposed to be here."

"Makes sense." Actually, I felt a little dumb for even asking.

I pulled on the gloves. They were tight but not bulky, and I could easily move my fingers around in them.

Alex slid the key into the deadbolt first and then the door-knob lock, letting us inside.

The place was a disaster. Black fingerprint dust covered

nearly every surface, and every cabinet door and drawer hung open, their contents removed and tossed to the floor.

"Was this from the murder?" I asked.

Alex shook her head. "This was the police. It actually appears everything was in pretty good shape before they got here."

"You'd think murder victims would struggle more."

Alex shrugged. "Hard to say. None of the murders took place in this room, so who knows."

"How did the cops even know to come over here?"

"9-1-1 call," she replied. "Abby called in saying she thought someone was in the house, then the line went dead. Cops will always respond to that sort of thing. The front door was unlocked, so the cop went in and called out a few times before finding the bodies in the individual rooms. Let's check those rooms out."

"Is there going to be a lot of blood?" I asked.

"Nope. That's why you're here. Maybe you'll see something I can't."

"If there isn't anything outside, what makes you think...?"

I trailed off as we entered one of the rooms.

It wasn't a stretch to assume this was Abby's room. Posters blanketed the walls displaying an unhealthy obsession with Robert Pattinson. Just like the front room, I was greeted with open drawers and fingerprint dust everywhere.

But none of that was what stood out.

On the floor at the foot of the bed lay residue in the image of Abby Smith. Flat, but in the way a good drawing makes you see depth. The image resembled her in every detail, but in a dark purple hue. Her face was locked into a scream—one identical to the one I'd seen on the outside of the house. That normally would have been enough to send me running away like a little girl, but I couldn't tear my eyes away. I froze in place. Next to her right ear was a residue stain that looked like pooling blood.

Sweat beaded on my brow and my stomach heaved.

I've seen my share of movies and TV shows where a person comes across a dead body for the first time. They always seem so shocked and horrified. I understood that now. I wasn't looking at a dead body, but this might have been worse, because little waves of terror emanated from the image. The way she had died was so horrific it had stained a perfect, psychic image of her corpse on the floor.

I wasn't sure the residue would ever go away. Maybe this was how houses became haunted.

I felt a hand grasp mine. Alex. Under other circumstances I might have been excited by the prospect. But not now.

"Tell me what you're seeing," she said.

My eyes closed in an attempt to shut out the vision. "I see Abby. The residue is like the most life-like drawing ever made. She's screaming her lungs out from pain... and fright..." I swallowed to control my nausea. "I don't think I can do this, Alex. This is too much."

"Tell me what you see."

"I can't."

"Jack, you're the only one seeing this," she said. Her voice remained completely calm, and some of it rubbed off on me. "If you can think of anyone else who can do better than you and me with this, then we'll go ask them for help."

The problem was, I *did* know someone who could do better.

Two someones. But one had died the day I had been born, and one had been missing for a week.

That left me and Alex. She knew it, and I knew it. But knowing we were the only ones who could figure this out didn't make me feel any better. Instead, the responsibility lay like weights were being loaded on my shoulders.

Alex squeezed my hand. "Take a deep breath."

Deep breath in, deep breath out. *You got this*, I said to myself.

I opened my eyes and stared at the 2-D residue image on the floor. "It's kinda weird," I said, keeping my voice as steady as possible. "There's a pool next to her head like she bled out, but I don't see any actual bloodstain."

"There wasn't a bloodstain," Alex said. "The medical examiners are still trying to figure out the cause of death. As of this morning they still don't have anything. What do you think?"

"I don't know," I said, but something in my voice must have hinted I did have something. My mind circled an idea, and Alex must have heard it.

"Give me your best guess," she said. "Crazy doesn't matter."

I turned to look into her eyes. They were filled with confidence. "I think something in her bled out," I said. "Psychically. Not blood. Like her... her *soul* or something. I don't know. Honestly I'm just spitballing here, Alex. But it feels right."

She nodded and returned her gaze to the spot where the body had been found. "That actually makes sense. I wish a camera or something existed that could take pictures of what you're seeing."

"How does any of what I just said make sense?"

Alex shook her head. "I try not to share theories until I'm at least partially sure I'm right. Let's go check the parents' room."

I nodded and followed her down the hall. My complete revulsion faded, replaced by anger and even curiosity. What did Alex know? What had killed these people?

And how could I stop it from happening again?

I peeked into each of the rooms as we moved down the hallway. To the right, a bathroom, no obvious residue. To the left, another room that appeared to be a spare, again no residue. And none in the hall seemed to point to anything having happened here in the past day. Pictures of the family hung on the walls. Abby had a younger brother who had been away. Lucky for him, I guess. Of course the other side of that was he was without a family now. I could sympathize with that more than others.

I paused at one picture showing the whole family together on a park bench. I didn't recognize the area. They all looked so happy. It was one of those pictures that caught the family at the perfect moment where they'd all been about to break into laughter. I didn't have any of those pictures with my whole family.

I tore my eyes away from the family portrait and walked through the door to the parents' room where Alex waited. I could tell from the look on Alex's face that she purposely chose not to say anything about my thoughts, even though she'd been listening.

She just stepped aside so I could enter the room and gave me a look of encouragement.

Abby's room should have prepared me for what I might see, but the scene still hit me like a punch to the face. Like the other rooms of the house, this one was a wreck from the police scavenging for evidence. On the bed, a residue image of Abby's mom—I didn't even know her name—lay face down with one arm hanging off the side. But I saw this with more than just my eyes. I *sensed* what had happened to her. She'd been thrown there, cast aside like a... like a chicken bone with all the meat picked off. A purple stain pooled around her head and dripped off the side of the bed, spreading on the floor.

At least the image was clothed. It wasn't one of *those* types of murders.

Abby's father's image lay slumped in a corner, head lolling to the side. He had some marks on him suggesting he had put up a struggle. I could see the afterimages of scratches on his hands and face. A similar pool of psychic residue dripped from his ear to the carpet beneath him.

Something about his ear seemed odd. It sported a wound of some sort.

"Explain the wound to me."

Alex had read my mind.

I kept my distance from the bed and walked closer to the father's image to look at the ear where the residue had leaked out. I caught myself reaching out to roll the head to the side to get a better look. A dumb impulse. If this had been a real body I would have expected to find some sort of gunshot or stab-wound to explain the bleeding out. Around the front of the ear, and presumably circling around behind, was a series of small puncture wounds. Not real ones, but psychic.

They reminded me of teeth.

Oh, man.

"Teeth," I said quietly. "Like something latched on to the

person's ear and... sucked." I swallowed hard. This was wrong. I was sickened, but I wanted nothing more than to make whatever had done this pay. "I'd bet the other afterimages have the same marks, but I can't tell because of their positions. Were any of those marks visible on the actual bodies?"

"Not that were reported," Alex replied. "I'd have to examine the bodies myself. Might be kind of difficult, but I think I can swing it. You see anything else? Sense anything else?"

I shook my head. "I think the images I noticed before were like a leftover scream. An echo or something. I saw Abby's screaming face as clear as day outside the door. Maybe she witnessed what happened to her parents after she called 9-1-1, then whatever was in the house got her. The residue on the walls before seemed so *frantic*." I sighed, frustrated. "I'm not explaining this very well. How can I explain what I barely understand?"

"You're doing fine."

"Those images I saw were temporary," I said, struggling to find a decent explanation. "Just an echo, or like the afterimage when you stare at a bright light for too long. The residue resembling each member of the family is more like a stain or a tattoo. But it's more than a mere visual copy of their last... poses. The images hold the emotion behind their deaths. Some of the cause. So when I study those images, I don't just *see* something. I *experience* it, too. It makes viewing them a hundred times worse."

"So what are you feeling?"

I gazed again at the residue stains; the faces etched in agony. "Whatever got them wasn't feeding off blood or anything. It fed off their psychic energy. Their soul, or whatever you want to call it. Whatever did this was starving like it had been locked..."

I didn't finish the sentence before things clicked into place.

"What got loose the night my dad was taken?" I asked.

Alex broke eye contact first, appearing embarrassed, guilty even. "An experiment. One of the first ones. The thing had been locked in a holding cell at Helix since before we were born."

"What is it?"

"It used to be human," she said. "I think I've told you a bit of this before. Maybe not. The original idea came up during the Cold War. Helix was contracted by the government to devise a way for a person to siphon secrets from people who were thought to be spies. I guess everyone was super paranoid back in the day.

"The inception of the idea came from vampires," she continued. "Vampires are virtually extinct these days, so this was taken more from concept than actual DNA. Somewhere in the process the idea of vampirism merged with sucking out a person's thoughts. The bosses, in all their wisdom, thought, 'Wouldn't it be great to get that same sort of ability in a human? But psychically? Then no one could hide anything from us.' Your grandfather said it was possible. He allegedly said he'd done a bit of it in Vietnam—don't quote me on that one. Maybe his journals can give us some clarity there.

"Anyway, a person can have some success at hiding thoughts on the surface, but not on a psychic level. So Helix began experimenting."

When I'd shoved Barry, I'd been flooded with thoughts, feelings, and images. I understood exactly what Alex was describing. I'd witnessed it firsthand. There was no hiding from that type of thing.

"All of this is from historical records, so I'm not sure how accurate the information is," she continued. "I looked up what I could after it got free the other day, but the information was incomplete. Helix scientists spliced creature DNA into the guy who volunteered—some CIA guy. The technology they used wasn't great at the time. It still isn't, except for the process used by Whyte Genetics. Apparently Whyte can somehow make any sets of differing DNA bond. Anyway, the experiments mostly involved injecting the host with genetic material from a random creature and from other humans with gifts. It went well at first."

The room around me vanished. I focused entirely on her words. The idea horrified and simultaneously amazed me. This wasn't science fiction anymore. Somehow this had become science reality. Mad science.

"What do you mean, 'at first'?"

"The subject went crazy." She shrugged. "He became totally addicted to the process of psychically pulling the truths from a person. He stopped being human. Became an... 'it.' He—it—began feeding on people's psychic energy rather than examining it. The stuff it'd been injected with started physically changing it. I didn't get a good look at the thing when it escaped, but I've seen a picture. Its teeth are all pointy now. Not like they've been filed down, but like they grew into that form. Looks like a demented kid. A kid and a leech of sorts. That became the name for it. *Leech*."

"And this is the thing that got free?"

"It was *set* free," she corrected, pointing at me. "Don't forget that. Someone *wanted* this thing out and about."

"I need some air." I walked out of the room.

"Head toward the back of the house," Alex said behind me. "I want to look around back there anyway."

Like most houses in Calm Waters, this one had a sliding glass door opening to the backyard. I unlocked and slid open the door, then walked outside, taking a series of deep breaths.

It was hard to believe just weeks ago I lived an average life. School, homework, a job, and friends. Now things were as far from average as possible. Monsters, psychic abilities, and a complete lack of family. People were being murdered in my town. Sure, Calm Waters had a few murders every year, but they were always distant. I would casually flip past them on the news or ignore the article in the newspaper.

Now I stood in a home where three people had been killed. I'd seen the residue imprint left behind. They had died, and they had done so in horrible pain and fear. I should have been worrying about Homecoming. About my job and the stupid amount of taxes taken out of my paycheck. Not murders. Not monsters. Certainly not psychic abilities I barely understood, and if I was honest with myself, still had trouble rationalizing in my head.

Could I actually help stop this thing? This Leech?

Could I find my dad?

"I don't get it," I said finally.

"Get what?"

"I just don't understand how all this works. I can sorta wrap my head around my mind filtering the psychic sense through my other senses. It makes as much sense as anything.

But why the images? Why do they even stick around? Back in the forest, by my dad's truck, why could I see the tracks, but only for a little while?"

"Your mind hadn't adjusted yet?"

"Okay." I nodded in agreement. "I can buy that. The Insider told me the whole purpose of my grandfather's psychic doodles was to reroute pathways in my brain to speed up my psychic development. Does that make any sense to you?"

"I guess." Alex stared off at the house without really looking at it. "It doesn't matter a whole lot, if I'm being honest with you, Jack."

"You don't care how this stuff works?"

"I grew up with it. It's as natural as breathing. Most people don't question or study the intricacies of how their lungs function. Have you?"

"Well, no."

"See? I don't care *how* it works, as long as it *works*." She looked at me from the corner of her eye. "But I can tell this matters to you. It isn't natural for you yet. I wish I had answers."

"Thanks for listening at least. I just want to know how the residue works. Even if it's theoretical mad science."

"You've still got three more journals to read back at your place. How about we delve into that a little later. I don't want to be at this house any longer than necessary."

"Right. Sorry." I refocused on the house. Our little chat helped calm me down. My brain now focused on the singular question: *why?* Why could I see things? Why had the Leech been freed. Why...

"Alex, why this house?"

"No idea. The police have been killing themselves over that question." She pointed around the yard. "But we really aren't far from the forest edge. The Leech probably got hungry like you said. Maybe this was the first place that got its attention."

"A random choice?" Somehow the idea made it worse for me. No reason or rhyme. Wrong place, wrong time. But still.

Why?

"The report put together by the police said they found some tracks out back," Alex said from behind me. "They assumed they were some old ones belonging to Abby."

"But you aren't so sure?" I didn't glance back.

"Only one way to find out." She walked past me. "Let's check out the back edge of their yard."

Trying not to sigh, I followed her out to an average grass yard lined on the sides with a fence and some trees and bushes.

"The tracks were over by the bushes at the back of their property," Alex said, pointing to waist-high shrubbery. "It backs up to another house that looks out over the forest edge. The neighbors were questioned but didn't see anything."

The bush she pointed to seemed different somehow. I walked toward it slowly, my eyes scanning the ground for any sign of residue. I almost missed it. If I hadn't been so used to seeing the color, I would have written it off as a trick of the light. But it was there.

Two footprints. Just two.

I crouched down and studied the bush and the ground below. The footprints were distinct but small, facing out from the bush toward the back of the house. Up close they looked kinda like a little girl's footprints, so it would have been easy for the police to assume they belonged to Abby. But I saw them differently.

The area inside the prints was a dark and inky purple. I thought of the wounds I had observed on the afterimage of Abby's dad. We needed to find this thing. *I* needed to find this thing. But how could I find this Leech-thing when I couldn't even begin to understand it?

"Take a picture of the tracks," I said. I had an idea. "Just in case I mess them up."

"Police already did." Alex's eyes narrowed as she took in what I was thinking. "You sure you want to do that? If it works..."

"If it works maybe I can give us an advantage." I shivered. "We need to find my dad, and this thing is somehow related to his disappearance. Alex, I don't know how else I can look for him. We're at a dead end. If we find this thing and put it out of commission, maybe that will give us some more answers. I've got to do *something*. I can't just sit around."

Before I could think about it too much and talk myself out of it, I stepped onto the pair of tracks. My thought was maybe I could get some sort of insight. Something more than just a pair of tracks to follow.

And did I ever.

As soon as my feet settled, I saw a whole different scene.

It was night, and light from Abby's home shone through the sliding back door. Laughter drifted from inside like an echo. Abby walked in front of the glass door holding a phone to her ear. The scene was surreal. I saw the expression of joy on her face in every tiny detail, such a contrast to the afterimage of her, screaming her throat raw. This was a happier Abby. It was kind of weird, but it made what I had seen earlier a bit easier to take. My last image of her wasn't going to be of her death, but instead of her life in a moment of happiness.

I found myself crouching down, like the thing that had stood here by the bushes watching the family. Alien thoughts drifted in and out of my head. Thoughts filled with naked hunger. The Leech was ruled by its need to feed. It had been deprived for so long. Alex had been right. Abby's family were the first living people the Leech had seen since it had been set free. The creature had hidden in the woods, hunger gnawing in its belly. But even then, it didn't want to rush in. It wanted to watch its victims. Observing them made the anticipation grow, and sucking out their essence would be that much sweeter.

It was disgusting.

It was addicting.

This was the sensation I had felt when I touched Barry, but on a whole new level. This was taken to the extreme.

The images shifted. Sped up like I'd hit fast-forward on the vision. No, not a vision, a *memory,* like my grandfather's memory I saw in my dreams. Soon the lights in the house went out. The stars above me moved in their paths. The sun began to rise.

The creature walked to the house. I watched as it walked slowly to the sliding door I knew would be unlocked. I felt myself being dragged after it. That was the last thing I wanted. I didn't want to see the murders committed. I didn't think I could handle it.

I forced myself to lift my feet and step out of the footprints.

It was day again. I took a deep breath. The house in front of me looked so much emptier than it had in the memory, like it too had lost its soul.

"What did you see?"

I related everything to her in as much detail as possible. She didn't interrupt me once.

"If you see the tracks here, why don't we see any others around that have the same residue in them?"

"Not sure." I shook my head. "Like I said, I don't understand why I can see the residue at all. But maybe I have a theory. The Leech waited here the whole night, fantasizing over what it was going to do to them. How they would taste. It was hungry, Alex. Maybe that's why. So much emotion over a long period of time burned the memory to this place. The steps in between weren't important to it, just right here." I waved back at the house. "And in there."

"If you could relive that memory, what about if we went back inside—"

I cut her off. "No. Not going to happen. Don't even ask."

Alex held up her hands in surrender. "Sorry, I won't ask. I thought maybe we could get some more information."

"You don't know what it feels like, Alex," I said quietly. "I felt the thing's emotions—every filthy and horrible desire. But the emotions felt *good* to me because I was the Leech standing here watching the family. Imagine how it would be if I were to go in and touch those dead memories. I can't. I just can't."

She let out a long breath. "I shouldn't have even brought it up. I'm sorry, Jack." She glanced around. "Let's take another look around the yard. See if we can find where the Leech left."

"Sure."

Alex took the side opposite the bush where I stood, and I

continued searching the area. Our paths naturally took us to a back gate which led into an alley of sorts between two other homes.

Alex opened the gate. "How much you want to bet this is where..." She trailed off as she stared down at a new set of tracks. They were odd, to say the least. Yet horribly familiar.

I bent down to get a better view. A person's hands and feet, but with something extra coming off of them. Claws.

"Alex, these look like the same ones I saw in the forest where my dad was taken."

An odd sound made me glance up at Alex. From somewhere she had produced a small pistol, and she was screwing a silencer onto it. She tightened it with a final twist, then held a finger to her lips. The expression on her face immediately quelled the question I had been about to ask. But then I had an idea.

I asked the question in my head.

What should I do?

Alex reached inside her jacket and pulled out a knife. With a quick flick of a finger, a four-inch blade flipped out from the handle. She held the weapon out to me, and I really had no choice but to take it. She motioned for me to stand behind her with a wave of her hand.

I peeked down at the track. There was the slightest hint of purple in it, and I glimpsed a faint trail to and from the fence line leading back to the alley. The alley itself was filled with large, black, plastic garbage cans and matching green ones for recycling. The trash wouldn't be picked up until the next day, so it was hard to get a clear view due to the mess. Those odd tracks led right into the cluster of garbage cans.

Alex lifted her pistol, keeping it aimed into the alley. It was a practiced motion and looked completely natural on her. I was no gun expert, but it was pretty easy to tell Alex was completely comfortable with a gun. I guess she hadn't been joking when she had been talking about guns earlier.

I let myself fall back a few paces, giving her space. Just in case.

Of the several garbage bins, only one was completely closed. I half expected Alex to lift the lid and jump back all dramatic like they do in the movies. Instead she approached the can in silence, keeping her pistol pointed at it, angling the barrel downward.

I jumped when she pulled the trigger twice in rapid succession. Her gun made a *chuff*ing sound with each shot. The noise seemed loud in this quiet alley, silencer or no.

Alex stood staring at the garbage can for a few moments, her face completely absent emotion. Then she leaned forward, one hand stretching to lift the lid. A slight movement above us caught my eye. If I hadn't edged myself back earlier I wouldn't have even noticed.

I didn't have a chance to shout a warning, but I didn't have to. Alex heard it in my head clear enough. She threw herself to the side in a roll as a *thing* pounced down where she had been standing a moment before.

The creature resembled a hairless werewolf crossed with a bony porcupine. The human shape the thing had once been remained, but it wasn't human anymore. Its front arms were longer than a man's, and its hands ended in claws. That explained the odd tracks.

A forest of quills like sharpened bones protruded from its

back. They didn't look like they had been grafted there. They looked natural, like they had grown out of the creature's spine.

The muscles on the thing's back rippled as it bunched up to leap at Alex. She rose from her roll and leveled her gun. I could see her finger tensing on the trigger.

Then she hesitated.

I realized I was in her line of fire. She couldn't shoot at it without risking a miss and hitting me, or a shot going through the creature and also hitting me.

But I couldn't move. I froze, rooted to the spot with a silly knife in my hand.

The creature would kill us both.

It leapt, claws slashing, and I knew they were going to rip Alex to pieces. She wouldn't be able to dodge in time. But somehow she was already moving. Her foot lashed out and hit the garbage can she had gunned down earlier, knocking it into the oncoming creature's path. It didn't do much, deflecting the creature a bit and slowing it down. The creature stumbled as it landed, crashing into another garbage can. Bits of rotting food, shreds of wrappers, and pieces of cardboard flew into the air.

That was all the space Alex needed.

She slid to the side and her gun *chuff*ed over and over. Blood spurted from the creature as the bullets tore through it, splashing the walls of the houses and the refuse on the ground with crimson.

The monster slashed at her again, weaker. Alex darted back out of reach from the claws. She shot into the creature until the gun's slide locked back, then in a smooth motion ejected the spent magazine and pulled another from her belt. The new magazine had scarcely been shoved into the gun before she fired again, taking a few steps back as she did so, circling around so she stood between me and the bleeding creature.

It wasn't moving anymore. It barely seemed to be breathing. It faced toward us, mouth still snarling and snapping with a mouthful of pointed teeth. Its eyes were the most human thing about it, and they glared at us with pure hatred.

"You need to get out of here," Alex said, her voice dead calm. "I'm going to make some calls to get this cleaned up, but you can't be here when that happens. Helix doesn't know you're helping. They can't find out, or they'll shut me down."

"You okay?" I managed.

"Fine. Just get out of here. If you see anything following you, run like your life depends on it. Use that knife if anything like this gets close."

I looked down at the knife in my hand. My grip on it all white knuckles. I hadn't been able to do anything with it before, so what made her think I could do anything with it should something start chasing me again? My hands started to shake. What good were all these powers I possessed if I froze? What good were these powers against something like that creature?

I imagined those teeth ripping into me. Those claws...

My head snapped to the side, and I felt a stinging sensation on the left side of my face.

"Snap out of it, Jack. You can't think like that," Alex said.

She slapped me!

"Go, Jack. We'll work out something later, but you've got to get out of here." She gave me a little push, and the next thing I knew I was running.

CHAPTER 18

Alex

Jack took off at a sprint. The jumble of thoughts coming off him in waves were all studies in terror. He was absolutely petrified of the "creature." And he wasn't only worried about it killing *him.* He was just as terrified it would kill *her.*

Jack was already too attached. *I could use that,* Alex thought, then felt immediate guilt. How else did she think he would react? If she'd been in his position, would she have acted any differently?

But Alex hadn't been in his position. Ever. She'd been raised knowing exactly what was really going on in the world.

Still. In a way it was nice that someone cared. Not about her ability, but about *her.*

She reached into her jacket pocket and pulled out her phone. She scrolled through her contacts until she reached her father's information. She hated talking to him. The phone rang once, and then he answered.

"What is it?" her father's voice questioned. Not "Hello." Never "Hello."

"We've got another Hound."

A brief moment of silence. *"Is it neutralized?"* Not *"Are you okay?"*

Alex gazed down at the still-squirming body of the Hound. It was a virtual twin of the one she had killed the night the Leech had been freed.

"It's dead," she lied. The lie felt good. It gave her control and kept her father from being control*ling*.

"Good. I'll send a team to pick it up. Did anyone see?" Meaning *"Did you screw up?"*

Alex pulled the phone away from her ear and had to resist the impulse to throw it against the wall of the house next to her.

The Hound made a small growling sound. She cut it off with a foot pressed against its throat. Its arms weren't able to move to do anything about it. Twenty 9mm rounds made sure of that.

"Alexandra, is there a reason you aren't responding? Were there witnesses?"

"Negative. I was alone."

"Doing what?"

"Following a hunch on the death of that family," she replied.

"And?"

It was like an interrogation. Every conversation went like

this. It had been so different with Jack's dad. He'd always listened, and when he did ask questions it was always out of curiosity. Never a demand. With her father, Arthur Gaines, she only received demands.

"It was the Leech," she said before she could stop herself.

A pause on the other end. *"How did you arrive at this conclusion?"*

She silently cursed herself. *Why can't I just keep my mouth shut? The conversation would already be over.*

"Tracks were mistakenly identified as the girl who lived at the home. They were the same size as the Leech's. The cause of death also suggests it. Plus the presence of a Hound suggests it was tracking the Leech."

She was just throwing stuff out now. It might or might not be true, but it would end the conversation.

"Supposition."

"Do you have any better ideas while you sit there in your chair?" she snapped. Alex closed her mouth with a click. What was she doing? Why did she bait him like this? It wouldn't lead anywhere good.

"I'll forgive your impertinence. You are, of course, doing everything you can. I'll leave you to it. Text me the location. And don't call me for at least a day. I will not be available."

Silence as he ended the conversation by hanging up.

Alex looked down at the Hound beneath her foot. It still clung to life somehow. She risked a glance around to make sure no one was coming or watching. The fact no one had come already suggested no one was home in the houses adjoining the alley.

Nobody and nothing.

She pointed the suppressed pistol at the Hound's face. *This is almost becoming a habit.*

For a moment she pictured her father's face in place of the Hound's as she squeezed the trigger.

CHAPTER 19

Jack

The knock at my front door nearly made me piss myself. My nerves were ragged. I hadn't stopped shaking since I'd gotten home after running the three miles from the Smiths' house.

Not that it was their house anymore. It was merely a shell.

I wasn't sure I wanted to answer the knock, but I thought maybe Alex had made it here after cleaning up the scene in the alley. Whatever that entailed.

Her push had flipped some sort of switch in my head, and all my body wanted to do was sprint away from the dead memories and the dying creature. No one was home to see me throw myself through my front door after dropping my keys five times. No one to see me sweating and freaking out.

The knock came again.

Rising from the couch, I set down the knife I was still uselessly holding. Before opening the door I took a deep breath.

I didn't want Alex to see me still freaked out. She'd already witnessed enough weakness and cowardice in me for one day.

When I opened the door, Alex wasn't standing there.

Barry was.

My last image of him flashed in front of my eyes—him colliding with his new friends after I'd pushed him—and suddenly his anger and jealousy became fresh and raw all over again for me. The sensation reminded me of when I had stepped into the footprints of the Leech. I hadn't just *seen* what set off those extremely potent emotions, I'd experienced the emotions too, as though they were my own.

And here he stood in front of me.

Barry looked terrible.

"Hey, Barry," I said cautiously. "I wasn't expecting you to come by... ever."

He shrugged, obviously exhausted. I think he tried to put a smile on his face, but couldn't manage it. I don't think he'd showered that morning, and his clothes looked like he'd slept in them. Dark circles around sunken eyes gave him a slight raccoon look.

"Can I come in for a second?"

He wasn't anything like the Barry who had taunted me like a schoolyard bully. It usually went something like this, with him coming by to apologize for being an idiot. But for some reason I'd thought this break would be permanent.

"Sure," I said.

He glanced at the spot on the couch he usually sat in before this whole mess had started. Back when things were simpler. Nicer. Calmer. Indecision showed in his body language. He wanted to sit down, but wasn't sure if he should.

And then I realized, more than just body language was in play. I was getting all sorts of weird... energy... from him. His aura—the same aura I'd seen when he'd tried to push me around—pulsed lightly. And I could *read* it, in a muted version of what had happened before.

"Sit down, Barry. You look tired."

He nodded and sat down heavily. He appeared skinnier. Paler. "I haven't been sleeping too well lately," he said. "Every time I do, I start seeing weird stuff."

"What, like nightmares?" I asked. What was this about?

"Nah."

He licked his lips nervously. He wanted to talk to me about something, but I could tell he thought I wouldn't believe him. That I would think he was crazy. He had mustered every scrap of courage to come and see me. He was braver than I had been today.

"Barry, what's buggin' you? We've been friends forever, so I can tell something's on your mind." I figured it would be best to keep our friendship current rather than act like it was done. He was hurting, and I felt responsible. "I've never seen you this screwed up. Something happen?"

"We've been friends forever," he agreed, ignoring my question. "Still, man, I don't know how to explain this all to you. Don't know that I can."

"Then why'd you come?" It was a cruel question, but I had to ask.

"I think maybe you're the only person who will possibly believe I'm not going completely insane."

Barry rubbed his eyes hard. I was about to say something—

what, I had no idea, but I didn't like the silence—when he held up a hand to stall me.

"First," he said, "I need to tell you I'm sorry."

I didn't expect an apology, but I could tell he meant what he said. His guilt over what happened seemed completely genuine, and I had a feeling it was all related to his state of mind. I felt the emotion rolling off him in waves.

"I shouldn't have said all that stuff to you," he continued. "I know now none of it is true, and that you've been dealing with some crazy stuff lately. I guess that girl is the only person you can talk about it with. I just wish you'd have trusted me."

My eyes narrowed. Those were some pretty specific words he'd used. A little too close to the truth behind everything. How could he possibly *know* anything?

But he did. I could sense it. His aura couldn't lie to me. Barry might as well have been an open book.

"What are you saying Barry?" I asked as calmly as I could manage. "I mean, I'm glad you aren't buying the trash being spread around by the media, but what wouldn't I trust you with?"

"Have you been seeing weird stuff lately, Jack?"

The question caught me off-guard. He was getting braver now. He'd committed to putting it all out there.

When I didn't respond right away, he added, "I don't think you're crazy or anything, Jack. I just... I just..."

"Yeah," I said.

"Yeah?"

"Yeah, I've been seeing some pretty crazy things."

He hesitated. "Were they, like, purple?" The shock must have been obvious on my face. He started nodding. "I knew it. That day at school when I was stupid and pushed you around, something happened. One second I was trying to shove you, the next I was flying backwards. But between those two moments, I saw... well, I saw *you*. It was like I was seeing and feeling what you'd been going through since your dad vanished. Please tell me I'm not crazy, Jack. Please tell me this isn't just in my head." There was a pleading look in his eyes. "I gotta know, man. I gotta know."

I was speechless. Just like I'd seen everything going on with him, he'd seen everything going on with me. A sudden thought overrode everything.

What if that's how it had been for Abby and her parents? What if they had seen all the horror of the monster being inflicted on them as it sucked away their souls? How twisted and sick would it have been if they felt some of the satisfaction the Leech enjoyed as it fed? The thought made my stomach do flips.

Barry stared at me with begging, tear-filled eyes. "You're not crazy," I said. "Where did you get the 'purple' thing from?"

He let out a long breath, one that sounded like he'd been holding it for weeks. "When I saw all that stuff, everything was tinged in purple. I was seeing through your eyes. You were seeing stuff. Tracks. Dreams. I don't know. It was all kinda garbled, like in the movies when they do the 'life flashing before your eyes' thing. But I could feel how bad this was all going for you. How angry you were with everything. And how Alex was on your side. How she believed you. Did you, you know..."

"See what you were dealing with? Yeah."

He winced at that. "It's been rough."

I didn't say anything. What could I say? Instead, "How about now? You still get any weird sense from me?"

"Nah." He waved it off. "I've just been beatin' myself up over all this. I was an ass."

So the whole episode had been a one-time deal for him. I wondered if this would happen with other people if I interacted with their auras. Not that I'd seen one since. And I didn't really want to.

"I wasn't much better," I replied, but my head wasn't in it. I knew I should be having a full-on conversation with Barry, but I remained too wrapped up in all the other insanity to really have a heart-to-heart. Maybe that made me a bad person, but how was I supposed to act?

"So what are we going to do now?" he asked. "I want to know more, but..."

But he was still trying to come to grips with the basics. I understood better than he could imagine.

I shrugged. "Not much we can do. I'm pretty much stuck here doing nothing." That was a lie, but I didn't want Barry involved in what was really going on. Especially after what I'd seen today. "I can't work—Helix won't let me—and I don't want to go to classes. I don't see the point. Alex is keeping an ear open for news when she's doing stuff at Helix. I'm just trying to keep things low-key until this all blows over."

Another knock at the door prompted Barry to get up. "I'll split. Look, man, I'm sorry. If you need to talk to someone about crazy stuff, give me a call."

"I'll do that," I lied. *Sorry, Barry, I don't want you getting hurt by all this.*

He opened the door to let himself out. I didn't go with him, but tossed a wave as he opened the door. Alex stood there.

"Uh, hey, Alex," Barry said. He was clearly pretty ashamed about what he'd said about her too. "Look, sorry about the other day."

"Don't worry," she said with an easy smile. "Everything is pretty tense right now. I get it. We all have things weighing on us." She stepped aside so he could leave, then came in and shut the door behind her.

"So he came to apologize, huh?"

I nodded. "Remember how I told you about all the stuff I saw about him? Well, he saw the same sort of thing about me."

"I read him as he left. He still doesn't have a clue about me. So he must not have seen *everything*."

"I guess that's good." I sighed. "But now I can tell exactly how he's feeling." I told her all about the conversation, and how his aura was still visible to me.

"As long as he can't *still* read you, I think we're okay." She sat down next to me and leaned back. "I'm sorry."

"Been hearing that a lot lately. What are *you* sorry for? You saved us today with your gun stuff."

"I'm sorry you have to push everyone away," she said. "It sucks, but it's safer for them."

I let her comment go. I didn't want to have that conversation. Ever. Instead I asked, "What was that thing that attacked us? Was that what I think?"

"A Hound," she confirmed. Thankfully she didn't pursue her last comment. "I know. It's one thing for me too have told you about them, and a whole different thing to see them. Courtesy of Whyte Genetics. I hate those guys. They've been using genetically modified monsters like Hounds for the past couple of years."

"What does Whyte Genetics have to do with anything?"

She looked at me like I was dumb. "They're Helix's main competition. They used to be part of Helix but splintered off. Almost every major government contract in the areas of genetics or paranormal research goes to either Helix or Whyte. There are hundreds of billions of dollars on the line for each of the companies."

It's all about money, I realized, shaking with anger. "Tell me this is not just about money. My dad, the deaths, everything. Tell me this isn't about money."

"Everything is always about money," Alex said. "Or about control. Often they're the same thing in business." She leaned forward and pointed at me with a slender index finger. "But ultimately it's about power. Imagine if you could control this world that is unseen by nearly everyone. You could control all the psychics. The monsters. The paranormal sensitives. That is power. When you have access to virtually unlimited knowledge, you can shape the progress of *everything*."

"Is that what Helix wants? What Whyte wants?"

"It's the only reason they exist, Jack. The two companies are like two giant nukes ready to be shot off at each other. Whyte has taken the first shot by sending his Hounds."

I saw where she was going with this. "It's going to get worse," I said. "How bad will it get?"

"You've only begun to scratch the surface of what goes on under everyone's noses. What would happen if Whyte could engineer even a dozen people like you and me? We would have a war on our hands, Jack. No joke."

"Let's go get some food."

My suggestion managed to catch her off-guard. "You can seriously think about food right now?"

"I'm a guy. You know better than most that we constantly have a few things on the brain, and one of them is food. And right now, I want some good Mexican food." I stood. "I saw the memories of three murder victims today, entered the head of a monster, watched you shoot a different monster to death, and ran three miles home. That was all *today*, Alex. Food is normal. I need normal right now."

"All right." She smiled. "I can do normal. Let's go get some Taco Bell or something, and then I'll start giving you the basics on guns and stuff."

"Taco Bell?" I asked, confused. "Who said anything about Taco Bell?"

"You said Mexican food."

"No... just... no."

CHAPTER 20

Jack

The dream came every time I closed my eyes to sleep—whether for a nap, or drifting off, or actually trying to sleep. Tonight, like all the other times, I ended up in that forest, reliving it again. From the dark of the forest to the purple tracks I followed.

I shot at the creature again, and then I spun around as I was attacked. Only this time I could see the thing more clearly.

How could I not have realized what I was dealing with? It all seemed so obvious to me now. The monster's size. How when it bared its teeth, they were all pointed like a shark's. It was the exact pattern of the wound I'd been able to see on Abby's father. My grandfather's memory wasn't just some random one; it was of the Leech.

Apart from that additional realization, everything about the memory was the same. Just like before, my hand came up glowing in purple light. I reached out and grabbed onto the

Leech's aura and squeezed. The creature squealed in pain, slammed my head against the tree again, then ran off into the forest. I staggered after, or my grandfather did.

I went along for the ride as my grandfather staggered after the Leech. My grandfather was hurt but determined. He wanted to catch this thing, and though I knew he eventually would, I was wondering how it would go down. I needed to know. I needed to know how I could do the same.

But it wasn't just that. The only other person that could possibly understand my situation was my grandfather, and he was dead. But he had been able to control his ability and hunt things like he was doing in this memory, so maybe by watching I would learn something.

And then maybe I wouldn't feel so helpless.

But nothing more happened in the dream. I rode along in my grandfather's body as he chased the monster through the forest. He stumbled, but never stopped tracking the blood trail.

And then I woke.

With no more information than before.

In bed, I looked at the red glow from my alarm clock. 2:36 AM. I tossed and turned for another hour but couldn't get back to sleep. I finally gave up, turned on my light, and pulled out my grandfather's journals.

It didn't matter what I turned to, everything interested me. These writings were a window into the mind of a person I had never met, but with whom I had everything in common.

Well, aside from the part about me freezing in a fight, and my grandfather going at it guns blazing.

One passage grabbed my attention:

· · ·

Janison Whyte was finally fired today. It's about time. Sure, the man is brilliant—we wouldn't have been able to bond DNA at all without him. Sure he did us a lot of good. But he's also reckless. I caught him injecting himself with DNA samples taken from one of those lizard men that live underground. He said it wouldn't hurt him, that it was research. Said he could take that DNA and shift to resemble them. But I wasn't having it. We don't allow that kind of experimentation here.

This confirmed what Alex had said about Whyte splintering off from Helix. But what did that whole "shifting" thing mean?

As interesting as everything was, I couldn't find anything about the Leech. I found theories on how to splice monsters together. Theories on time travel. Even, curiously, a recipe for grilling steaks. But on the thing sucking out people's souls? Nada.

I sat back in my bed, frustrated. If nothing else, I could at least practice putting up a wall in my mind. I closed my eyes and pictured a room. I shut the windows. The doors. Everything. Those were easy now. But every room has places where stuff can get in. A tiny gap where wall and window meet. Vents. Cracks in the walls. I filled them all as I found them, but for every one I closed, two more became noticeable.

It was an annoying process, but there was no way I would quit. I'd already embarrassed myself enough the last little while. I didn't know why, but I needed to show Alex I wasn't sitting around doing nothing.

I took a break at 7:00 AM to shower and try to wash away my exhaustion. Afterward I stood in front of the mirror, wiping the layer of steam coating it. For a minute, I stared at the person gazing back at me in the reflection.

Who was I?

I certainly wasn't the same person my father had left behind that night when he went to go investigate the trouble at Helix. That person didn't exist anymore. I had no interest in sitting down to play a video game. Reading? It would be nice, but I knew I'd only be thinking of the various journals I'd liberated from Helix.

I was stuck. Maybe I could watch a movie. Try and let my brain relax a bit. Old movies—all movies in general, really—were therapeutic for me. Maybe I'd be able to sit there, enjoying the dialogue old movies are known for, and just breathe.

The movies triggered an idea.

I finished drying off and pulled on a pair of flannel pants and a Foo Fighters t-shirt before going back to my room. From under my bed I pulled out the old duffel bag I'd used to take the journals and grabbed the two film reels: "Field Tests" and "Discoveries." I love my old movies, but I didn't know jack about old reel-style movies.

That's what the internet is for.

Browsing the interwebs told me I needed something to play the films. Obviously. It needed to have another reel to spool onto. Less obvious. The old diagrams didn't help much. I did a quick Google search to see if there were any antique stores here in Calm Waters I'd somehow overlooked these past years. Nothin'.

Maybe I could ask Alex to look at Helix for one. They had the reels, so naturally they ought to have a machine to play them, right? But I threw the thought out as soon as I had it. It would be suspicious if she was suddenly searching for a machine to play the type of films recently stolen. In fact, I had to be really careful who I asked at all. For all I knew, Helix had people everywhere. And if what Alex had said about a blossoming corporate war between Helix and Whyte Genetics was true, Whyte could have people from Calm Waters in their pocket as well.

This sucked.

Unless my dad had a projector up in the attic...

Huh. The attic. Probably the first place I should have looked. My dad was a pack rat, never threw away anything.

When I was a kid, I'd always been afraid of the attic. I think most kids have an irrational fear of attics and basements. There's just nothing good a kid can see in those two places. You're either looking down some stairs into a dark and creepy basement, or you're looking up a pull-down ladder into a dark and creepy attic. But once you've seen Leech monsters, weird Hound-things, and psychic visions of people's corpses, an attic doesn't hold much fear anymore. After all, what's going to be up there? A bat? A raccoon?

The last time I'd been up in the attic was years ago when I was searching for a vintage *Star Wars* Halloween costume my dad swore he had. Darth Vader, of course. I think I gave up looking after a few boxes. Again, attics used to be creepy.

Sunlight peeked through the single window at the other end of the dusty space. But morning sun and all, I could hardly see a thing. Too many boxes kept out too much light. My dad had at least installed some real lighting up here, so I flipped the switch on the wall right by the hatch, illuminating the dusty space, and looked around. The boxes closest to me were the ones we used the most often. Our fake Christmas tree, lights, and ornaments. Tents and sleeping bags for camping in the summer months—no place better for camping than in Redwood National Park. I edged by and made my way to the window where the oldest boxes sat.

An open box ahead blocked my way. It was marked "Mom." Inside were photo albums and old VCR cassettes labeled with various old family gatherings from before I was born. The box didn't have hardly any dust compared to the rest in this section of the attic, which meant my dad must have been looking at these. He'd taken it harder than I had when she left. She hadn't even given any reason I knew of. One day we're having ice cream after a Little League game, the next she's out the door with a small suitcase.

We hadn't heard from her since. She hadn't even really said goodbye to me.

I was only ten years old at the time. Old enough to understand, but young enough to get over it without serious mommy issues. She and my dad had been married for fifteen years. Fifteen. And then she just leaves. I'd never even heard them argue. Not once. Crazy.

I realized gazing into that box—not touching it—my dad had never attempted dating again. Maybe he still held out hope. Maybe that was why he still came up here to reminisce.

I held no illusions that Mom would return. Honestly, I didn't even care much anymore. It was her loss, not ours.

I skirted around the box. I'd leave it for my dad to mess with when he got back. Seemed best to leave things as they were.

I searched through half the boxes in the attic before uncovering a bulky object covered in a sheet. I yanked it off with a flourish, which in hindsight turned out to be a terrible decision. Thick dust flew into the air, choking me. I could hardly even see.

When the air finally cleared, I was rewarded with an old but functional-looking film projector. It took some doing, but I maneuvered it downstairs. Thankfully my aunt wasn't around, or this whole scenario would have been hard to explain. In the living room I pulled some pictures off one of the walls to give myself a clean, blank wall to use as a screen. The instructions I'd found on the internet helped me get the thing going.

So now the question was, which one did I watch first?

"Field Tests" sounded more awesome than "Discoveries," so I went that route.

The picture flickered onto the wall. The first image on the screen was my grandfather's giant face as he peered into the lens of the camera.

"*This thing on?*" he asked. His voice was gruff, just like I expected from a guy named after Wyatt Earp. The sound was a little wobbly, but clear enough. I was lucky the film had sound embedded in it. "*I swear we've been fiddling with it for the whole damn day. We're an hour behi—what? It's on? Swell.*"

He paced in front of the camera, smoothed the front of his shirt, and adjusted the holster around his waist. It made me wish I'd taken it from that Helix storage room.

"*Well. Today is the eighteenth of April, 1975. I've been instructed to begin recording the field tests of our sensitives.*" He squinted at the camera. "*Danny, are you sure this thing is working? I really don't want to have to ask our people to work their magic twice. It's taxing, and they need to be focusing on progress rather than showing off for whoever's going to see this blasted recording."*

"It's working, Father," came a voice from off camera. It was my dad's voice, only younger. Just the sound of it made me smile. *"You don't need to worry."*

"Anyway, as I was saying." Wyatt quickly brushed at each side of his mustache with a knuckle. *"We're going to field-test a few of our sensitives. The first will be pyrokinesis."*

Huh. Pyrokinesis. This had a serious chance to be completely awesome. I leaned forward in anticipation.

The camera shifted to a boy—at least twelve or thirteen from size alone—with hands shoved in his pockets. To his right, off in the distance, was a series of straw scarecrows, each one a bit further than the prior one.

"We found young Lawrence here after a firestorm down the road in the San Joaquin Valley," my grandfather said. *"He was curled up in a ball in the only part of a farm that hadn't been reduced to ash. It was quite the mess, with the charred lumps we later identified as cows in the blast area surrounding his still form. When we measured, the burned area formed a perfect circle around him. Apparently his mother had just died after being kicked in the face by one of those cows, and Lawrence here literally exploded into fire. For the record, he's seven years old."*

Big kid, I thought.

"Lawrence," Wyatt called, *"go ahead and start with the closest."*

The boy nodded, then snapped his fingers.

The first scarecrow, nearly thirty feet away, burst into flames. He then snapped again, and the same thing happened to the next scarecrow, which was a bit farther away. More snaps, more burned scarecrows. The last had to be at least a hundred yards off.

I'd seen these kinds of videos before. In fact when I went looking for information on ESP on the internet, I'd come across a number of videos showing how so-called psychics could game a video camera to make the viewer buy into the lie.

As if reading my thoughts, I heard my grandfather yell, *"Okay, Lawrence. Give us the grand finale. We want to make sure people believe you."*

Lawrence took a deep breath and held his hand out toward the flaming scarecrows. The fire instantly vanished from the dummies and appeared as a standing flame in his hand.

He let the fire crawl up his arm. Then over his entire body. Soon Lawrence resembled the Human Torch. He began juggling fireballs.

"Well done, Lawrence!"

There was applause in the background. Obviously other people were in attendance. The boy clapped his hands together, and the flames vanished.

Of course, so had his clothes.

"We need to develop some flame-retardant clothes," I heard my dad say. An aide of some sort ran out with a towel and covered the boy. Lawrence grinned like a fool and gave the camera a thumbs-up.

My mouth hung open as they escorted the boy off-camera. This film was made before any of Hollywood's modern tricks with computer-generated effects. What I'd just witnessed should have been impossible.

A thirty-something-year-old man wearing a faded-green Oakland Athletics baseball cap walked out to take his place. He was ridiculously tall, his dark hair sticking out from under his hat, and he sported a precise black mustache.

"*Terry here was found at a circus,*" Wyatt said. "*He was their floating objects magic act. Turns out his telekinesis was legitimate. Unfortunately, he is not able to levitate himself.*"

Terry appeared slightly bored, but behind him the still-smoldering scarecrows began to lift off the ground. They floated closer to him, then spun above his head faster and faster until they were a blur.

"*Okay, Terry,*" Wyatt shouted. "*Three... two... one... go!*"

The dummies froze in midair, then exploded in slow motion. At first I thought something was wrong with the reel. But my dad commented on the film, and his speech was normal speed. "*He's gained much more control these past few weeks.*"

The fragments of the straw dummies began slowly pulling back together again, this time into the shape of a smiley face in the air.

The crowd off-camera again clapped and laughed.

"*I think we're running out of film,*" said my dad's younger self. "*We maybe have a few more sec—*"

The film ended.

Never before had I been so riveted by a film of any kind. It was insane. I got back to my feet and immediately pulled off the reel and followed my trusty internet instructions on how to rewind it so I could watch it again. I was standing for the second watch-through, equally riveted. I watched it two more times, pausing it to study individual frames. By the time I finished, most of the day had passed, and it was almost dinner time.

It's one thing to know you have abilities most people don't.

It's amazing and terrifying at the same time. Suddenly a whole different world is visible, with new possibilities and infinitely more potential. But at the same time, with these new abilities came new horrors and a new pessimistic way of viewing things.

I'm typically an optimistic person, but after everything I'd gone through the past week, even I had trouble keeping things light and fluffy as I expected the other shoe to drop, ruining my good mood.

Part of me reacted to the two examples of power I had just witnessed and said, *Nice! I'm not alone. I should totally get together with these guys and make some real-life X-Men!* But the other, more cautious part of me, scoffed and said, *You think that hasn't already been tried? Why do you think there's this growing conflict? Why do you think people are dying in your stupid unimportant town? Control of these people, Jack. Control. Money. Power. Just like Alex said. Imagine how things are going in bigger cities.*

As cool as the powers were, it was hard not to imagine the destruction they could cause.

Of course, I wondered what kind of damage *I* could cause. As I'd found out with Barry, I could still read him like an open book. If things stayed this way, he would never be able to lie to me again. He'd never be able to hide his true intentions. I didn't like those implications. People needed to be able to keep things to themselves.

I supposed that was the whole purpose of Helix making the Leech in the first place. In their paranoia they wanted to make sure they had someone—or something—that could tell with absolute certainty if a person spoke the truth.

I shivered at the mental picture of the Leech's teeth. Could I end up like that creature? Ruled by the hunger?

The other question nagging at me was about this Project Sentinel the Insider had mentioned to me. I still hadn't been able to find anything in the journals about it, but what would happen if Helix or Whyte Genetics found out about me?

Or a more chilling thought: *What if they* already *knew?*

There was no way to prove it short of walking up to Alex's father, or to one of these Hounds saying, "Hey guys, you looking for me? Check out what I can do!" That didn't seem like the most intelligent decision.

But I couldn't get the doubt out of my head.

I picked up the other film reel. After how crazy the first one had been, my expectations for the second one were insanely high. It was labeled "Discoveries," after all. How could it not be awesome?

My stomach rumbled, so before starting the film, I heated up some leftover chicken my aunt left in the fridge. Dinner in hand, I returned to my impromptu theater, I set things up, and started the movie.

I had no idea what to expect. While the prospect of seeing different people showing off different powers seemed awesome, it was the unknown that tantalized me.

At first, that's exactly what it looked like I was getting. It opened with Terry, the guy with telekinesis, sitting reclined in a chair. He was wearing only loose shorts—far shorter than they had any reason to be—while a man in a white lab coat attached dozens of circular pads at various places on his body. Each pad had a thin wire running from it into a machine covered with hundreds of knobs and dozens of small screens.

I noticed Terry appeared a little older in this reel, and more worn. Dark circles rested under his eyes.

An unfamiliar voice narrated from off-screen. *"The day is November first, 1981. This is Doctor Arthur Gaines speaking and overseeing this trial."*

Arthur Gaines. The CEO of Helix... and Alex's father. Where was this going? I took a small bite of my chicken.

As Gaines narrated, his assistant pointed on the various pieces of equipment to what was being discussed.

"The purpose of this experiment is, first, to determine that a sensitive—whether minor, or major like Terry here—has a higher baseline brain wave pattern than a mundane, unimportant person."

The contempt for non-sensitives was clear in his voice, and from the assistant's flinch, I had a hunch he wasn't a sensitive.

"The top line on the far left of the machine shows the standard wave function of a normal human brain. I believe this specific reading was taken from my assistant here, Mr. Wells. Is that true, Daniel?"

The man in the white lab coat looked just to the side of the camera. *"Yes, Doctor."*

"I thought as much," Gaines said. *"Below Mr. Wells's line you will notice the current baseline for Terry."* The camera zoomed in, showing another wave function, the spikes on which peaked far higher. *"As you can see, Terry's base pattern has much higher peaks than that of my assistant's. In layman's terms, this is showing how much more active, and very likely, how much more* efficiently *our telekinetic uses his brain than the normal, boring, and average person. The results are not much different among other non-sensitives.*

"The next thing I want to show is the difference between a sensi-

tive's baseline, and when a sensitive uses their abilities." I leaned forward in my chair. *"Very well. Terry, I want you to lift the pencil from the front of my assistant's breast pocket. In three, two, one... go."*

Terry made no movement, but on cue, a yellow pencil smoothly drifted out of the assistant's pocket.

"As you can see from the active brain scan, the height of the peaks more than doubles when his ability is utilized. We recently tested this theory on several other subjects, and the results were nearly identical.

"My hypothesis," Gaines lectured, *"is that sensitives unlock a section of the brain allowing these abilities—telekinesis, pyrokinesis, mind-reading, shapeshifting, et cetera—to manifest. What triggers the development is still not known for certain. My personal theory is the phenomenon stems from trauma, and the mind's wonderful ability to adapt to trauma. So my next logical thought is, naturally, what if a subject who has already developed abilities is put through even more trauma? Are further developmental breakthroughs possible? Food for thought."*

Something about the way Gaines said "subjects" left me feeling dirty, like I had oil covering me. There was something sinister behind his words.

The film cut away from the scene and resumed from a different one outside a large window into a room.

In the room, the pyro-kid—though he wasn't much of a kid anymore—sat in a chair. He looked like he had one foot in the grave, and had a heavy bandage wrapped around the top of his head. Thin wires also seemed to be coming out from his skull. My stomach sank.

"The date is December twenty-fifth, 1981. Doctor Arthur Gaines

speaking and conducting the experiment. A full month has passed since we introduced a piece of our telekinetic's brain into the brain of Lawrence. The purpose of this experiment is to see if direct assimilation of tissue from another sensitive will cause manifestation of multiple powers.

"*Side note to the experiment,*" Gaines added. "*The telekinetic, Terry, did not survive the inverse procedure. Another telekinetic will need to be found.*"

I almost threw up the few bites of chicken I'd eaten. This was monstrous.

"*You'll notice inside the room is a table. On that table are two blocks of wood. First, Lawrence will light one of them on fire to show he retains his pyrokinetic ability.*"

Off to the right, barely in the field of view, stood the same assistant, though he looked somewhat ill and appeared to be enjoying his job far less than before. He reached over and hit a key on the wall where an intercom system was mounted.

"*Please light one of the blocks on fire, Lawrence.*"

A slight delay ensued before the block on the right became surrounded by fire. The fire appeared much weaker than it had in the first film reel.

"*Next,*" Gaines said, "*we're going to see if he can lift the other one with telekinesis.*"

The assistant keyed the intercom again and relayed the request. I waited for the cube to lift, much like I assumed Gaines did.

But it never moved.

The assistant shifted nervously, like something was coming that he wasn't looking forward to.

Inside the room, Lawrence's eyes were wide. Sweat poured off his face. His eyes pleaded.

Gaines' voice broke into the silence, hard and flat. "*It is worth noting the reason Lawrence is behind a window made of the same materials as an airliner window is because since his... procedure... his range has become significantly limited. In his current state, he cannot get upset and set us all on fire. So by having the subject behind the glass, it means that when we run thirty thousand volts of electricity through our subject, we stand less chance of an accident happening to ourselves.*

"*The viewer will recall my earlier hypothesis that additional trauma will induce an additional development of psychic abilities. Combined with a piece of another sensitive's brain grafted to his own, I feel strongly this will yield the results we want.*" His voice shifted, prideful at his train of thought. It made me want to shower and scrub myself clean. "*Wells,*" said Gaines, "*let's give Lawrence here a jolt of encouragement.*"

The guilt and grief shone plain on Wells's face as he reached to his left and flipped a switch. A slow whine of energy built up, then Lawrence's body rocked as, apparently, electricity was pumped into him through his brain.

I wanted to cover my mouth with both hands to hold in the scream and nausea. And try as I might, I couldn't tear my eyes away from the screen. Alex already wasn't a big fan of her father, but if she saw this she might actually murder him. And I wouldn't stand in her way.

The whine of electricity cut off, and Lawrence's body slumped down in the chair he was strapped to.

"*Mr. Wells,*" Gaines said. "*Please inform our subject we will continue this process for the next three hours unless he can develop telekinesis."*

With the command relayed through the intercom, Lawrence wept. It was hard to believe this was the same boy who had once commanded fire with ease.

"If we cannot make our plans work through breeding, then we will engineer them through experimentation," Gaines said. *"I will have my results."*

The film ended abruptly following his pronouncement.

I ran to the bathroom and heaved what little I'd eaten throughout film. And then I heaved some more. The rest of the chicken went into the garbage.

Should I call Alex and have her watch this? She would read my mind regardless, so the first time my thoughts went in this direction, she'd know what was up. But I couldn't talk about it right now. I needed time for the filth of what I'd watched to dull. Or maybe for me to grow desensitized.

Somehow I doubted I'd have that kind of time.

The medicine cabinet in the kitchen contained a bottle of sleep aids I had been prescribed for dealing with migraines. It didn't matter what time it was, I wanted to be knocked out *right now*. I popped one in my mouth, washing it down with a swallow of water.

Remote in hand, I sat on the couch flipping through the channels until I found a movie I didn't hate. Any movie, really. I found *Armageddon*. That would do. I'd seen it a hundred times and it was already half over, past the crappy love story part and into the space action.

I was passed out before it ended.

CHAPTER 21

Jack

The sleep aid only knocked me out for a few hours, and had the opposite intended effect of leaving me wide awake. I spent the rest of the night trying to forget the second video. It didn't work. To keep from freaking out, I read the journals and practiced walling off my mind. I could do it more quickly now, but I still wasn't convinced I had it right. The only person I could really test my technique on was Alex, and she'd looked like she was about to freak out the first time I showed her what I learned.

Every so often, I tried going to sleep. The dreams seemed like they would be a great escape, but I could never stay asleep long enough for the dreams to come. How was I supposed to learn anything if I couldn't be in my grandfather's memory?

Not getting anywhere frustrated me.

The only positive from my studying all night was a passage

from one of the other journals. I'd picked up the thinnest of the journals, and while thumbing through it, the words "record player" popped out. My dad had a huge collection of vinyl, older bands mixed with current stuff. What could my grandfather actually have to say about music?

Turns out, nothing, but his words were better than I could have expected.

I've put a lot of thought into the mechanism for my ability. Ever since returning from 'Nam, I've had the luxury of thinking things through without worrying about falling into a pit of pungi sticks or getting stabbed in the throat while sleeping. The question on my mind is "Why?" Not because I need to know. I don't. My ability saved my life in the jungles more times than I can count, so I don't have the slightest sliver of disbelief.

I reckon I've just got a curious mind.

It really started when I tried explaining my ability to Danny. Since he doesn't have the gift, he wanted to know what it was like.

Damned if I could give him a good answer. And that didn't sit right with me.

I spoke with a few other folks who have abilities in the same wheelhouse as me, and none of them had a good answer, either. Most didn't care. They aren't curious, and they don't have sons or daughters who look up to them.

Something about my grandfather's words brought a smile to my face. My mind could have been playing tricks on me, but I swear my ability let me feel a little of the love and pride Wyatt had for my dad. My dad was the same way with me. Always had been. I blinked away a tear, grateful these words helped wash away some of the disgust from the film.

I found my answer on accident, the journal continued. *I don't rightly know if it's the end-all, be-all answer. But for me, it was enough. And Danny-boy seemed to think it made sense. Which is good enough for me.*

Basically, my ability is like a record player needle on the vinyl of the world.

I'm not a music fella, but Danny is. What I am is a lover of history, and science fiction and fantasy novels.

I almost laughed. From pictures of Wyatt, I never would have guessed he was into that kind of stuff. I fell more on the side of movies, but Barry couldn't get enough of the stuff he called "speculative fiction." How I wished at that moment that I'd had a chance to get to know my grandfather. I think we would have gotten along.

In my reading a few years ago, I stumbled on a short story called "Time Shards" by a guy named Gregory Benford. The skinny on the story is it's about a guy trying to listen to conversations from ancient times based on sounds captured in the grooves on pottery. Well, I got interested in the ideas of the story, fell down a rabbit hole, and found an area of theoretical study called "Archaeoacoustics." Apparently that short story was based on some actual theories.

The stuff seems shaky at best, but then, so was ESP for a while. The idea is that sound can be captured by objects, and by running frequencies over them—pottery, walls, buildings—you can supposedly hear conversations from the past. The discipline goes deeper than that, but for my own purposes, it clicked.

Grooves on a piece of pottery that can emit sound? Sounds like a phonograph or vinyl to me.

And then I thought, "What happens when a person's psychic energy is released into objects?" Well, it gets recorded in them. The stronger the energy, the better the "recording." And me? I'm the needle that picks it up.

I ran it by Danny. His words were, "Yeah. I can dig it. That's pretty fantastic, Dad."

It ain't a perfect answer. But not all of them are.

If it worked for my boy, it's good enough for me.

Maybe I was admitting to some personal biases, but my grandfather's words resonated with me. The world captured people's psychic energy, and since I was attuned to that world now, I could see it. The sharper and higher quality the needle on a turntable, the clearer the music. My grandfather's papers had helped upgrade me as a needle, so to speak. And the more I practiced, the "sharper" I got.

He couldn't have known it, but my grandfather, even in death, was a perfect mentor.

I closed my eyes for a minute, letting Wyatt's words settle over me. Their comfort, while profound, couldn't completely banish the horrid images from that old Helix film.

My phone rang. Lying on my bed, I heard it buzzing on my

desk. I couldn't see the caller ID on its display, nor did I want to. A spike of anxiety shot through me. These days, every time someone called, bad things happened. I'd either end up at an old crime scene, robbing a building, or forced into explaining more than I wanted to in a conversation with Barry. Call me crazy, but none of those options sounded appealing.

I let my phone ring through to my voicemail.

Thank goodness, I thought in the following silence.

But it immediately rang again.

Nope. Not going to do it, I thought. *Let someone else get bugged this time.*

Voicemail again.

A third time, the phone buzzed.

"Come on!" I yelled as I pulled myself off the bed. I grabbed the phone and saw Alex's picture. I sighed, then hit the button to answer the call.

"What?"

"Why aren't you answering your phone?"

If I didn't know any better, I'd say she sounded a tad worried. Of course, she hid the emotion with anger.

"Please tell me you're calling with some boring normal news," I said. "You have some classwork to deliver to me. Or you accidentally got some extra fries and thought I'd be the perfect person to share them with."

"I don't share food," she said. *Of course not.* "I do actually have some schoolwork I was told to give you. But that's not why I'm calling."

Please don't let it be a murder. Please don't let it be a murder.

"Oh?"

"There was another murder last night. I need you."

Two sentences I wish had been separated, and the first never uttered.

"I don't know if I should go, Alex. Look what happened last time."

I heard a knock on the door downstairs.

"Seriously?" I asked. "Maybe I just won't answer the door."

Downstairs, the door opened. "Well hello there, Alex," my aunt said. Apparently she'd gotten home while I'd been lost in the journals all night or trying to get some rest. Then, "Jack! Alex is here for you."

I hung up, pulled on a pair of shoes, and walked downstairs. Sure enough, Alex had a stack of papers for me—an English assignment was on top. I also caught a glimpse of papers with information for a project from our Music Appreciation class. She handed them to me and put her phone back in her jacket. It was the same jacket she'd been wearing the day we'd been investigating Abby's home. I imagined her pistol hidden underneath. As I took the stack, I noticed the assignment was already filled in. I flipped through the other pages and saw they were filled in too. I peered a little closer.

"Why does it appear all my assignments are done ... and *in my own handwriting*?"

She had the decency to look a little embarrassed. "I figured you wouldn't want to deal with the work. It's mostly just busywork from the professors anyway. Last time I came by you were neck-deep in reading those journals... so I thought maybe I'd take care of all this for you."

This was unexpectedly awesome. I felt my eyebrows rise in surprise. That still didn't explain how the answers were in my handwriting.

"Don't ask," she said, reading my mind. "Plausible deniability."

Okay...

I blew out a breath. "Thanks. This must have taken you a while." I rubbed my eyes, and looked at the wall clock. It showed a time of 2:00pm. I'd spent all night, the morning, and part of the afternoon trying to sleep, or lost in Wyatt's journals. Time flies when your life is hell.

Alex shrugged uncomfortably. It was like she wasn't used to receiving compliments or something. "You *look* like hell," she said, reading my thoughts and responding to them. "While you were dealing with all that last night, I broke into the professors' offices. Getting all the answer keys took a little longer than I thought."

"Really?" A laugh burst out of me before I could control myself. "Aren't they going to notice?"

She appeared confused. "Door locks are no big deal. And the JC's security system is older than we are. Combined. I bypassed it in a few minutes, and I barely have any experience hacking. Give me a little credit. Though, I may have left a little surprise in Terrier's office. She might be going through some stuff, but how she treated you was a bridge too far for me."

"Well all right then. Wait. There've been some rumors about some pranks played on the professors, Ferris Bueller style. You wouldn't happen to know about those, would you?"

Alex smirked.

The laughter that erupted from me felt good. Real good. An easy comfort had formed between the two of us. My insecurities were all still there, but they didn't seem so brutal and obvious around her.

"So what did you leave for her this time?"

She shook her head again. "Remember, plausible deniability... but I once overheard a stray thought that she has a *terrible* fear of mice. Petty? Maybe. But so was the way she treated you. If she didn't have tenure the college would have fired her years ago for incompetence. She gave me a low score on a paper right at the beginning of the year. You know why? I wasn't 'feminist' enough for her."

I got another chuckle out of that. When the laughter faded, I decided to get back to the point of her visit.

"All right," I said. "There was another murder. Where are we headed?"

"All I have is an address." She pulled a sticky note from her back pocket. "I literally just heard about it on the way over."

"Where's the address?"

She glanced down at the sticky. "I was going to look it up on the way, but my phone was being stupid. Uh... 53 Juniper Street."

All my good humor vanished when she read the address. I was out the door and running toward Alex's car before I even realized I'd moved. Alex ran after me, having read my mind.

53 Juniper Street.

Barry's house.

CHAPTER 22

Alex

Over the last few days Jack had been through a lot. Alex recognized the fact, but it wasn't until this minute that she'd truly worried about him. It was hard to believe this was only Friday night, and everything had started last Sunday.

She'd read Jack's mind enough to know he was having trouble dealing with everything. Jack had experienced more horrible things lately than most people did in a lifetime. He was on the edge of depression, starting to become paranoid, and beginning to lose hope in ever finding his dad.

Yet he kept pushing forward. It was admirable. Likable. Maybe even... attractive? Alex knew plenty of people that couldn't even touch the level of determination Jack had recently displayed.

But this news might break him.

Don't let him be dead. Don't let him be dead. Don't let him be dead.

Over and over. The only thought in Jack's head. In Alex's experience, it was rare for a person to be so consumed with one thought such that all others were gone.

The Peters's residence—Barry's home—stood a few miles away from Jack's place. It only took five minutes to get there, but those minutes seemed to drag out into an eternity. Or maybe it was residual anxiety spilling over from Jack. Alex always worried about becoming too close to any person for that reason. Would she start thinking, and therefore feeling, like that person if she spent too much time with them? Would she start losing a bit of herself?

But she didn't need Jack's anxiety to feel bad; she felt terrible enough as it was. She'd gone over to Jack's home knowing she'd have to manipulate him a bit to get him out of there. The already completed assignments and class project had been the metaphorical carrot. Divulging the details of the prank hadn't been part of the plan, but a nice bonus. To see him laughing again made her feel good. Then uncomfortable. Was she getting too close?

Alex recognized her life had turned into a jumble of questions she didn't have answers to.

Like a *normal* person.

She hated it.

It made her want to shoot something.

But the moment when she read that address to Jack... well, things had gone poorly. He hadn't screamed out loud, but there had been plenty of screaming in his head. And the expression on his face left little to be interpreted.

Now, his hands were clenched together, knuckles pure white. His right leg bounced up and down anxiously, and his eyes stared straight ahead without focus.

She wanted to reach over and grab his hand. What that would accomplish was anyone's guess, but it seemed like the thing to do.

But she couldn't make herself do it. Her hands stayed firmly locked on the steering wheel of her Civic.

She turned right onto Juniper, and there, a few houses ahead and to the right, sat the Peters's residence. Police tape marked it off, just like the last house they'd searched. She pulled up to the curb rather than into the driveway. It would look less suspicious to the casual onlooker, and if they needed to escape they'd be able to get going quicker.

"Do you know who all was... killed?" Jack asked.

Those were the first words he'd spoken since getting in her car.

Alex shook her head. "I just heard there was a murder. The thing that caught my attention was the cause of death, or rather, the medical examiner's inability to figure out the exact cause of death. The police were gone by this afternoon."

He stared at the house, his face gray, and drew in a shaky breath. "Okay. Let's go in there."

"You want to wait a minute?" Alex asked. "It's fine if you want to."

Because it's not like they're going anywhere, Jack thought. The morbidity of the thought shocked Alex.

"No," he said, shaking his head. "What if we wait and some of the residue vanishes? We can't really afford that, can we?"

He forced a smile, trying so hard to be strong. He was thinking about... not letting *her* down.

Guilt threatened to crush her, but Alex gave him an encouraging nod.

"Hey, I don't have much information on this one." She got out of the car and walked to the front door, Jack only two steps behind her. She pulled on a pair of latex gloves like she had at the previous crime scene and handed another pair to Jack, then pulled out her lockpicks. "So, we need to be extra careful. I don't like walking in blind, but you're right. I don't think we can afford to wait." The lock clicked open for her with little effort.

She went in, pocketing the picks and unzipping her jacket. She wasn't going to wait for signs of trouble this time. She pulled her Sig P226 and attached the suppressor. She'd even brought three extra magazines instead of her customary one. No one ever survived a gunfight and thought, *Gee, I wish I hadn't brought all that extra ammunition.*

Her recent encounter with the Hound had left her with the shakes after talking with her father. Almost getting killed, and having Jack killed along with her only added to the fear. She didn't feel that emotion often, but wasn't fool enough to take it for personal weakness. Jack's dad had taught her that.

She'd be more prepared this time. And if there was nothing here, then she'd be ready for the *next* time.

Because there was always a next time.

She glanced over her shoulder and noticed Jack still hadn't stepped inside. The door gaped open, an easy sight for anyone that happened to be looking. She walked back and took his hand. It felt cold and shaky.

"You need to come in, Jack," she said, as encouragingly as possible. With a gentle tug she pulled him inside. This time she did manage to give his hand a little squeeze before releasing it to close the door behind them.

"I hate this," he whispered. She half-expected his thoughts to turn to fear and anxiety—and she wouldn't have blamed him if they did. Instead, the next thing he thought, then said, was, "We have to stop this. I'm so sick of people—innocent people—dying."

Jack

Alex gave me an odd look as the words left my mouth, but I meant them. This situation was so... terrible. So frustrating. So disgusting.

What had Abby and her family done to deserve their murder? Nothing. What had Barry's family done? Nothing.

They were just caught—like the rest of the town and all the *normal* people—in a crossfire they didn't even know existed.

"Barry came over and apologized," I said to no one, but I guess the words were directed at Alex. "He was such a mess. Thought he was going crazy."

"Most people's minds can't rationally deal with all the paranormal stuff out there," Alex said. "They don't know how to justify the explained with the unexplained. I'm honestly surprised you've been able to cope as well as you have. Insane asylums are full of people who see more than they're able to process."

"But Barry wasn't going insane," I said, not really

responding to Alex's words. "All he needed was for me to tell him he wasn't crazy. He just needed to be reassured."

She nodded. "He was in a good place when he left your house yesterday. His thoughts were calm. Whatever you said made a huge difference."

Her words made me feel a little better. "Maybe if... if..."

"Jack," she said softly. "Nothing you could have said or done would have stopped this from happening."

"So I should take comfort in that?" I asked. It felt wrong. "While I was trying to get some sleep and feeling sorry for myself because my life was *hard*, Barry was getting his soul sucked out through his ear."

"It isn't fair," she said. "But neither is it your fault. You can heap blame on yourself all day, but isn't that a similar thing to what you said you were just doing sitting on your bed?"

She had a point.

"Let's go see if we can find anything." I sighed. "Maybe something will give us a clue."

I looked around. The first thing I noticed—and felt—was the sparseness of the place. The feeling of emptiness. This wasn't the same atmosphere as in the Smith's home. That was a soulless feel brought on by what had happened. That feeling existed in Barry's home as well, but it was an undertone to the hollowness I felt. I hadn't been to Barry's place in a long time, I realized. It was so barren, and things had changed.

Paintings were missing from walls. The TV wasn't the forty-six-inch flat screen I was used to seeing. Instead it had been replaced by a squat, thick, twenty-something-inch. Even the kitchen table had been switched out, in favor of a cheap card table.

In the living room was a single recliner, the back facing me.

Spin it toward me, or walk around to look at it?

Either way it was like a horror movie.

I settled on walking around the recliner. A few steps took me to the front, and I was greeted with the dead image of Barry's dad. The image—all inky shades of purple—sprawled out in the chair as though he'd been sleeping. From his left ear spilled a stream I recognized as the psychic leftovers from his soul. It looked like the majority had been sucked out, then the remains had dripped down the side of his face, down his shoulder, and down the chair opposite the side I'd walked around.

Barry's dad had always been nice to me. Whenever my dad had a business meeting to attend to at night—and before I was old enough to watch over myself—I'd always been welcome here.

Now he was reduced to an afterimage of his corpse. I felt so empty staring down at him, like a hole had been carved out of my chest.

"Tell me what you see," Alex said.

I shut my eyes to blot out the image, but the vision of the body remained. "Just read my mind."

"No," she said. "Well, I am. Can't really help it. But I need you to focus. Talking will help that. I can't see what you see, and your thoughts are all over the place."

I opened my eyes and talked her through what I saw as best I could. I'm not gonna lie, I almost had to run outside and throw up. I *knew* Barry's dad. No matter how I looked at it, this was personal to me.

"Try to keep personal connections out of it," Alex said,

reading my mind. "I know it's hard, but sometimes you have to view people *not* as people."

Easier said than done.

I kept my eyes focused on Mr. Peters's chest—or the residue image of it anyway. If I looked at his face, it would be over.

"There aren't any scratches or anything."

"Good," Alex said. "The Leech came in at night, so it makes sense. He was probably dozing. Anything else?"

"No."

"I'll give you a minute to breathe, but then we need to go look at the other rooms."

"I know."

Breathe in. Breathe out. Breathe in. Breathe out. I turned away from the chair, trying to get the sight of the afterimage out of my head. Memories of Mr. Peters taking Barry and me camping, or out for ice cream, or even just sitting with us while we watched TV, haunted me.

Now he was just... gone.

It was time to go to Barry's room.

I walked down the hallway to the back room on the right, past the bathroom and his parent's master bedroom. Like in the front room, any adornment that wasn't a family picture had been removed. Barry's mom had a thing for lighthouses, and the hallway used to be her personal gallery of paintings and photos. They were all gone. Sold so the family could pay bills, maybe?

I hadn't seen this in Barry's memories. Maybe he hadn't realized—or bothered to notice—what was going on.

My hand strayed out and my finger trailed lightly on the wall. I must have run down this hallway thousands of times.

Barry and I had been friends forever. And our parents had been friends, too.

A quick glance in his parents' bedroom showed stacks of boxes. I stopped short and moved to the doorway. No psychic residue assailed me here, but the boxes were in the process of being filled. Moving boxes.

Barry hadn't said anything about moving. Even if he hadn't been killed, I would have lost him anyway—a macabre, but realistic realization. I could almost feel weights being piled on my shoulders. I didn't know why it hurt me right now to think about Barry moving, but it did.

No matter what I did, I kept on losing people.

Who would be next? Alex? She was really the only person I had left. A lonely feeling, that one.

"Don't worry about me," Alex said from behind me. "I'm not going anywhere."

Strangely, that helped a little.

I walked past the hall bathroom. The psychic image of Barry's mom was in the tub. Her image weaker than the one of Mr. Peters, already fading. I didn't go in there. Her image wouldn't be clothed, and she deserved some privacy and respect, especially in death. She'd been more of a mother to me these last few years than my own mother had been before abandoning us. She made the best cinnamon rolls.

The last room was Barry's. How many nights had I stayed here? The ever-shrinking optimist in me was saying he could still be alive. The pessimist knew the reality of things.

Barry's residue image lay on his back, arm hanging off the bed like he'd collapsed there and gone to sleep. But he hadn't gone to sleep. He'd been killed, then left on the bed like a rag doll. His wound was clearly visible, with psychic energy pooling around his head.

My best friend, dead in front of me. It was worse for me than for anyone who actually saw the body, or at least I imagine that was the case. The police saw a body with no marks. The cause of death mysterious. They'd point to a poison, or breathing in too much gas. Natural causes or something.

They didn't have to see things the way I did.

I shoved part of a closed fist into my mouth and bit down to keep from screaming, choking back anger and despair. My dad going missing was harsh, but even the pessimist in me couldn't discount he may still be alive. But Barry? He was gone. Forever.

I scanned the room, then walked from place to place, picking up weird odds and ends that wouldn't have meant a thing to anyone but me. A doodle here, ticket stub there. His favorite book, *Dune*, on the nightstand—brand-new, but only because he'd worn out at least two other copies. He'd supposedly been saving up for the past year so he'd have the money for a rare, signed copy. I opened the drawer of the nightstand and found the beat-up paperback copy he'd read previous to the new one. A dark purple residue stained it, so I reached down and picked it up. I didn't get the sense of anything strong, just the tiniest hint of boyhood glee. I stuck the copy in my jacket pocket.

Posters of various rock bands he'd wanted to go see live covered the walls. Foo Fighters. U2. Rise Against. I used to give him a hard time about it. *Who does rock band posters, man?* I'd say. *Isn't that reserved for girls? At least get some supermodel posters or something...*

I stood right next to his bed. His afterimage was deep purple and strong. This had been bad for him. Worse than for his parents. They'd gone quietly. Not Barry. He'd been scared out of his mind.

Why is Helix letting this happen? I wondered. *Why are they just letting the Leech kill people in the town?*

"I don't know," Alex said, answering my thoughts. "I've been getting the run-around on that topic."

I gazed back at Barry's image, hearing Alex, but not truly listening to her.

He was my best friend, and... I had to know.

Before Alex could say anything, I reached down and put my palm on the afterimage right where the wound was...

... and I saw what he saw.

It was similar to grandfather's memory-dreams, but more hazy and ethereal. The emotions and thoughts were stronger, though, like when I had stood in the Leech's steps.

The vision sucked me in, and Barry, with me invisibly in tow, reached for his new copy of *Dune*. His parents were asleep, so he had all the time in the world to read. He'd helped them pack since getting home from my place, and he couldn't decide when to tell me they were moving. He'd just found out himself, and the thought ate him up inside.

This was brutal.

A noise sounded from down the hall, loud enough to be heard over his dad's television. Barry assumed the sound was his dad popping out the footrest on the recliner. I knew better, but there was nothing I could do about it. I wanted to scream at Barry to shut his door, lock it, and shove his desk chair under the doorknob.

But I couldn't. This had all already happened.

The closest equivalent I could come up with was when I would watch a horror movie, knowing something was about to happen. With most films, I knew the tropes, and the filmmakers usually telegraphed the approaching horror. Occasionally, for fun, I would even yell at the actors not to go down that hallway or into that forest. But they don't listen. They can't.

They're doomed no matter what.

I doubted I'd ever be able to watch a horror film the same way again.

The noise came again, and Barry set down his book, feeling uneasy. He figured he was just feeling leftover paranoia from his experience with me. He listened for a long moment then reached to pick up his book again.

He heard the bathroom door down the hall opening, then the splash of bathwater. Had his dad gone in the bathroom while his mom was bathing? He didn't want to think about that. Wherever they were moving to, he knew his first priority would be moving out of the house into a dorm or apartment. If he even could. His parents might need him at home, working to keep them all afloat.

But his feeling of unease returned, stronger now due to a rising sense of animalistic panic. Something in the home had changed at a deeper level. The atmosphere felt... wrong.

He mulled the choice over in his mind. He could either stay here and hope he was just feeling some paranoia, or he could go see if everything was okay.

"You guys okay?" he yelled. *"You better not be doing anything freaky in there."*

No response.

He got up from his bed, and to me it was like he was swimming in a purple haze. His heart hammered, and he felt sweat beading on his forehead. Barry took a hesitant step toward the door...and heard an ever-so-slight creak of hardwood from just outside.

"Dad?" he squeaked.

In my head I begged and pleaded for Barry to run.

A figure stepped into the doorway, and for a moment Barry thought a kid had broken into their house. Then the "kid" opened its mouth and bared a set of teeth that could have been transplanted from a shark.

Barry screamed, and I screamed with him. His terror swirled around me and engulfed me. His fear and panic so intense they overrode my sanity.

It got worse from there.

Over the Leech's stained teeth another set appeared, these a writhing black and purple. They were *psychic teeth*. I didn't know if Barry could see them or not, but it didn't really matter. All I felt was Barry's pure fear, and I added to it with my own. I knew what those teeth—both physical and psychic—were going to do.

Barry tried to turn and run, but the monster raised its hands, and its aura flowed from them like purple writhing tentacles, reaching out to grab Barry by the head. Even as the terror hammered me, I couldn't help but wonder how the Leech was doing it. How was he extending his aura like that? It seemed so easy. So natural. More psychic tentacles appeared, thinner, undulating forward with lazy menace. They stabbed into Barry's aura, piercing his soul.

Barry screamed again, this time confused because he couldn't see what held him in place.

Then the emotional feedback started.

The Leech took a deep breath and *tasted* the fear radiating from Barry. Barry's aura pulsed rapidly like a scared rabbit's heart. Immediately I felt my friend growing weaker, and I sensed his aura being drained by the Leech's psychic tendrils. The Leech drank it in, and with it, Barry's fear. My earlier suspicions were horribly confirmed. This was an enjoyable experience for the Leech.

Worse, *Barry* felt the enjoyment the monster was having, as did I. Barry pissed his pants and sobbed uncontrollably. He wanted to shout for his mom, but couldn't. His swirl of emotions consumed me, and for a moment I thought I would drown to death in it. When I finally surfaced, I saw more of the memory.

The Leech moved up close and personal, its otherworldly tentacles slowly turning Barry's head so the creature could clamp down those psychic teeth around the ear. The last thing I saw were those teeth flexing out like a hundred sharp, little appendages.

And then pure pain, white-hot, like dozens of knives shoved slowly into my head.

I thought Barry had screamed before. I thought *I* had screamed before.

That was *nothing* compared to this.

This was the sum-total of every other pain I'd ever experienced *or even imagined* all rolled up into one, then magnified a thousand times.

That was the last thing I saw. My last memory of Barry.

When my vision cleared, I was staring up into Alex's face. Her expression was panicked, and there was even a little redness in her eyes.

"Jack! Jack! Can you hear me? Snap out of it, Jack!"

I took in a deep, ragged breath, which prompted a relieved sigh from her.

"You scared the hell out of me, Jack! I thought you weren't going to see if that sort of thing worked? Are you okay?"

And suddenly, everything was clear as day. I knew right then I liked Alex as more than a friend. More than just the person I relied on because I didn't have anyone else. Her face paled, and I guessed she had just read those thoughts. But I didn't really care.

Instead of doing anything impressive, tears blurred my eyes and spilled down my cheeks. I couldn't stop them, no matter how hard I tried.

Alex

Alex did the only thing she could think of: she pulled Jack into a hug.

She hadn't trained for this sort of thing, and she couldn't even remember the last time she had hugged anyone. Had she *ever* hugged her father? Doubtful. Her mother? A faint memory lingered in the back of her mind, from when she had been just a little girl. Her mother sweeping her up into a consoling hug after she'd fallen off of a bike.

That was also one of her only memories of reading a person's mind who was legitimately concerned for her out of love rather than responsibility.

Until now. With Jack.

Alex tried to hug Jack the same way her mother had hugged her. It was awkward, and she didn't think she was doing any good until he clutched back at her.

Her father had always told her crying was weakness, especially when others could see you doing it. It let them see into your heart and mind. And of course that wasn't acceptable. That was a right reserved for actual mind readers like them. Alex had embraced this school of thought. Lived by it. But now, as Jack sobbed into her shoulder, and she read the completely raw thoughts of sadness he experienced, she wondered if she had been wrong this whole time. Had she cheated herself?

In Alex's opinion, people were generally scum. Not just scum, but *lying* scum. Except... sometimes people were good. It didn't happen often, but every now and then she would find one. Jack's dad had been one, and the more time she spent around Jack, the more she was sure he was cast from the same mold.

And she thought she had lost him.

When Jack reached down and put his hand on the bed to see, Alex hadn't been able to see anything, but from reading his mind she could sense he was seeing the psychic residue of his friend's corpse.

Jack had only held his hand there for a few moments when she had been flooded with two sets of thoughts projecting from his head. Two sets of thoughts... and two sets of screams. They were muddled, but she remembered the flavor of Barry's mind from her earlier run-ins with him. Both the voices filled her mind, frenzied, and their volume increased by the second.

She'd lifted her hands to cover her ears as the two screams rose to piercing levels.

It was the first time she had ever wanted to *stop* hearing the thoughts around her.

Hearing other people's thoughts was like breathing, completely natural. Essential, even. But this had been like being stabbed through both eyes simultaneously.

Her brain had felt like it might explode from the mounting pressure. She wanted to claw at her ears to make it all stop. Then it got worse as a third, more alien flow of thoughts piggy-backed on the other two. The Leech's. They were barely intelligible, but carried an inherent impression of hunger and delight at the suffering and fear in Barry's mind. The thoughts came more as pictures. Gut-wrenching pictures of Barry in horrible pain were followed by the image of psychic teeth sinking into the boy's psychic energy. Those teeth ripped into Barry like a wolf tearing into a corpse, except the teeth seemed alive. The images came from two places at once: from Jack's mind and the alien vision of the Leech. The combination of thoughts and feelings and images formed a disjointed nightmare.

Then, without warning, all the sound cut out. Alex was left with ringing in her ears. No, not in her ears, but in her *mind*.

Once upon a time, Alex's father, in one of his moments of "brilliance," had thought it a good idea to make her feel the effects of a flash-bang grenade. The concussion and light flash had been enough to bring her to her knees. She'd been completely disoriented for a few minutes, and it took another fifteen to feel totally fine again. Through it all, she hadn't been able to hear anything with either her ears *or* her mind.

The psychic concussion, brought on by reading the tortured

thoughts of Jack, Barry, and the Leech all at once, was on par with that grenade.

She shook her head attempting to clear the disorientation, and after a few minutes her senses had begun returning. She found herself lying on the floor, having collapsed at some point during the experience. Jack was on the floor beside her, the position of his body and awkward angles of his legs and arms made him look like a puppet who'd had his strings cut.

She couldn't hear his thoughts.

Was that because she was still screwed up from the effects of the psychic vision?

Or because Jack was gone?

She stared down at him for what seemed like an eternity. She checked his breathing, but couldn't focus enough to get a pulse. She'd talked herself into believing his breathing was so shallow she couldn't see or feel it in her current state.

Her eyes burned from tears she forced herself not to shed.

Whispers began floating into her mind, louder and louder until they were at the volume she was used to. She realized she was shouting at Jack, asking him if he was okay. Then he'd opened his eyes, and she'd never felt relief so strong in her life.

Crystal clear, focused and strong, came his thoughts—about her—as he gazed up at her. Then he had dissolved into tears and pain as the reality of his friend's death crushed him.

Alex held him for a long time, there on the floor of his dead friend's bedroom. Most people their age worried about what clothes to wear the next day, their jobs, or money. She and Jack worried about people dying, friends and strangers alike. They worried about a world full of crazy things that would drive most people to insanity.

After a time, Jack calmed down and gently pushed away from her. He gave her an embarrassed smile and got to his feet. After he took a series of deep breaths, he seemed almost calm. He didn't say anything about his earlier thoughts, and his mind focused on what he'd witnessed in the vision.

Alex felt oddly... disappointed... he wasn't thinking of her. Then she felt ashamed. *How can I be so self-absorbed at a time like this?*

"I couldn't have stopped it," he finally said. "It was just bad luck. Or maybe the Leech was drawn here by the hopelessness Barry's family felt. I don't know. Regardless, even if I had been here, I don't know what I would have done against that thing. I feel like my insides have been cut out of me with a dull knife."

"I know," Alex said. He needed to talk it through. "So what are you going to do?"

"I'm done sitting around." She could sense the anger in his thoughts. The determination. "We need to find this thing. I can't let it kill anyone else. I can't lose anyone else, and I don't want anyone to feel what I'm feeling."

"What about finding your dad?" Alex asked, and immediately wished she could take the question back.

Instead of freaking out, Jack said, "If—*when*—I find him, I don't think I could face him if I let this Leech run around killing people. I can't face anyone—not him, and especially not *you*— if I don't try my best to stop it."

Alex found herself nodding along with his words. It was a start.

CHAPTER 23

Jack

I was beginning to think I'd made a terrible mistake.

The gun seemed to weigh more than it should, and I was extremely nervous. Alex said it was her favorite pistol: a Sig ... something... blah blah... whatever. The gun metal was dark, but I could swear I saw the psychic purple tint to it. I filed the detail away.

The morning after the craziness at Barry's house, Alex drove us twenty miles east of Calm Waters along an old service road. There were hardly any trees out here, and even fewer animals or tourists.

Shooting guns. What a terrible idea. Even worse—this had been *my* idea. Definitely not how I normally spent my Saturday mornings.

"It's okay to be anxious," she said. "It happens to most

people when they shoot for the first time. Honestly, I'm a little surprised you haven't shot before. Your dad was one of the better shots around. We used to have competitions in the range under Helix."

"Who would win?" I asked, trying to keep my mind off the fact I held something that could kill someone.

She let out a quick laugh. "Me, of course. Well, about eighty percent of the time. So are you going to shoot that thing or what?"

I was pretty sure she was the worst instructor ever.

"Probably," she said after reading my mind. "Doesn't change the fact you asked to be taught how to shoot. Point the gun at the can over there." She pointed at a Coke can sitting on a stump. "Line up the sights like I told you and pull the trigger."

I straightened my right arm, gun in hand, and brought my left up to steady my aim. I leaned forward slightly.

"A tad more," Alex said. "The lean will help your body absorb some of the recoil. Put your feet out a bit wider to make your base steady. Good. Not don't straighten your arms quite so much. There you go. Shoot when ready."

After a few breaths to try and calm my nerves, I aimed as best I knew how, and pulled the trigger. At first I thought I did it wrong, because nothing happened. Maybe the safety was on. It seemed like I kept pulling the trigger back further and further, yet the gun wasn't going off—

The gun roared and bucked in my hand, and the bark of a tree trunk three feet to the right of the can exploded outward. It was loud even through the ear protection Alex had insisted I wear.

"Okay, now do it again," Alex said, leaning in by my ear.

My actions were far less sure this time around. Partly due to adrenaline and also with the knowledge of what the kick felt like and how the roar sounded.

"Uh... why don't we use that silencer-thing you used before?" I asked. Maybe that would help a little bit.

"You need to get used to the sound. Hardly anyone will be using suppressors when they're shooting around you or *at* you because the government, in all their infinite ineptness, thinks suppressors are a public safety hazard. Idiots. Though the suppressor would save you some hearing loss, I suppose. That's the reason I like them and use them."

"So I *can* use the silencer?"

"No. Shoot the can."

I let out a breath, disappointed, then aimed again and squeezed the trigger. I figured I should be prepared this time for a long pull on the trig—

The pistol roared again and jumped. I didn't even see where the bullet struck this time, but the soda can still stood there, mocking me.

"Sorry, I kinda forgot to mention the trigger pull," Alex said. I was pretty sure she was snickering behind my back. "The first pull is a lot longer than the subsequent ones."

Aiming again, I squeezed and saw the bullet hit right below the can on the stump. Feeling better, I shot again and was rewarded with the Coke can jumping off the stump.

Alex had me set the gun down on a TV tray she produced from the trunk of her car while she placed three more empty cans on the stump. She also set up a metal target stand that held a large piece of cardboard on it, onto which she'd spray-glued a target.

"Okay," she said with a grin, "time to go through a pile of ammunition."

"Isn't there a smaller gun I can start with?" I asked. "You know, one that kicks less?"

"The size of the gun isn't the issue. In fact, the smaller the gun, the snappier it is. Girls my size always get recommended tiny 'girl' guns, but they're harder to deal with. For you, you just need to grip the gun harder with your off hand. Don't turtle. Don't completely straighten those arms. You need the recoil to get absorbed rather than fighting against it."

"Why not shoot a smaller bullet? Wouldn't that help? In the movies, all the assassins say they use .22s."

".22s don't have stopping power against most supernatural creatures running around out there. What's the point of shooting at something if you can't stop it completely?"

"Uh... there isn't one?"

"Exactly." She slapped me on the back. "See, you're learning already."

She directed me to replace my ear and eye protection, then motioned to the cans. "I want you to shoot until you knock off all three cans, then fire at the paper target. When you get there I want you to aim for the center of the target where you see the circle with a '10' in it."

I nodded my understanding and hoped I didn't appear too shaky.

It took me six more shots to knock off the cans. This was a lot harder than I'd imagined it would be when I asked for some lessons. I knew I wouldn't always be able to rely on the psychic abilities I was developing, and though I had the knife Alex had given me a few days ago, I also wanted to be passable with a gun. Not that I looked forward to the idea of shooting anyone or anything, but I was done being underprepared.

But why was this so difficult? I was aiming pretty good... or so I thought.

"Because you're anticipating the noise and the recoil," Alex said in my ear. "Block it out. It doesn't matter. It's like the beep on the microwave. It only serves to tell you the action has been completed."

The noise didn't matter. The kick didn't matter. Just accept that they're going to happen. It made sense. "All that matters is the aim and the trigger?"

"For now, yes," she said.

I fired twice, one hitting the edge of the center circle of the target, and one the ring outside of that one. The gun's slide locked back.

"Nice!" Alex pointed to the button that made the magazine —a magazine, not a clip; she'd been adamant about that— slide out. I shoved another one in and went right back to firing.

When I focused on aiming down the barrel and almost letting the gun shoot itself, I seemed to do better. I kept my grip tight and shoulders down. Soon I hit the target with every shot, and the "spread" was becoming more and more grouped.

"You're doing really well, Jack," Alex said. "Put the gun down, and I'll go move the target back a little bit. Five to ten yards is where a majority of your shooting will take place, but I'd like to make sure you can hit from a bit further away."

Once she was back, I loaded a fresh magazine in her pistol and took to firing again. My grouping wasn't as close, but I still hit the target more often than I expected. Alex changed the target once, then twice. I continued shooting, and she continued loading empty magazines for me.

When I reached down for another magazine and discovered there weren't any, I set the gun down and looked back at Alex. She gave me a thumbs-up.

I wondered how well she could shoot.

Alex's eyebrows raised a fraction, and she waved at me to bring the gun back to her.

She stood a good ten feet behind where I'd originally shot from. After handing over the gun, she took a magazine from a belt she wore and walked me back several dozen yards further away, and waved me behind her. "Do you see the upper portion of the outer ring? Where you see the '5'?"

I squinted downrange and was barely able to make out what she was talking about. "Yeah," I replied. None of my shots had hit there thankfully.

"Okay. Right on the number."

Alex let out a quick breath, brought up the gun, and rapidly pulled the trigger twice. When she holstered her pistol and walked toward the target, I followed, curious how she'd done.

She pulled the target down and pulled a dime from her pants pocket. There were two connecting bullet holes right where she'd said she would put them, and they both could be covered by her dime.

Nodding with satisfaction, she pulled her ear protection down around her neck. I did the same as she started talking.

"One of the benefits of being part of a rich company is a virtually unlimited ammunition budget. I practice a lot, and I'm better than most other people. Not just with pistols, but with shotguns and rifles too. Since I turned ten, I've shot at least two hundred rounds of ammunition every day. Sometimes that takes an hour, or sometimes only a few minutes. Depends on the drills I'm running.

"Some girls do cheerleading and dress shopping," she said with a dazzling smile. "I shoot stuff."

There was something undeniably sexy about it all. Maybe cheerleaders were overrated. Mostly.

She laughed at my thought, but blushed a little as well.

"The unfortunate thing is I can't just take you out shooting whenever I want," Alex said as she took down the target stand. "I had to pull some strings at work to take this much ammo offsite. Helix has strict inventory controls. I'll do this as often as I can, though. If you want."

My hand was numb from the shooting, and the reek of gunpowder burned my nose. My hands shook, not from adrenaline, but from using muscles I didn't even know existed. Even so, I still had about a dozen reasons to say yes. Some of them were rational. Some... not so much.

"I'd love to."

"Awesome," she said with another smile.

I was helping her load everything into her car when I felt my phone buzz in my pocket. She waved at me to take it while she set about cleaning up the shell casings with a dirty broom and dustpan. I had the feeling this wasn't the first time she'd snuck off to shoot out in the woods.

I suppose I really shouldn't have been expecting anything

different. My number of contacts had shrunken significantly over the past week. The blank caller ID was the give-away.

"How was your morning shooting session, Mr. Bishop?" the Insider asked. *"It's my understanding that she is* quite *the excellent shot. I have always wondered if that translated into being an excellent teacher. Tell me, does it?"*

CHAPTER 24

Jack

How had he known our plans? I hadn't even fully realized what we were doing until we were almost here.

"Alex is a great teacher," I said.

Alex stiffened, dropped her broom and pan, and came over and put her face right next to mine to try and listen in on the conversation. *Very* close to mine. My mouth was suddenly dry. She shot me an annoyed look before turning her attention back to the phone.

"I'm glad to hear it." The Insider sounded like he was in an amazing mood. *"I was also heartened to discover your psychic abilities have been progressing. Tell me, have you been able to completely shut out another person's attempts to enter your mind yet?"*

Such an awkward question. He knew the only person I could attempt that with was Alex.

"I haven't really attempted it," I said. "Been a bit busy with murders and the whole not-getting-killed thing."

"*You disappoint me, Mr. Bishop,*" he sounded far less pleased than before. "*I suppose there is nothing for it. It is my job to know everything about everything. Did you know that?*"

"I don't know much of anything about you," I retorted.

"*Well, I suppose that is true. And guess what?*"

"What?"

"*I don't care,*" he said, his voice flat. "*I risk everything by calling you. So when I do, I expect a little more respect than you are showing. Or have you forgotten that most of your knowledge—which I certainly hope has been increasing by the day—is due to my help? That said...I think it is time for us to meet.*"

"Why?" Alex blurted.

"*Ah. Hello, Miss Courtney. I should have assumed you would be listening in. Though, a man in my position should never assume. We need to meet,*" the Insider continued, "*because the game has changed. Things have been put into motion that require direct intervention on my part.*"

The game had changed? "What's changed?" I asked.

"*Simply put, Mr. Bishop,*" came a tired reply, "*everything. I have new information about you, your father, Helix, and Whyte Genetics. The stakes are now much higher than they were before, and keeping you in the dark would be stupid of me. So I can either be a walking cliché, and tell you 'there isn't time' to properly educate you on your now-dire situation. Or I can just tell you what you need to know in the hope it will give us all a better shot at living.*"

My dad? My heart instantly began hammering in my chest. I wanted this new information *now*.

"Why can't you just tell me over the phone?"

"*Because I'm going over on my minutes for the month!*" Sarcasm dripped from his voice. Then I heard a deep breath. "*Seriously, what happened to the day when a kid would just do what an adult requested? Is it too much to ask that you trust me?*"

He was really starting to piss me off. "I'm not a kid. And I'm a little short on trust these days," I said, my voice getting louder with each word. "Considering I psychically experienced my best friend's murder, I think I'm entitled to ask *any question I want!*"

My words echoed off the trees around us—and earned me an approving nod from Alex.

"*Fair enough, Mr. Bishop. I can't discuss it over the phone for several reasons. Mainly my paranoia. I suspect people are always listening in on my conversations, no matter how careful I am. In person, I can somewhat limit the number of ways I can be eavesdropped on. What I have learned is far too much, and too detailed, to only discuss verbally. I've prepared physical documents for you, and I always deliver things in person. Besides... I feel it is time to get your measure, face-to-face.*"

"If you're worried people are intercepting your phone transmissions," Alex said, "then now there is the potential scenario those same people know you are going to be delivering us something."

Us. I liked the sound of that.

"*There's no way around it, Miss Courtney,*" the Insider responded. "*No matter what solution I reach for, the consequences are equally damning for all of us.*"

"Where do you want to meet?" I asked. We could sit here all day going back-and-forth. If things were really as bad as he insinuated, then we needed to get this ball rolling. I had things I needed to prepare.

"I am delighted *you are willing to give me the benefit of the doubt,"* the Insider said. *"The best place is somewhere populated with a bunch of civilians. Preferably somewhere loud, but where you know as many of the people as possible. Calm Waters is limited on these types of places, but I'm sure if we take a moment—"*

"I know a perfect place," I cut him off. I turned my head and raised an eyebrow at Alex.

"You've *got* to be kidding me," she said, eyes wide. "No way. Not a chance."

"If you two are done with your cute, silent conversations," the Insider said, *"I'd love to hear your supposedly 'perfect' place."*

I smiled and spoke into the phone. "Tonight is Calm Waters High's Homecoming Dance."

CHAPTER 25

Jack

After outlining the extent of my plan to the Insider—meeting at the dance was about as detailed as the plan got—Alex dropped me off and rushed off to "go shopping." She might have been the toughest girl I'd ever met or even heard of, but she was still a girl.

"I don't like or support the stupid tradition of new college students going back to our old high school's Homecoming. But if I have to go, girls get new dresses for dances, Jack," she had said. *"It's practically the only rule we all try to follow."*

My aunt Martha was out running errands, claiming she'd fallen woefully behind on everything. I'd grown used to her quiet presence, but I needed a moment to myself. I was tired. Exhausted, really. I went upstairs to get some sleep.

Yet the moment I got to my room I got distracted by Barry's copy of *Dune*. It sat on my bed where I'd left it the night before.

The purple residue still covered it. In the aftermath of Barry's death, and mixed with some of the stuff I'd read in my grandfather's journals over the last couple days, the earlier passages I'd read had solidified in my mind. The more attached a person was to *something*, the more likely a permanent psychic connection would be formed. I thought back to the psychic residue on Alex's favorite gun and on Wyatt's journals. If the strong emotions of fear and dread could be recorded on the world, then logic dictated love and joy could as well.

I'll make this right, Barry, I thought as I looked at that battered and well-loved book. *I promise.*

Reverently I set the book back down.

I wanted to read more from my grandfather's journals. I wanted to see if there were any more ESP tricks I could learn. It was pretty clear from what I'd read—and from the videos I didn't ever want to watch again—that unless I let myself get experimented on, I'd be limited to the power I had.

The videos...

I hadn't really thought about them since first watching them. All the chaos had distracted me. I wouldn't learn anything more from rewatching them, but that didn't mean there weren't ways to learn more about what I *could* already do.

It was a good idea.

It was a great idea.

But I had barely slept in two days. I lay down on my bed, and before I knew it, I was asleep.

Relief. I was back in the dream. Strangely, it had become a source of comfort to me.

I saw the old-time sign again, and went through all the same motions of stalking the Leech from within my grandfather's body in his memory.

I'd circled around the question long enough, probably worried about the potential answers. Why did I experience Wyatt's memory? And why *this* memory?

Was this the only one I'd ever see, or was there more behind the curtain? And what would happen when I got to the end of the memory? This Leech was obviously the same Leech as the one terrorizing the town. It seemed too convenient for me to be witnessing a memory related to the very thing plaguing the town right now.

So was it actually a coincidence?

Maybe the Insider's paranoia had rubbed off on me, but coincidences didn't seem likely to me anymore.

I chased after the Leech again after it jumped me. This was where I'd been kicked out of the dream last time. I followed it further into the woods, using the blood trail and the psychic residue of the creature's footprints as an easy guide.

My grandfather didn't worry about tracking the monster. He worried about what to do when he caught it. The people at Helix—Gaines, specifically—had ordered him to take it alive.

Though, now he wondered if, maybe, that order would get conveniently forgotten.

I knew that was a pointless thought. It wasn't going to happen.

The trail went on forever. Wyatt moved on pure adrenaline and willpower. He knew he had a concussion, and his left arm

STEVE DIAMOND

hurt far more than it should. Was it broken? He pushed the thoughts and pains away, his mind singularly focused on finding the Leech.

The forest opened up about a hundred yards ahead. A cabin stood barely visible in the moonlight, and the monster's tracks led to it.

Gun leveled—though it wavered due to the blow to the head—Wyatt took those last hundred yards with extreme caution. No twigs crunched under his boots, and he kept his breathing low and quiet. He paused to lean against a tree for a few minutes, hoping to regain his wits. Didn't work, but he went on anyway.

How could I *not* admire him?

On the flip side of that admiration, this was usually the part in the movies where things went real bad for the guy who doesn't call for backup.

Broken shingles and shattered windows made a mess of the cabin. Around it hung the stench of decay, the source being a heap of corpses near the front door, stacked like a grotesque collection of firewood. They were both human and animal.

The front door to the cabin stood partially open, blocked from closing by a bloody leg of a corpse. My grandfather circled to his left, gun steadier than it had been a short time ago, his adrenaline pushing away the fog. When he came into full view of the open door, I saw the Leech sitting in the doorway, slumped against the frame. I couldn't tell if it still breathed.

Wyatt's aim steadied, and his finger tightened on the trigger of his revolver.

The choice weighed on him. Shoot it and call it a day, or render it completely unconscious and drag it back to his truck?

His finger tightened a fraction more.

Then let off completely.

I'm not a murderer, he thought.

He walked up slowly, gun still trained on the creature just in case.

When he was standing right over it, the Leech lunged, psychic tendrils exploding out from it like I'd seen in the vision of Barry's death. They tried latching on to my grandfather, but his aura flared outward into a bubble, stopping them. I felt Wyatt—weak from blood loss and mild concussion—willing himself to stay upright, desperate to keep those psychic tentacles from touching him. Even now he forced himself to not pull the trigger on his gun. He was a good man. It was impossible not to feel a little humbled.

He forced himself to take a step closer. Then another. The Leech tried to move, but it was too feeble now. My grandfather swung his gun like a club with all his strength, hitting it with a *thud* in the side of the head.

The monster collapsed, unconscious.

Wyatt let out a deep breath, cursed himself for not shooting the Leech in the face, and pulled some twine from his pocket to tie the creature's hands and feet.

This time the memory didn't end abruptly like it had before.

It faded out like a song, everything losing clarity until gone.

CHAPTER 26

Jack

My eyes snapped open. I yanked my phone out of my pocket to check the time. 2:00 PM. I'd only been asleep for an hour and a half.

It was enough to give me an idea.

If the Leech had used that cabin in the past, then why wouldn't it go back there? It seemed reasonable enough. Well, as reasonable as could be expected for a monster.

The Leech was almost an animal now, living on instinct and driven by hunger. A quick internet search didn't find any record of any cabin in that area of the forest. But I knew it was there.

I checked my phone every three minutes to make sure I hadn't missed a call or text from Alex. *Where is she?*

Another thought from the dream spun around in my head. That pile of corpses at the front of the cabin. That was a lot of murders to cover up. If that many people had vanished, wouldn't the FBI have gotten involved? Wouldn't it be part of at least some sort of urban legend around Calm Waters?

It also suggested the Leech needed to feed on far more than the few people he'd recently taken here in the town to survive. Had he taken more than I knew about?

So where were all the reports of missing victims? The earlier TV news report about missing animals took on a different light—but from my glimpses into the Leech's twisted mind, I was left with the impression it needed humans after a certain point.

After working the problem in mind, I did have one idea on how to track the monster. That sign I always saw at the start of the memory could give me a good idea where to start. From there I could potentially follow the steps from my grandfather's memory.

I wanted to head straight there, but if I ran on by myself, Alex would kill me.

And she still wasn't returning my calls.

Where the heck was she?

No sooner had I formed the question when someone knocked on the front door.

Alex was already letting herself in with a key by the time I'd run down the stairs to open the door. When the heck did she have a key made?

"A key seemed like a good idea," she said in response to my thoughts. "I actually made a mold of it a while ago, but you've always been home, so I never needed it."

Okay then.

"So... I've been calling."

"I know, I know," she said, holding up several bags. She started up the stairs toward my room. "I had a lot to get done to prepare for our meeting with the Insider. And thanks to your *terrific* idea," she continued, and it was impossible to miss her sarcasm, "I had to go find a dress for the stupid dance."

"You didn't already have one?"

Her expression was withering. "I already told you the rule. Besides, do I look like I have a closet of dresses?"

She looked like she *should*, but that probably wasn't the point. It was a bit hard to imagine someone that looked like her *not* wanting to get all dressed up.

"It's not a matter of desire," she said. Was she blushing a little? "I've just always had stuff going on. I've never bothered with the dances."

Wait a minute. I thought back on all the school dances I'd been to. I didn't remember ever seeing her there, but I never really thought about it before.

"You've never been to a dance?" I was blown away. "Why wouldn't anyone ask you?"

"Easy there," she said pointing at me with an accusing finger. "I *always* got asked. Always. In fact, I get asked *several* times to each dance. I just always said no. I'd rather be shooting... or something."

I could tell she kept something back, but I didn't press the issue and said nothing. She had her reasons.

"Thanks," she'd turned her back to me and was staring into one of the bags.

"For what?"

"You don't push me for answers," she replied. "I swear,

everyone pushes and pushes over every little thing. And it's even worse with anyone who knows I can read minds. Suddenly I should have *all* the answers. And worse, I should share them with everyone." She turned back around, a short, black dress in her hand. "Do you realize that I know *everyone's* secrets? But I don't share them. I'll use what I hear in everyone's skull to my advantage whenever possible, but I don't go around blabbing. If I'm not divulging their secrets, why should I let everyone know my own? Why should I give them an advantage over *me*?"

As her miniature rant carried on, she walked towards me. I sat on the bed, now leaning back as she towered over me. I had run out of room to back away from the tirade.

Alex blinked and looked down at me. "Oh. Uh. Sorry." She took a few steps back and glanced down at the dress in her hand.

"You're welcome," I said which drew the tiniest hint of a smile from her. The dress in her hand was much smaller than I had anticipated. "So. I see one dress and several bags."

"I wasn't sure what to get, so I bought five. I'm going to try them all on and see which one gets the best response from you."

Was this the *best* thing ever, or the *worst*? I had a hard time deciding.

"And you're going to start with... that one," I said, nodding at the dress she held.

"Yeah. Why?"

"Well, where are you going to put your, uh... gun?" Or *anything*?

She reached down and picked up a smaller bag and pulled

out a tiny holster. The question weighing heavily on my mind was a simple one.

"It goes on the inside on my thigh," she said.

Oh.

Clearing my throat, I said, "It looks a tad smaller than your gun."

She shook her head in obvious sadness. "I know. I had to downsize specifically for this situation. Luckily, I pretty much have unlimited funds through the company, and I ordered an expensive Rohrbaugh R9 for Helix's armory a while back just in case a situation like this popped up. It doesn't have great stopping power, but it's better than nothing."

"A situation like this?" I raised an eyebrow. "You've been preparing to come armed to a dance?"

"Of course."

"Do you have a scenario for a zombie outbreak in a convenience store too?"

"Obviously."

I shook my head in amazement, but she went on like I hadn't interrupted her.

"Anyway, the gun is narrow enough to not get in the way of walking. It's more of a 'slow dance' gun rather than a 'jump around' kind. But don't worry, I'll have several other guns in the trunk of my car just in case. I always have a rifle of some sort in there, plus a few extra pistols and several hundred rounds of ammunition. I like to be prepared."

Right. Because that was exactly what I was worried about.

Alex looked down at the dress and sighed. "You have a point though. This was the dress I was rooting for, too. I drove into Eureka after dropping you off. Broke several laws getting there and back this fast. This was the first dress I found. Now what am I going to do with it?"

"I'll tell you what," I said. "Once this whole mess is done, we'll go out somewhere and you can wear that dress. Hopefully you won't need a gun."

Alex's eyes narrowed. "Are you asking me out?"

Uh-oh. How was I supposed to respond? I *was* asking her out, but what if that wasn't what she wanted? Of course, if I backed out, what if she *did* want me to ask her out? This wasn't the best thought-out situation.

And she had just read my mind through this whole thought process.

Usually she would comment on my thoughts, bailing me out. This time she stared at me with raised eyebrows and folded arms. Was she actually going to make me answer her? Seriously?

"Seriously," she said.

This was more pressure than I was used to feeling when dealing with the fairer sex. I started sweating.

"Yes," I said finally. I thought I sounded firm in my decision. Mostly. "When things calm down, let's go somewhere nice. Maybe even drive down to San Francisco and make a day trip out of it."

I held my breath.

"Deal. But not San Francisco. That place is a pit." She grabbed the other bags and walked out of my room to the bathroom down the hall.

Alex

Alex slid into a long, pale blue dress with a slit up the center to allow for walking. It also allowed for the drawing of her gun strapped along her left inner thigh, as well as the knife on the inner right. She hiked it up a little and took a few practice steps running in place. Not the best, but it would do.

She opened the door and returned to Jack's room. His mouth fell open just a little as he saw her. *Excellent.* She soaked in the jumble of thoughts running through his mind. His eyes ran from her feet up to her eyes to meet her gaze. For a moment his reaction was slightly uncomfortable, but then the admiration felt good.

Recognizing and evaluating her own strengths and weaknesses had always been one of Alex's strong points. She knew enough about herself to see the severe trust issues, the streak of stubbornness she'd been developing the past few years.

Faking legitimate social interactions was easy for her. But dealing with someone else's attraction was not her strongest suit. More often than not, that attraction had nothing to do with *her*, and more to do with the way she walked and her chest size. Most guys were pigs, and in reality, girls were no better. It was hard to be around such blatant duplicity all the time. Such disingenuousness.

But with Jack...

Sure, he'd always admired her looks. But he was actually a really decent guy under all the jokes he used to compensate for his own weaknesses.

Alex assumed it had a lot to do with the amount of growing up he'd been forced to do this last week.

Jack liked her. More than liked her. But it was *all* of her that he liked, not just her looks. He respected her for what she was rather than comparing her to any of their other peers.

It was refreshing.

She'd loved watching him squirm when he'd asked her out. There were some definite unexplored benefits to reading minds —especially when the other person knew what was happening. But the shocking moment for her had been the realization that she *wanted* him to ask her out. This was going in a direction her father likely wouldn't care for.

And Alex found she didn't much care what he thought.

She pulled out another dress, similar in cut to the blue one she currently wore, only red.

"Nope," Jack said and his mind echoed at the same exact time.

"It's the same dress," she replied, confused. "Just a different color."

"Exactly. It's red. Red is cliché. All damsels in distress either wear red or white in the movies. You are not, and are not likely to ever be, in distress. Every other teen at this dance will be in red because that's what they see all the movie stars in. They're dumb. You're not.

"Besides," he said, looking sheepish, "the blue just seems made for you. Perfect."

She couldn't very well argue with that.

She gazed down at the other two bags. One held a white dress, and the other a deeper blue rather than the pale tint she wore.

"Dark blue?" she asked.

"It'll look great on you," he responded. "As will any of the other ones you try on. But I'm having a hard time imagining anything looking better on you than what you're wearing right now."

And he meant every word.

Under any other circumstance, or with anyone else, she would have automatically fought the issue. No one made any decisions about her except her.

But...

"Well," she said. "I guess that settles it."

"What about tickets?" Jack asked.

"I made some. No one will be able to tell the difference." They were exact replicas of the ones they'd given out to those students who had wasted their money. *Honestly, who pays forty dollars to go to a dance in the school gym? Worse, what college students paid money to go* back *to their old high school dances, tradition or not?*

"So we're all set," Jack said, then frowned. "This is gonna be awkward, isn't it? No one is going to want to talk to me when we show up at the school tonight."

"Does that bug you?"

Jack thought for a moment, then shook his head. "I guess it doesn't. I don't really have anything in common with anyone around here anymore. I just don't much see the point of school at the moment. Their problems just don't rate."

"Welcome to the club," Alex said.

"Where do you think the Insider will show up?"

Alex pursed her lips in thought. "If it were me, I'd try to do it in the gym where all the kids are dancing. Not too many teenagers are going to have guns hidden under their dresses. Nor should they. The event, for the most part, is safe and controlled.

Noisy like he wanted. That will make audio surveillance extremely difficult. He'll probably pose as a chaperone or something. Who knows? We won't know him until he approaches us."

There wasn't much else to talk about at that point. Alex returned to the bathroom, where she changed back into her cargo pants and long-sleeve t-shirt. When she came back, Jack spoke.

"Alex?"

"Yeah?"

"I need to test something."

She searched his mind and knew exactly what he wanted to do. She hated that he was suggesting it, but she understood. Alex knew better than anyone that she wasn't the only person who could read a person's mind.

"You want to try to shut me out," she said.

He was apologetic, but firm. "I need to try, Alex. Please."

With a sigh, she nodded her agreement.

Almost immediately his thoughts quickly faded away. It was so much more controlled than the first time he'd attempted the technique. He kept his eyes open, studying her reactions.

And then there was nothing.

She had a brief moment where she was back in Barry's room, with Jack sprawled on the floor looking dead. No thoughts came from his mind.

It wasn't natural. Everyone had thoughts... right up until the moment they died.

The moment stretched out longer and longer. Jack didn't even sweat. She rubbed her hands together. Alex didn't hear *anything.* With no one else in the house, she couldn't even get a whisper from the neighbors.

She wanted to scream just to have some noise.

Then it was all back. All his thoughts.

His forehead wrinkled with concern. "You okay?" he asked after letting out a deep breath. "I could tell you were starting to lose it."

"I was that obvious?" *Not good. Not good at all.* She always had outward control over her emotions. Always.

"You looked like you were going to run out of the room screaming."

"Don't ever do that with me again. Please." The pleading she heard in her voice shamed her. "The last time you were that silent was at Barry's place when I thought you were dead."

Her heartbeat finally began to calm down. She took in a series of deep breaths.

Sudden understanding dawned on his face. "I'm sorry, Alex. I didn't even think of that." He ran a hand through his hair. "But you know I can't promise to never do it around you. If it's just us, I totally promise. But what if someone else can read minds? Like your father. He's about the last person in the world I want hearing my thoughts."

He swore in his head, and his thoughts automatically turned to violent and grotesque visions from some film he'd seen. All the visions came with a built-in sentiment of stark fear anytime he thought of her father.

"What is this film you're thinking about?"

"One of the films I took from Helix," Jack said. "You're... going to have to see it for yourself."

His one constant thought was that her father was a

complete monster. In his mind, whether he realized it or not, he'd put her father even above the Leech in terms of awfulness.

"Tell me what you saw, Jack. Give me the short version."

"I..." He hesitated, his mind trying to intentionally avoid going there. But Alex got enough to know the gist of it. "I think it's better if you watch it yourself. Go downstairs, the projector is all set up. My aunt seems to think I'm just going through some sort of phase, so she didn't even question it being there. Just... just go watch it."

When he didn't make any move to rise from his seat on the bed, she asked, "You aren't coming?"

"If I never have to see that film again, I will die happily."

A half hour later she returned and sat down next to Jack on his bed. She was shaken. No matter how much she detested her father, she'd never thought he could go that far. That film had been enough to make her want to take a gun and shoot her father until the magazine ran dry. Then reload and do it again.

This was a part of Helix she'd never actually witnessed. She wondered how many people *had* witnessed it. She didn't think Jack's dad had—or if he had, he was far better at guarding his thoughts than she had given him credit for. She'd heard the occasional whisper in a random person's mind while wandering the halls at Helix, but had always dismissed them as vivid imaginations. Now she could see how dumb she'd been. How naïve.

She knew Helix ran experiments, but the argument was the experiments were run on *monsters*.

In that video, her father had *been* the monster.

Her father had always spouted the stance Helix was *ethical* about their experiments. That they just wanted to make the world safer. But last time she checked, human experimentation like on that film wasn't ethical. Helix—and therefore her father —was no better than Whyte Genetics.

She had no idea what to do.

They sat there on his bed for a long time, unmoving and in silence other than their thoughts.

CHAPTER 27

Jack

Rap music thumped from inside the gym, advertising this dance would be no different than any other in the school's recent history.

There weren't that many people in Calm Waters with a full set of DJ equipment, so everyone hired the same DJ for their events. And yet, I couldn't even recall the guy's name.

I wore my nicest pair of jeans with a button-up shirt—no tie, because ties should never be worn by anyone—and one of my dad's old sport coats that was still somehow fashionable in our town. I had the knife Alex had given me inside one pocket, with a half-dozen of her spare magazines in the various pockets of my jacket and pants. She didn't exactly have places for them. All the ammunition was a lot heavier than I expected.

Alex looked even better than she had when she'd tried on

the dress a few hours earlier. She'd pulled up her hair stylishly, but also tightly, she said, so no one could grab her by the hair and yank her around. She worried about having to wear heels rather than running shoes. How was she supposed to run? I told her the girls in spy movies always ran in heels. Her response was, *"They also sometimes beat their partners to within an inch of their lives."*

Alex walked slowly. Apparently having a gun and a knife strapped to the insides of her legs made things more difficult than she had anticipated. On the plus side, it also served to let us—mostly her—take in the scenery better.

My nerves were raw, and the first time two girls screamed for no other reason than they were teenage girls, I nearly jumped into the nearest bush. But Alex had her arm looped through mine and held me in place. She said we needed to blend in, and I was more than fine with that arrangement.

A huge sign hanging in front of the gym's entryway welcomed everyone to the dance, and specifically welcomed back "last year's senior class." Someone's bored mom and dad took our tickets without even a second glance. Inside the gymnasium, the music nearly blew out my eardrums. Students bounced up and down to the beat, which sounded exactly the same as the beat from the last song. At least I think it was a different song. Maybe it was the same one, and was just really long. The crowd mainly centered around one girl who wore a crown. The Homecoming Queen, I presumed, but I couldn't see much other than the tiara. She looked like the girl who had served Alex and I at the restaurant several days ago. Maybe she was.

I wasn't in any mood to dance, and neither was Alex. We weren't here to have fun.

Other students gave us constant, disgusted looks as we passed by. By "us," I mean "me." The glances thrown Alex's way were more confused than anything else. I didn't need to read minds to know what they were thinking. I already knew pretty much everyone hated me because of what they falsely thought my father had done. They wondered what someone like Alex was doing with a complete tool like me.

For her part, Alex's expression became more and more angry. I had to pull her back when she took a murderous step toward a group of gossiping teens near us. It wouldn't do for a college student to come back to high school and beat all the mean girls to death. Probably.

We waited by a wall through the next three monotonous songs. Everyone on the dance floor seemed to enjoy them-selves, though I imagined if their parents knew *how* they were dancing with their dates, they would be enjoying themselves far less. That was the whole point though. If this had been a normal dance for me, I'd have been right out there with them.

My phone vibrated in my pocket, and I almost missed it over the vibration caused by the massive speakers. The caller ID was blank. I didn't even need to nudge Alex, since she read my mind. She turned me so my back was to the crowd and she could see everything behind me.

I answered the phone and shoved one finger into the oppo-site ear. Just as I was about to yell "hello" into the mouthpiece, the music died down into a slow-paced song. Another series of delighted shrieks erupted from the crowd. I glanced over my shoulder and saw every girl pulling their date onto the dance floor. I felt so detached from all the excitement. A month ago, I would have been part of that crowd. Now I couldn't have cared less.

"*Mr. Bishop*," the Insider said. "*I'm glad to see you made it. Tell the lovely-looking Miss Courtney to get nice and personal with you. I need an excuse to approach you.*"

I repeated everything the Insider said in my head so Alex would hear it. She looked hesitant, but took two steps closer and wrapped her arms around my neck. She was nearly my same height, and for a moment our faces were only an inch apart.

She "accidentally" stepped on my foot to get me to re-focus on the situation. My mind had been blissfully elsewhere.

Alex moved a little closer then, pressed completely against me, her head to the side of mine. While I imagine this was so she could still see around me, I'd never wished more than right then that we were two normal people dancing together. My right hand strayed down and wrapped around her waist, then my left, phone still in hand.

I could have stayed like that forever.

From the corner of my eye I saw someone approaching. Where he'd been hiding was anyone's guess. Alex tensed and pulled away just a little so she could look in that direction.

The man was a shade under six feet tall, thin, with dark hair receding into a widow's peak. His round glasses reflected the lights from the DJ's stage and from the disco ball spinning endlessly above us. His suit—a full three-piece, four-button, black suit with light pinstripes—looked tailored. I suspected the bulge under his left arm was a gun.

"Here is how this is going to go, Mr. Bishop, Miss Court-ney." It was the Insider, without a doubt. Somehow I'd expected him to be more imposing. Maybe he normally used that misconception to his advantage. "As we stand here and talk, I am going to make very exaggerated and angry gestures. I want everyone to think I am scolding you for *whatever*.

"As I do this," he continued, pointing angrily out into the crowd. "I want the two of you to appear appropriately ashamed. As far as any of the other delinquents here can tell, I'm just one of the chaperones giving you a hard time. Why? *Because I can*. It sounds perfect to me. A new song should start shortly. DJ Lee—you'd think he'd pick a better name—uses the same playlist at every event."

As he finished talking the slow-song transitioned into yet another bass-thumping rap anthem.

"Perfect," the Insider said. "Not only is this song exception-ally loud, but it is one of my favorites. Now, Mr. Bishop, you should probably end that call on your phone. It will conserve your minutes."

As I followed his instructions, he began to angrily count off on his fingers. The movements were large so they drew anyone's attention if they were looking.

"I will have to talk quickly," he said counting off his index finger then, pointing at the both of us. I ducked my head as if embarrassed, and Alex did the same. "I know definitively that Mr. Bishop's father is held at Whyte Genetics in Sacramento. They are interrogating him, and they want the details to Project Sentinel, of which fortunately he only has minimal details.

"The bad news is that even those details are enough for a smart man like Janison Whyte to piece things together." He counted off a second finger and pointed at the thin straps on Alex's dress.

"This means they know enough to have a good idea who Project Sentinel's main subject currently is," he continued. A group of girls were edging closer to attempt eavesdropping. The Insider leaned to the side and fixed them with a malevolent stare to send them scurrying away.

He then grabbed one side of my jacket and pulled me toward him. With the other hand he produced a thick envelope from his pocket and slid it into my inside jacket pocket.

"Are you carrying *ammunition*, Mr. Bishop?" His face continued the charade of anger, but his tone was light and pleased. "How delightful and how very paranoid. You should take that as a compliment. Paranoid men stay alive longer. And it isn't really paranoia if they are actually out to get you. Speaking of which..."

His eyes flicked over our shoulders, and his expression went flat. "As they said in my day, 'The jig is up.'" He put a hand on each of our shoulders. "I assume Miss Courtney has a gun. Perhaps a 9mm? Good. Mr. Bishop, you are therefore her pack mule. I want you to reach into my jacket and pull out the .45 I have holstered there."

"What's going on?" I asked.

"Some of Whyte's minions are here. I just saw someone get jerked through one of the exits people are using to go get air. Anyone that has gone in that direction has yet to return.

"I would normally run that direction to hold them off with the guns holstered on my ankles, and the one at my back," he said calmly, "but I fear it is too late for that. On the bright side, maybe we can use this opportunity to see how far you've come in your skills. Like a field test!"

He sounded... cheerful.

Behind us, screams of terror cut over the relentless beat.

CHAPTER 28

Jack

I pulled the gun from the Insider's shoulder holster and spun around to Hounds bursting through the door. The reflected light from the disco ball revealed their faces already wet with blood.

They came through the door, more and more, until I'd counted thirteen. Not the most comforting number.

The two at the head of their group were larger than the others. These two raised their distorted human faces into the air and sniffed. Even over the clouds of cheap perfume and cheaper cologne, their heads swung directly toward us.

"Run!" I found myself screaming needlessly.

Our path took us toward the only other open door in the gym. The original entrance. Unfortunately, everyone else did the same, and the press of teens was thick. Alex had already kicked off her heels and hiked up her skirt. In her other hand she had her small pistol. The Insider had another gun of his own in hand.

He turned, aimed at the group of monsters, and pulled the trigger.

I didn't see if the bullet hit, but the roar of the gun made everyone in the room flinch as one, and only increased the level of panic. The ringing in my ears made concentration difficult.

"Gun!"

It didn't matter who screamed, but it was perfectly timed to happen in between the lull of two songs. DJ Lee had been too absorbed in the music to realize the screams he'd been hearing weren't in appreciation of his "skills." The result was instant and chaotic. The mass of teens split in two halves, one-half running toward the same exit as us, and the other half toward the back exit...

... where the killing machines waited.

A stampede of overly tight dresses and bad suits enveloped us. Masses of high school and college students now stood between us and the Hounds, but those same people also prevented us from using our guns—not that I would be any good with mine.

Adrenaline surged through me. My focus tunneled in on the area in front of us as the blood pounding in my ears began blocking out the shouts of panic and the screams of pain behind us.

I risked a glance toward the back exit and knew I'd never forget that sight. The Hounds literally ripped their way through the teens that had mistakenly run toward them. Someone flipped the lights momentarily blinding everyone. The sudden illumination showed everyone how completely screwed we were in a vision that would make Hell look on proudly.

Bodies were thrown through the air to hit the walls where they rebounded, leaving red splotches and smears. I saw a series of body parts hurled into other teens. A severed head arced over the crowd and hit the Homecoming Queen a few feet to my right. She fell to the ground, trampled under the feet of the dozens of other students surrounding her.

One of the larger Hounds jumped to one of the walls and hung there like a spider, surveying the crowd until it spotted us. We were still fifty yards away from it, but it made a guttural bark and leapt toward us, covering a third of the distance in that one leap. Blood sprayed over and over where it landed. The other Hounds followed the first one's lead and made their own leaps into the masses of students. Dozens were already dead. Hundreds would follow unless they got out.

All because the Hounds were searching for us.

For me.

We were only ten feet from the exit, but the bottleneck had slowed our movement to a crawl.

A smaller Hound jumped up to the wall a few feet to our left. Alex freed her arms enough to bring her gun up. She punched a boy in front of her with her other hand so he would stoop down in pain, then quickly shot twice over him. Her rounds caught the Hound in the head, and the creature dropped lifeless to the floor. A student next to her cried out in pain as a burning hot shell casing ejected from Alex's gun hit him in the face.

Five feet to the door.

The screams behind us grew louder and closer.

Three feet.

I felt a spray of blood from some unlucky kid hit me across the back of my head and neck.

One foot.

Then we were in the parking lot.

Alex shoved me forward into a run as she blew past me. The Insider ran past on the other side, quick for a guy his age.

We sprinted through the spaces between cars, and I held my jacket closed as tightly as I could manage so it didn't get caught on the side mirrors.

The screams behind us came less frequently now, which either meant there weren't very many people left alive, or the Hounds had left the survivors alone to chase us.

I heard a crash right behind me, but didn't pause to look. I cut between an old pickup and a Kia as the Insider turned and shot three times, his gun sounding in a continuous roar.

I didn't look back.

Ahead I saw the lights flash on Alex's Civic. I was relieved that in her paranoia she'd parked facing out.

"Sprint!" the Insider screamed. He planted himself ten yards ahead of me and the muzzle of his gun flashed in repeated two-shot bursts. Farther ahead—I'd never been the fastest runner—I saw Alex steadying a gun on the top edge of her car door.

And by gun I mean a matte-black rifle straight out of an action film.

The end of the rifle lit up in a giant orange flash each time she fired. I had no doubt that if I'd had time to turn and see what she was shooting at I would have been equally horrified by how quickly the Hounds moved, and impressed by her accuracy.

Instead, I wisely focused on willing my legs to take one running stride after another. My lungs burned and my legs felt like jelly. I wasn't going to be able to last much longer at this pace. I held the Insider's gun in a death grip, finger off the trigger. I hadn't fired a shot.

Alex stopped shooting and ducked inside her car to open one of the back doors. She slid over to the passenger side, leaned out the window with her rifle, and began shooting again. I reached the car four steps later and practically dove into the driver's seat. The Insider was only a step behind me, and he jumped into the back seat.

I still held the gun, so I shoved it in a jacket pocket. It was bulkier than the one I'd practiced with. Alex had already stuck the keys in the ignition, so I started it up. Her car was a stick shift, and I mentally thanked my father for the painful lessons a few summers ago.

The vehicle's tires spun as we shot forward. The front headlight on my side of the car scraped against the rear bumper of the car across from us. We were doing fifty by the time we rocketed onto the road in front of the school. I looked in the rearview and saw at least six of the Hounds, including both of the larger ones, loping after us. On flat ground they moved quicker than they had any right to. They were actually keeping pace with the Civic as I hit sixty.

I swerved, narrowly missing a girl in a pink dress as she ran in front of the car. In the rearview I saw one of the large Hounds casually toss her twenty feet through the air when she froze in front of it.

Then another Hound appeared on the road in front of me.

"Ah hell!"

Alex turned and saw the monster on the road, then grabbed my right knee and shoved my leg down, flooring the accelerator.

The speedometer jumped to seventy miles per hour, then seventy-five.

I thought I caught an expression of shock on the Hound's face as the car plowed right into its mutated body. It left a solid dent in the hood, then hit the windshield hard, cracking the glass, which shattered inward. It was a miracle my face wasn't cut to ribbons. I looked in the sideview mirror as the Hound hit the street behind us and lay unmoving.

Steam began to spill out from under the hood, but I kept the gas pedal floored. The car wouldn't last more than a few more miles at this pace.

There was only one place close enough that came to my mind.

Behind us, the remaining Hounds slowly lost ground, but gained it all back whenever I slowed down for turns. All the while Alex leaned out the window and shot controlled bursts from her rifle. The Insider leaned out his own window and did the same.

"Hold on!" I yelled, then stomped on the brakes.

The Civic came to a halt at the first place my panicked brain had taken us.

My house.

CHAPTER 29

Alex

The Hounds were several hundred yards behind them, but gaining fast. Alex looked up to see where Jack had stopped the car.

His own freaking house.

Unbelievable.

"Open the trunk, Jack!" she yelled.

It popped open, and she ran around to it, pulling out a duffel bag with enough ammunition for her rifle to last twenty minutes in a siege-like scenario.

Sirens wailed in the distance, but she knew they'd have their hands full helping those injured at the school.

Alex was on her own.

"We need to get in the house now," the Insider said, his manner calm and collected. A professional.

Jack was already running to the door. He was much calmer

than he should be, likely due to the adrenaline pulsing through him. His driving had been surprisingly good. She tucked that observation away for the future.

If there is a future.

Jack unlocked the door on the first try. *Small miracles.*

She left her car running and rushed into the house after Jack, with the Insider right on her heels. He went straight to the back of the house, and she heard the scrape of the kitchen table presumably being pushed against the back door.

"Couch!" she yelled at Jack.

He responded without question and helped her shove it against the front door. Suburban homes were never good places to repel an attack, but better than being caught in the open. Her silver lining was the relatively few windows the home contained. On the other hand, the Hounds only needed a few. Alex ripped open the black bag and yanked out a stack of magazines for her gun and two sets of noise-dampening earmuffs. They had microphones in them to amplify normal sounds, but still cut out the loud report of most of the gunshots. She shoved one into Jack's hands and pulled a pair over her own ears.

Gunfire from the back told her the Hounds had already made it to the house. A loud thump from above made Jack look up. At least one of the Hounds was on the roof.

Glass exploded in through the living room window and one of the two larger Hounds appeared three feet in front of her. Alex brought her weapon up on instinct and held the trigger down. Bullet after bullet stitched a line of carnage from belly to neck on the monster. Blood exploded with each shot. A haze of burnt gunpowder hung in the air.

Shots from behind made her swing her rifle. Jack fired up the stairs, his eyes open as wide as they would go. His face completely pale, he pulled the trigger as fast as he could. The slide on his gun locked empty, but he kept pulling the trigger while he screamed unintelligibly at the top of his lungs.

A Hound slowly rolled down the stairs, a single bullet wound in its head. One shot of his twelve wild ones had been a winner.

More gunfire from the back of the house. The Insider was still alive.

Alex never saw the Hound that hit her from the side. It must have lunged through the already broken window, tackling her like a linebacker. The air *whooshed* from her lungs, and she was sure some ribs cracked with the impact. Her rifle flew from her hands.

She shoved her left forearm into the monster's neck and drew the knife sheathed on her leg with her right hand. Her dress had ridden up to her waist, making the draw fast. She brought the blade down, stabbing as fast as she could pump her arm into the Hound's neck. She lost count of her strikes, but they were enough. The Hound clawed at her side weakly and fell away from her.

Alex shoved it away with her left arm and took the brief opening to bring the knife around and bury it in its left eye.

The Hound jerked and collapsed.

Another Hound appeared over the top of it, teeth bared.

The unmistakable sound of her rifle being fired shattered a brief moment of quiet, and the Hound flew to the side in a fountain of gore.

She pushed the Hound the rest of the way off her. Silence

hung heavy in the room, mingled with the odors of blood and gunpowder.

The Insider leaned against the doorframe leading into the kitchen, holding Alex's rifle. He appeared completely at ease and uninjured. That'd he'd made it through all of this without a scratch was amazing. But he'd held the back door, which was all that mattered.

Then she saw Jack slumped on the floor, unmoving.

Covered in the blood of the Hound, Alex rushed to his side. He wasn't dead, but the entire left side of his face was a giant, already-forming bruise. It looked like he'd been hit by one of the Hounds, which likely planned to take him away after killing Alex and the Insider.

He opened his eyes almost instantly.

"What the heck happened?" he asked. "I feel like I got hit by a sledgehammer."

"Worse than a sledgehammer. A Hound," said the Insider, nodding to a corpse not far from Jack. Apparently the Insider had come to Jack's rescue as well.

"Did we get them all?" Jack asked.

Alex gazed around at the massacre. "Five in this room, how many in the back?"

"Two," the Insider said.

"We took two down in the gym," Alex counted on her fingers. "And I got one in the parking lot."

"Same," the Insider added.

"That's eleven. The one I hit with the car makes twelve," Jack said, pushing himself up.

"There were thirteen," Jack said, rubbing his head. "Did we get the ones on the roof?" He blinked a few times, then his eyes widened when he saw Alex. "Alex, you are *covered* in blood! Are you okay?"

"I'm completely fine, by the way," the Insider smirked.

Alex ignored his comment. "I'm fine. It's not my blood. Is there still one more?"

"Unless you killed another one from up there," Jack pointed.

"The last one I killed was one that passed me," the Insider said. "So I think we still have one in the house." He glanced around at the disaster. "Or what is left of your house."

Alex took her rifle from the Insider, checked the rounds left in the magazine, then replaced it with a fresh one. She then reached into the bag and pulled out her Sig, which she handed to Jack. "You're better with this gun."

He took the weapon with a grimace. "I guess you want to hunt it down?"

"Most definitely."

"I'll be down here," the Insider said. "Think I'll put a bullet in each of these Hounds, just in case. Can't have any of these alive. Who knows what kind of trouble that could cause Whyte Genetics? I think I'll also place an anonymous call to Helix mentioning some keywords that will get one of their *special* teams here to make this mess go away before the police arrive."

"How much time do we have?" Jack asked.

"Helix's standard response time is fifteen minutes in a situation like this," Alex replied. "We shouldn't be here when they get here."

"Okay then," Jack said. Every thought in his head was laced with exhaustion. His face hurt more than he let on. And seeing what had happened to his house was more painful still. But overriding all those thoughts was concern for *her*. Jack felt woefully inadequate in his ability to help or protect Alex or anybody.

How was she supposed to feel about that? No one had ever shown that kind of concern for her. At least, not since her mother had died when she was little. But she realized it felt... *good*. Good to have someone genuinely care.

Zip it, Alex, she told herself. *Monster first. Guy later.*

Walking up those stairs was about as far from Alex's best-case scenario as possible. She didn't want to leave Jack with the Insider, who she didn't trust in the slightest, regardless of his help so far. She could read his mind, of course, and his thoughts were legitimately concerned with making sure Jack stayed safe. But she hadn't had enough time with him to determine if those were thoughts he forced himself to think, or if they were natural.

Besides, everyone's definition of "safe" differed. Alex was pretty sure her father thought he was making the world a "safer" place by performing inhumane tests.

The worst part about was in realizing she could do nothing about it. For all her power and skill, she was just a spit in the ocean as far as her father was concerned.

So she either left Jack with a man she didn't trust completely, or she took him with her upstairs with her to hunt a monster hell-bent on taking him away. Not to mention Alex had given him a gun. She hoped she hadn't made a terrible mistake.

No great choices here.

She started up the stairs, motioning for Jack to go ahead of her. Not ideal, but he knew the house better than she did.

As they walked, she focused on Jack's thoughts, picking out the latent thought patterns tied to the home. How he stepped only on certain steps because they didn't creak. His childhood fears of places he couldn't see clearly in the house. She used the thought relays in his mind to get an idea of where he looked when his gaze went to a different place than her, and to pick out something he recognized as different that she wouldn't normally notice.

The entire process taxed her mind far more than just reading someone's thoughts. She didn't employ the method often because of the mental fatigue involved, and because she would learn more than she ever wanted to about another person's way of perceiving things. That perception could be damaging or misleading.

But here she didn't have much choice.

A wide spray of bullet holes marked the wall at the top of the stairs. Jack saw them, and Alex heard his embarrassed thoughts. A pattern of blood and brain-matter on the wall marked where his one good shot had taken the Hound down. He was numb towards the violence at the moment, but once things had calmed down a bit—likely the next time he went to sleep—he would feel it. Monster or not, a person still had to deal with causing a death.

She heard *chuffing* sounds from downstairs as the Insider put an insurance bullet in each of the Hounds. Apparently he'd been concealing a suppressor on him. Why was he bothering to keep the sound down after the gunfight that had just occurred? She made a mental note to ask him later.

She passed Jack on the stairs, motioning him to stay behind her.

She heard no sounds upstairs. Aside from the bullet holes at the top of the stairs, this level of the house was like a different world than below. She moved down the hall, passing Jack's room on the left and the bathroom on the right. Both were quiet, with no Hound in sight. The door to the spare bedroom on the left where Martha normally stayed—Jack's aunt thankfully absent tonight—stood closed.

At the end of the hall was Jack's father's room, which was slightly ajar. She swore she heard wind coming from behind it. She edged forward. From Jack's mind she kept track of the space behind them. His mind hyper-focused on his father's door. It shouldn't have been open. It was always closed—

His thoughts were cut off in a panicked half-yell.

Alex spun, rifle ready, and found the last Hound—one of the two that had been larger than the rest—holding Jack in front of it, its elongated arm wrapped around Jack's throat. His face was turning red. His gun lay on the floor, somehow removed from his hand without making a sound. The hatch to the attic hung open above the Hound's head. Alex felt stupid for not having noticed it.

A window sat at the end of the hallway behind them, and the Hound edged towards it, dragging Jack.

Jack wasn't a scrawny kid, which made it impossible to get a clear shot without risking hitting him. Her aim was almost always perfect, but she couldn't account for the Hound's unpredictability or intelligence. A small feeling of panic wormed its way into her consciousness, but she shoved it down. This wasn't the time. Alex focused her mind.

Options flew through her head. She couldn't read the monster, its mutated thought process too alien to get an accurate picture. She could shoot through Jack and into the Hound. *No.* There weren't many places where that would be able to work, and again, the need to be *absolutely perfect* made her reject the idea.

The Hound was only a dozen feet from the window, and she knew she wouldn't be able to catch it once it left the home. It was too fast, and there were too many places it could go. It would—

Alex, came the clear thought from Jack's mind. *On the count of three, I'm going to jerk my head to my left. You're going to shoot it in the face when I move.*

All of Alex's plans evaporated. Jack made the choice for her, taking any control from her hands. She wanted to shake her head no, but that might give their communication away. And the truth was... she didn't have a better idea.

The Hound backed away another step, then another. It *huffed...* like it was laughing at her predicament.

You've got this, Alex, Jack thought to her. *Three.*

Alex steadied her rifle, but kept an expression of helplessness on her face to keep the monster unaware of her intentions. She had one chance at this.

Two.

Alex slowly let out a breath. *Please let this work,* the thought floated in her head. She didn't know if it was hers or his.

One.

Jack jerked his head to his left. The Hound's head was exposed for just a moment.

Alex pulled the trigger.

CHAPTER 30

Jack

I'm never going to be able to go into an attic again.

I reached up and rubbed at my right ear. There was a small, round notch in it where Alex's bullet had grazed me. It had stopped bleeding, but still stung.

We drove—if you could call it that in a car leaking steam from the hood and making weird thumping sounds—away from my house as fast as Alex could take us. I had two duffel bags in the back seat: one with some clothes I'd managed to hurriedly throw in, the other with my grandfather's journals and the two film reels. I'd been tempted to leave the one labeled "Discoveries," but somehow that felt wrong.

There'd been no sign of the Insider when we'd returned downstairs after Alex's bullet tore through the Hound's head. We didn't care to look for him, and were out the door five minutes later.

Alex suddenly pulled over at the side of the road. She looked pale, and her hands trembled. It was an odd sight. She'd almost always been so calm and cool that seeing her start to freak out made me want freak out.

She opened the car door and barely managed to get her head outside before puking her guts out. She wiped off her mouth with the back of her hand. Distantly, I considered it a good thing she still had her hair tightly wound up.

She pointed back at me without looking up. "Water. Glove box."

I reached in and found a bottle of water. I opened it for her and handed it over. She took a swig, rinsed it around in her mouth, then spat. The process repeated until the bottle was empty.

"I need a place to change," Alex said weakly.

I looked down at her dress and bare feet. The dress would be a complete loss, covered in so much blood that I couldn't see the original blue I thought looked so good on her. Her feet were cut up and bruised, and one of her toes appeared to be broken. She definitely couldn't go out in public like that.

I checked myself over too. Apart from the sticky blood on the back of my neck and head I looked okay. The mess from the Hound having its head blown apart next to me would need to come off, but I could wipe that off, change shirts, and no one would be the wiser.

Well, aside from the massive bruise on my face. I touched it with a tentative hand, wincing as it already stung.

All of that should have bothered me, but it all blurred together in my mind like memories out of focus. Maybe it was a coping mechanism. Or maybe I was just in shock, and it would all hit me later.

"A hotel?" I suggested. They had showers.

Leaning back into the car, Alex sat back. I had a feeling her car needed a deeper cleaning than we did. Alex nodded. "Okay. I've got some cash in my gun bag. We need to keep this off-grid as much as possible."

She closed her eyes for a few moments like she was trying to collect herself. When they opened again, she was back to business. I envied her ability to compartmentalize.

"I know a hotel at the edge of town," she said. "Tourist trap. It's, like, fifty-nine dollars a night. I saw it on my way out of town to buy my dress."

There wasn't really any need for me to reply, so I didn't. Without another word she pulled back out onto the road, dirt swirling in our wake.

We finally reached the hotel close to midnight. The name on the side read "The Vacancy Inn." It was every horror movie cliché wrapped in a neat little bow. But like Alex had mentioned, it was out of the way and only fifty-nine dollars a night. HBO was extra.

Alex parked, fished some twenties from her bag, and handed them to me. I took off my dad's sport jacket and my shirt, and used the latter to scrub the blood from the back of my head and neck. I took a t-shirt from my bag and slipped it on.

I looked to Alex. "Do I look decent enough?"

She didn't look convinced but said, "For this place? It'll do."

"Be right back," I said and hopped out of the car.

The night clerk was half asleep when I went through the reception door. Tall and rail-thin, he typed away at a laptop. Calm guitar music—instrumental—played from his tiny laptop speakers. He looked up at me and let out a sigh and a half-smile.

"Hey there," he said. He ran his hand through thin hair, which served only to make it stick up wildly in every direction. His nametag read "Rob."

"Hey," I said back. I figured the less I spoke the better.

"Room?"

"That'd be great."

"Sixty-three dollars and thirty-four cents." He checked his watch. "Since it's after midnight, we give you all day tomorrow, then make you check out the day after that at by eight. Sound good?"

"Sure."

I handed over four bills. As he made change, he finally seemed to really notice me. He kept glancing at my face.

"You okay, man?" he asked. "You get in a car accident or something?"

"Or something," I said.

He nodded slowly. He seemed to be considering something, then as he handed back my change said, "You need anything?"

"You have an ice machine?"

He pulled a face. "Not really. I have an ice maker in the back room." He pointed to the door behind him. "We charge ten bucks a bucket."

Looking at the change he'd just given me, and thinking of Alex's battered feet, I asked, "How big are the buckets?"

The night clerk pulled one from under the counter. It would fit one foot. Barely. "Tell you what," he said with another smile. "My boss won't have any idea how much ice is gone. It's not like he checks water levels or anything. How much do you want?"

"I could use three buckets," I replied.

He went into the back room. I heard a rumbling, then, and a short while later he returned with three buckets of ice. He passed them over the counter to me, and pulled a key from a rack on the wall next to him.

"Room number three," he said. "It's at the end on your right. And the ice is on me."

"Thanks," I said with a genuine smile.

The clerk was already turning back to stare at his computer screen. "No worries, man. You look like you could use a little help." He sat down and resumed typing.

I walked outside, struggling a bit to carry the three heavy buckets of ice, and saw Alex watching me from the car. As I walked to the room, she followed and took a spot just outside. She waited in the car until I'd unlocked the door, then hurried in.

She went straight for the shower, and I unloaded her bags from the car, taking them two at a time into our room. They weighed at least twice as much as my own. I slid one that had clothing in it—her "go bag" she said she always kept in the trunk—next to the bathroom door, along with two buckets of ice.

Only then did I really look around.

There was only one bed in the room.

Hopefully Alex would be alright with the arrangement. I looked around for a cot, but didn't find one. One night on the floor wouldn't bother me.

I took a washcloth I hoped was clean and wrapped some ice pellets in it. My cheek hurt bad. Getting hit in the face was far worse than the movies pretended. The ice felt amazing, and I slid down the wall to sit on the floor.

My eyes were closed, my head resting against the wall—which I prayed nothing was crawling on—when I heard the bathroom door open.

Just in case, I kept my eyes closed.

"Is this ice for me?" she asked.

"Yeah," I replied. I was exhausted. "The night clerk told me I looked like I 'could use a little help.' Apparently my face is a spectacle. I figured a little ice for my face, and a lot more ice for your feet, which have got to be killing you."

No response. I waited a couple of minutes before daring to peek through a cracked eyelid. Alex sat on the edge of the bed, wearing a pair of short running shorts and t-shirt, staring at me. She had one foot in each of the buckets of ice, though the ice was more of a watery slush now.

The next thing I knew tears spilled down her face.

The way I figure, a person can only hold in that kind of stuff for so long. It sucks when it all comes out. It sucks even worse when someone else sees you lose it. Been there, done that.

I quickly rose, sat next to her, and pulled her into a hug just like she'd done for me only a couple of days earlier. We stayed like that for an hour while she cried her eyes out. I didn't know all the reasons behind the tears, and I didn't need to. Sometimes things just get to a point where one little thing makes it all spill over.

No words were said. Nothing I could say would likely do any good.

When her tears stopped, we were lying down on the bed next to each other. She gave me a peck on my throbbing cheek, then relaxed against me. She was asleep within a minute.

My own eyes closed right after, and for the first time in forever, I didn't dream.

CHAPTER 31

Jack

I woke up in the exact same position I'd fallen asleep in, with Alex still curled against me. She smelled like generic soap and cheap shampoo. It was amazing.

I levered myself up as carefully as possible, trying not to wake her up. The digital clock next to the bed showed almost nine-thirty.

Alex stirred and opened her eyes.

I expected a freakout. Instead she leaned into me with another hug and smiled. Despite everything, to me, she still looked fantastic.

I, on the other hand, was a complete disaster. My face hurt even worse than before, and my right eye had swollen half-shut. Reluctantly I pulled away from her and shambled to the shower. I grabbed my own bag of clothes and brought them in with me.

Forty-five minutes later I felt somewhat better. I used the rest of the shampoo in the little bottle the hotel provided, then took some time to be sure all the grime, blood, and Hound brains went down the drain.

When I came out of the bathroom, Alex was fully dressed and had all our stuff packed. She'd put our torn and bloody clothes in a garbage bag after emptying my pockets and leaving their contents on the table.

Ammunition magazines, my wallet... and a rumpled envelope.

The documents the Insider gave me. I'd forgotten all about them.

I wanted to open that envelope badly, but we had something else we needed to take care of first.

"I have an idea," I said. "Let's go for a drive."

I had Alex stop the mostly-wrecked car near the sign marking the entrance to Calm Waters. The sign was updated from my grandfather's time, and now a rest stop sprawled here, but I knew it was the same place from my dream.

During the drive, we'd had the radio on, listening to the news reports.

Calm Waters was a disaster.

Between sixty and seventy-five dead. Another twenty estimated missing. A majority of the dead, unsurprisingly, were high school kids and college students. Descriptions of the incident, however, were unclear. Reports ranged from wild animals on the loose to a terrorist attack.

I reached forward and turned the radio off.

"You sure you want to do this right now?" Alex asked.

"I'm worried if we wait, things will get worse," I answered.

"Okay. Lead the way."

We got out of the car. I wore a normal pair of jeans and a t-shirt with a track jacket over the top. Alex was in her usual cargo pants and long-sleeved shirt. She walked a bit gingerly, but not too badly.

Alex carried her normal gun, and I'd refused the one she'd offered me. Some cheap, XD something-something. I just wasn't good with it, and I was probably more of a danger to us *with* the gun than without it.

We crossed the road and continued straight into the woods. I circled us around until we were at the approximate spot where in my grandfather's memory I had seen through the trees as headlights had shone across the "Welcome" sign. The sign looked different, and the foliage around us had also changed, but not the redwoods. They don't change much over a few dozen years. It was that very trait that made them an attraction year after year.

The going was slow, and every so often I would stop and close my eyes to recall the dream. It almost wasn't even a dream anymore, since I'd lived it so many times. It was more like a memory implanted in my head. My *own* memory now.

The path was clear in my mind. Every so often Alex would point out something she noticed while reading my thoughts, but mainly she let me guide us, not distracting me from the goal.

There were enough similarities in the larger trees that we were able to move steadily along. We took a small break for water and for Alex to rest her feet. The further we walked the less we talked.

Three hours passed, and then, just like in the memory, a hundred yards ahead I saw the forest open into a small clearing.

Alex drew her pistol.

Just like my grandfather before me, we took those last hundred yards with extreme caution.

At the edge of the clearing I studied the collapsing remains of the same cabin. Half of the roof had caved in, and the wall facing us appeared unstable. It looked like a piece of history time had abandoned.

Except for the pile of corpses. They were obviously recent.

The Leech had been here.

No movement gave away the Leech's position. Maybe it wasn't even here right now. It could have been stalking another family for all I knew.

I circled to the left to get the best angle on the door, but this time the Leech wasn't lying there against the doorframe bleeding.

The stacked corpses consisted of a few animals, but mostly humans dressed in ragged clothing or plastic bags. Homeless. That was how the Leech had avoided pulling attention. I wondered if the Leech had just grown tired of preying on the homeless, or if the "supply" had begun to run out.

Cautiously, I entered the cabin, Alex at my heels. This looked to have been the main living room, and for the most part it remained intact, though it reeked of mold and filth. In one corner a pile of newspapers and foliage looked like it had been used as a bed. The back of the cabin wasn't accessible due to the collapsed roof.

A shadow passed across the broken window, and Alex's gun came up in an instant. I suddenly regretted not taking the pistol she'd offered.

But nothing happened. Maybe the shadow had been just a tree branch moving weirdly. My nerves felt like they'd been run across a cheese grater, and some of that rubbed off on Alex as she read my thoughts.

Sorry, I thought.

She lowered her gun and turned toward me, waving it off.

Another flicker of movement, and the Leech appeared behind Alex in the doorway. Its pointed teeth were bared in an animalistic snarl. Alex began to spin back toward the door when a writhing, purple spike jutted through her chest. She shuddered and dropped her gun, psychic energy bleeding from the wound as she slid off the spike.

She didn't even make a sound as she hit the floor.

No. No. She can't be... No...

The world trembled around me. I couldn't scream. Couldn't cry.

The purple spike withdrew into the Leech's arm. It smiled at me—a terrible smile that made my lungs freeze with fear—then sniffed the air. A look of recognition played out across its face, like it knew me.

Or it smelled a memory in me. Of my grandfather.

What could I do against this? Alex lay in a heap on the floor, maybe dead. She was the one person who had kept me from coming unglued since my dad vanished. But she couldn't help me here. Everyone was gone.

The Leech held up its hands, wreathed in purple tendrils that elongated and crept toward me, just like they had when it had come for Barry. It had such control over its psychic ability. I had nothing.

I promised Barry. The thought was random in my head. *Am I gonna let him down? That thing just killed Alex, and now I'm waiting for it to kill me?*

No.

I brought up my hands in front of my face and saw them wreathed in a lighter purple than the Leech's.

Everything slowed down, then stopped.

All that mattered was the Leech.

Dust particles froze in midair. No wind. No sound. Nothing. The only movements came from me and from the Leech.

Its eyes narrowed in concentration. Its psychic hands reached for me, flexing open and closed in their desire to choke the life from me so it could feed on my psychic essence.

No.

I did what felt natural. What I'd seen my grandfather do in the memory. I pushed out my psychic energy, wrapping it around me in a protective bubble.

The Leech's tendrils shot forward. Dozens of them. They flared out from its aura and struck like snakes. Up close, the things looked like giant versions of the creature's psychic teeth which I'd seen when it had attacked Barry. I struggled just to keep them out, and even then, a few got through my guard. They stung where they touched me, and I could feel my strength draining with each nip.

The Leech seemed to grow stronger.

Was it feeding off of me? Using my own psychic ability against me?

For the most part my shield held. But all that did was stall. I didn't know how to use my aura to attack, and I could only hold out so long against the Leech's assault. My breathing grew ragged, and on my arms dozens of tiny snake-like bites wept psychic essence. Exhaustion already clawed at me. My aura stuttered, letting even more of the tendrils through. I didn't have much more left in the tank.

The Leech threw its aura at me again. I wouldn't survive this. Couldn't. I thought of my grandfather in the vision, and how his will had been iron. How, even bleeding and with a concussion he'd held.

Maybe I didn't have the raw strength yet to face a monster like this straight on... but that didn't mean I was helpless. It didn't mean I should just give up.

I calmed myself like I had in Alex's gun lesson. *Just think of the target. The rest doesn't matter.* I poured every last tiny scrap of power I had left into the bubble. Or... *almost* every bit of power. I also sent one, small, thin tendril of my own snaking through the shadows to my left toward the Leech. Then I forced my legs to move, closing the gap between us until I stood over Alex's unmoving form.

More and more of the Leech's psychic tentacles hammered into my psychic barrier, and I fell to my knees at Alex's side, next to her outstretched hand. A few more of the tendrils slipped through and pulled energy from me.

It hurt. More than anything had ever hurt me before. I

wanted to cry out, and I had to blink away the tears forming in my eyes.

The Leech laughed at me, thinking it had won. It actually licked its lips in anticipation.

My own singular, tiny, insignificant tendril burrowed into the Leech's foot, and I felt the slightest trickle of energy coming from it.

The monster looked down in shock. That momentary hesitation cost the Leech its focus, and its feeding tendrils retreated just an inch away...

... giving me all the time I needed.

I dropped the bubble, grabbed Alex's gun, raised it, and pulled the trigger without thinking. The weapon was just an extension of my hand, like Alex had taught me.

The monster's eyes widened, and it tried to redirect its energy.

Far, far too late.

The first bullet hit it in the leg, and the next its arm. My aim wasn't great, but at this range it was hard to miss, even in my exhausted state.

The Leech screamed in pain.

I let my psychic aura surge, copying the way the Leech had tried to feed on me. How it had fed on Barry. Now *I* fed off the Leech's fading aura, drinking in the energy until I thought I might burst.

It tried to fight back, but I swung my very real fist at its face, and the monster's nose gave beneath the punch. Red blood spurted, mixing with the psychic energy it leaked like crazy.

With the psychic hand not holding the gun, I reached out to

the Leech's throat and squeezed its aura until every bit of the monster's energy was snuffed out.

The Leech collapsed like a rag doll. Dead.

I'd finished what my grandfather had started. He'd let it live, but I couldn't. Not after everything it had done. I was brimming with power, intoxicated. This was what the Leech felt every time it killed someone. It was *this* feeling it hungered for.

And yet I had a hollow feeling in my gut.

I looked down at Alex. Psychic energy bled from her still out of a gaping psychic hole in her chest.

If the Leech's power could hurt her, could my own power heal her? Could I *close* the hole? Seal it up? What if I could fill it back up with what had been lost? Like... like a blood transfusion, but with psychic energy.

It was a stupid, crazy, desperate idea. But it had an outside chance of working.

I quivered with power. Power that would make me hunger for it every time I saw another's aura.

I knelt down and brought Alex's head into my lap.

The wound was ugly, though only I could see it. To everyone else, the cause of her harm would be a mystery. I held my hand over the wound and *willed* my super-charged aura to drip into her.

Drip. Drip.

Nothing.

Please, Alex. Please come back.

Drip. Drip.

She took in a breath.

I almost choked in relief, but kept letting my psychic energy drip into her. At the edge of my vision, black began creeping in.

Just a little more.

Drip.

Drip.

Just a little more.

Drip.

I couldn't see anything, and soon I swam in darkness.

CHAPTER 32

Jack

A hospital bed. Here I was again. Only this time the hospital was a lot quieter than before.

I blinked a few times, then brought up my arms to check their damage. No sign of any wounds, psychic or otherwise. But my head pounded.

It took three tries to sit up, and when I did I was surprised to see the sleeping form of Alex in a chair next to my bed. She looked fine. Beautiful. Alive.

My crazy, stupid gamble worked.

A cup of water sat on a tray next to me. I was still pretty weak, and I discovered this when the cup fell from my fingers. Alex jolted awake, her hand reaching for a gun that wasn't there. Her eyes blinked in confusion, then she broke into a huge smile.

"You're awake!" She flew across the room in a blur and

hugged me.

This was way better than the last time I'd woken up in a hospital.

"What happened?" I asked.

She didn't answer right away, just kept on hugging me. I was only too glad to return the embrace.

When she finally pulled away, her eyes were wet. Geez. Twice in just a couple of days. I was a bad influence on her. Well, at least I thought it had only been a few days.

"Alex—"

She held up a hand to interrupt me. "Don't say anything. Not yet. Just give me a second." She took a long series of deep breaths, wiped her eyes, and laughed in relief.

"I thought you were done," she said, shaking her head.

"Done?"

"The doctors thought you were a goner. After the fourth day—"

"Whoa, whoa, whoa." It was my turn to interrupt. "Fourth day? How long have I been out?"

"Ten days."

No wonder I felt like complete garbage. I probably stank like garbage, too.

"A little," Alex said with a smirk.

Awesome.

"They had no idea what was going on with you," she said. "I didn't either. I woke up on the floor of that cabin and you were unconscious next to me. It was hard to even tell if you were breathing. I made a litter and dragged you to the car, then drove you to the hospital."

Her eyes widened as she read my memory of saving her life. I shrugged uncomfortably at her expression.

"I told them I found you on the side of the road," she continued after a moment. "And I insinuated you might have been a victim of the violence at the dance." She shrugged and curled back up in her chair. "It wasn't hard to lead them there. That's all anyone has been thinking about. All anyone *can* think about."

"It is that bad?" I asked. "I know a lot of kids died..."

"People are picking up and moving," Alex replied. "Not just one family here and there. Everyone. In a couple of weeks no one will be here. Helix is closing this location."

"Where are all the employees going?"

"Wherever they want. Helix is offering paid transfers to anyone who wants to stick with the company."

The important question. "Where are *you* going?"

"I'm going to our branch in Sacramento."

"The Insider said my dad was in Sacramento," I said.

"What a coincidence."

She reached over and pulled an envelope from her jacket lying on the room's table. The envelope the Insider had given us.

She tossed it in my lap.

"You read this?" I asked.

"Yep. You're going to want to read it too."

I didn't open the letter. Instead I set it aside and looked at Alex. "It might be lonely in Sacramento for you."

"I won't know anyone," she agreed.

"I suppose I should be a good... friend... and make sure you have someone to talk to."

She smiled at me before I could verbalize my next thought. "Plus," I said, "I promised you a date."

EPILOGUE

Alex

The room was dimly lit and furnished with only a round, polished oak table surrounded by six high-backed, expensive chairs. Every chair was filled but one.

It's like those movie clichés Jack always talks about, Alex thought.

Despite being in the presence of four other people, her mind remained silent other than a low buzzing. A tiny orb rested on the table. A dampener. *More like a silencer.* As Alex gazed at it, the sphere seemed to writhe just beneath the surface. The movement pulled an involuntary shiver from her. As long as that... thing... was here, no one's abilities would work. Besides, no one wanted their minds read in this setting.

Especially not the person whose seat remained vacant.

As if summoned, the door to the room slid open. The brighter lights from the subterranean halls of Helix cast the newcomer as a silhouette. He was always the last to arrive at these meetings. *Always make them wait*, he'd told her once.

He took his seat. Arthur Gaines. President and CEO of Helix. Alex's father.

Alex was grateful no one—not her or her father—could read minds here. She didn't want her father to know any more than she gave him.

"Give me an update," Gaines said, taking a seat.

"All our assets are being moved to our Sacramento facility," said the man to her immediate left. Richard Path. Her father had often referred to him as a manager of perception. He could make a person perceive him as whatever he wanted. A deputy. A teacher. A manager. Whatever.

"How many of our... normal... employees will be coming with us?" The briefest flicker of distaste crossed Gaines's face at the world *normal*.

"Five percent," Path replied.

"Well done." Gaines nodded. "It is *so* much cheaper to hire new people than move existing ones. What about public perception?" This question was directed to the man on Alex's right, Mel Smart.

Smart smiled as only a lawyer could. "They will believe whatever I tell them to believe."

"Is that what I asked?" Gaines said in a low voice.

Smart's smile faltered, and Alex took a bit of satisfaction from it. The man was... greasy.

"The high school attack has been blamed on rabid animals," Smart answered. "We bought some wolves, killed them, then passed them off as the source of the attack rather than Whyte's Hounds. Then we burned down the gym to get rid of any actual evidence. The world will believe we are moving our facilities simply as a further result of Daniel Bishop's made-up ineptness, and the terrible tragedy at the school. They'll believe anything I say."

Gaines nodded at that, then turned his eyes to Alex. "And how are things progressing with Jack Bishop?"

"He's set to move to Sacramento," she replied. "I've already set him up with an apartment and a job."

"Good," her father said. "We need to continue to observe him. Martha, I trust you will be going with him?"

Sitting to Gaines' right was Jack's aunt, Martha. She nodded once, saying nothing. Alex was convinced Martha was the only person here—besides herself—who genuinely cared about Jack.

Gaines nodded as well, but added: "I wish your loyalty to me were as absolute as it is for Daniel and his son."

"Loyalty is earned with trust," Martha replied. "Not fear."

Arthur's expression darkened. "Your opinions matter little. You'll get a minimal stipend for your efforts, but expect nothing beyond that. You've made your allegiances clear."

"I should hope so," Martha said.

Alex fought to keep her expression neutral.

Jack had no idea how much of his life had been monitored and directed, even before his dad had been taken.

Alex had been officially observing him for years now. In high school, she manipulated his scheduling to match her own, and their first year at CWJC had been similarly adjusted. She made sure he saw her when he worked at Helix. Went to the theater when he did. Ate at the same restaurants. Shopped at the same stores. Most of the time he never knew.

For the longest time she'd had no idea why her father had tasked her with surveillance of Jack. She simply did as she was told. It was safer that way.

Then she'd received the call from the Insider about Project Sentinel. Careful searches on the company server had yielded quite a bit more information.

As far as Alex could tell, Jack was just one in a series of people being observed under the scope of Project Sentinel.

Her father hadn't objected when she'd asked to be more involved in Jack's surveillance.

Hopefully her father felt she did her job well enough to keep her involved. Because now the job was more complicated. Alex was smart enough to realize her feelings for Jack were strong. They were real. She wasn't about to let anyone—or anything—hurt him. That desire to protect him and be close to him made her heart beat a little faster.

It felt... fantastic.

"Good, good," her father continued as he pushed himself up to standing. "It is now time to move forward. We are officially canceling all other Helix experiments. Project Sentinel is now our *only* priority."

What?

Everyone appeared as shocked as Alex felt.

All except the man to her father's left. Alexander Jones. He never went by "Alex," to her relief. Always "Alexander." Or "the Doctor." She wanted nothing to do with the small man. He was in charge of all of Helix's experiments, including those of the more clandestine variety she'd seen on the films stolen by Jack.

Gaines pulled a small remote from his pocket and tapped a button. The wall behind him shifted and slid apart to reveal a huge screen, which blinked to life. First it showed images of Jack, then shifted to images of prior participants in the program. Alex didn't recognize any of them, with the exception of an old photo of Wyatt Bishop.

Interesting.

The images shifted again, this time to blank silhouettes of six other people. Who were they? No names were provided, just the labels "Subject One" through "Subject Six." She needed to get the names of these people.

"Effective immediately," her father said, "all extra surveillance on Subjects One through Six will be terminated. We will no longer consider them viable subjects, and instead will focus all our attention on Subject Seven, Jack Bishop. Admittedly, both the Doctor and I were most keen on Subjects Four and Five. But here we are. The Doctor and I plan to jump-start his progress over the next six to twelve months."

"What's going to happen with the other Subjects?" Martha asked.

"What do you *think* will happen?" Gaines asked sharply. "They will be educated and taught how to use their powers for the benefit of Helix. If they become a danger, they will be eliminated. Like usual. However, I always have backup plans.

"Now if there's nothing else," Gaines continued, "some information recently came to my attention that will help put things into perspective for our direction on the project. First, Hounds have been reported at the locations of all our Subjects. That, in itself, is worrying. It screams of inside information.

Second, to go along with that suspicion, I tracked some rather interesting data requests on our servers.

His eyes met Alex's. She kept her face calm, but inside she panicked. *He knows!* Worse than that, he'd followed Alex's queries to come to the answer. She should have been more careful. *What have I done?*

"These requests were quite sophisticated, and masqueraded as internal requests from the heads of our other facilities across the country. However, these requests had a spy program piggybacking on them. Our data security team is finding artifacts of the program throughout our systems, regardless of how secure we *thought* they were. We have to assume we have been completely compromised, and that Whyte knows everything."

Whyte? Alex thought. *Not me?* She kept the relief she felt off her face.

"How can you be sure it's Janison Whyte?" Smart asked. "It could have been anyone."

Gaines's smile was cold. He pressed a button on his remote, and a new image appeared on the screen. "Because he was in town, personally observing Jack Bishop."

Alex blinked several times, trying to clear her eyes. They had to be mistaken. The photo was from one of the many surveillance cameras Helix had covertly installed around the city. It showed a clear image of a man looking right into the camera, cheerful grin on his face. The man her father said was Janison Whyte.

She recognized the man, not as the CEO of Whyte genetics...

...but as the Insider.

The Insider is Janison Whyte. They're the same damn person.

The realization felt like a punch to her throat. All this time, they'd accepted help from the man, and he'd just been manipulating the same way Gaines had.

A sicker thought took hold in her stomach.

The Insider—Whyte—had told her and Jack that Daniel Bishop was being held at the Whyte Genetics facility in Sacramento.

His own facility.

His own Hounds.

His own... games.

Alex forced down her shock and fury at the manipulation.

The Doctor spoke up. "He shifted again. Our facial recognition software didn't pick him up until he made contact to gloat."

"He made contact?" Alex forced herself to ask.

Gaines nodded. "He left a message on my personal phone."

He clicked his remote again, and a voice came over the speakers in the room. She recognized the voice of the Insider immediately.

"Hello there, Arthur. It's been a while since we last spoke, hasn't it? I trust you are doing splendidly, and that your preparations to move your headquarters to Sacramento are progressing efficiently. Yes, yes, I know, you have yet to make that knowledge public, but when has that ever stopped me from knowing your business?

"I am just calling to congratulate you on Jack Bishop's progress. He is indeed the key to Project Sentinel. Who would have thought that after all these years you would finally have the project catalyst nearly within your grasp? It's just like you dreamed back when I was

your terrified assistant. Those were interesting times. Before I came into my own abilities.

"Ah, but I digress. I just wanted to let you know that I personally made sure Jack survived all those Hounds I sent. Truth be told, he didn't need much help from me. Between your incredible daughter— give her my regards and best wishes—and Jack's developing powers... well, let's say my field test of your 'Subject Seven' went perfectly.

"Oh, Arthur! If you could have seen the battle he had with the Leech. It was exquisite! For a minute there I was sure I would have to intervene, but he did so much better than his grandfather did.

"Do you miss Wyatt like I do? Do you regret what you did to him the day he died? The day Jack was born? Arthur, you may have killed Wyatt that day, but I'm almost positive he is still around.

"I'm sure you know what I mean.

"I look forward to our meeting again in Sacramento. I'm sure it will be... explosive.

"See you soon, Arthur."

AUTHOR'S NOTE

There you have it. You've finished reading my "Author's Edition" of *Residue*, and I hope you enjoyed the ride!

I feel like this is the appropriate time to give you, the reader, a little insight into the madness that has surrounded this book. You see, it's been quite a few years since *Residue* originally released, and the path to this point was filled with more than a few bumps and potholes.

Residue was initially published by a small publisher called Ragnarok Publications. I was extremely excited. But it became pretty apparent early on that they didn't know what they were doing. I never saw a content edit for the book—and *every* author needs a good edit—especially the new ones! Worse, I never saw a copyedit. Then the company botched my release date, which screwed up several events already planned.

Thankfully, one of my best friends, Larry Correia, saved me from complete disaster and got his whole, amazing fanbase to buy copies.

Shortly thereafter, I met Robert McCammon and Terry Brooks, two of my heroes. Terry got me into reading fantasy back in the '80s, and Rick cemented my love of horror in 2006. They both read *Residue*, loved it, and offered me cover quotes.

The original publisher refused to put those quotes on the cover of the book.

Yeah. I still don't understand that one.

Ragnarok went out of business shortly thereafter, and I fortunately got my book back. A new publisher bought Ragnarok's assets, then bought *Residue*... and things basically went the same. Within a short time, my novel was orphaned again.

Enter Wordfire Press. Kevin J. Anderson—with Wordfire's Acquisitions Editor at the time, DJ Butler—saved the book. I love Kevin, and Dave (the "D" in DJ) is still a good friend of mine.

But after a few years I began feeling like I should take control of *Residue* and wondered if I should fix a bunch of the issues in it.

So here we are.

What did I change? Well, I fixed and changed stuff on literally every page. Mainly, I increased the age of the two main characters. I initially meant for this book to be YA, but it already straddled the line between that slightly younger readership and adults.

If you've read the original version of *Residue*, this one will feel roughly the same, just a lot smoother and with more content. I put a lot of effort into this redo, so I hope you enjoyed it.

The main question I get about *Residue* is: where did you get the idea for this book?

Like most authors, I'm constantly influenced by the things I read and the shows I watch. In this case, I was reading the novel *Necroscope* by Brian Lumley. To this day, it and the sequels are among the most influential works on my writing. It's dark, and it's straight-up horror. I adore it.

While reading this book, my wife and I started watching a TV show called *Chuck*, and the humor and characters collided with the horror novel.

Thus *Residue* was born.

I knew I also wanted a few other elements. I wanted the main character, Jack, to have a good relationship with his dad, because I'm sick of most fictional dads being deadbeats. Additionally, I didn't want Alex to be a perpetual victim who only agonized about which boy liked her. So I made her the professional of the story, and Jack the newbie.

Here are some other fun facts for you readers.

Alex carries a Sig P226. Why? First, when I use guns in fiction, I like to be detailed and accurate (as long as it's relevant to the character). Often times this becomes a reflection of my favorite guns, or what I *feel* the character would use. I happen to love the Sig 226 and 229. In fact, the first gun I really recall shooting was my dad's service weapon—a Sig P226. I love the full metal frame, which keeps the recoil down.

As Alex mentions in the "gun teaching" scene, women often get sold on buying little tiny guns. It's stupid. Of the female competition shooters I know, they go for heavy guns, because it reduces muzzle flip from recoil.

As for that instructional scene where Alex teaches Jack to shoot, that was basically how my first shooting experience went. You see, the Sig 226 is what is called Double-Action/Single-Action. The first trigger pull is long, and the first time shooting it seems odd. But after that, the next trigger pulls are much shorter. Hence the comical scene. On a personal side, I don't really like Double-Action/Single-Action. I like Single-Action only (SAO). But the 226 and 229 get passes.

My Sigs are still my favorite pistols, especially my Sig M18. Once I get a gajillion dollars, I'll buy a Sig P226 SAO. I love those things.

Next, I love mad-science. I love shows like *X-Files* and *Fringe* that blend science with the supernatural. All the monsters in this book—and in this series—are mad-science versions of classic monsters. The Hounds, obviously, are werewolves. The Leech is basically a vampire. Jack's journey with his power is very similar to the classical temptation of mortals when given the chance to embrace vampirism when offered to them.

I mention "archaeoacoustics" when Jack is reading Wyatt's journals. This was added into this version of *Residue* at the suggestion of M.A. Rothman. This actually exists, and the short story by sci-fi legend Gregory Benford also is a real story. Now, the idea of actual words being recorded into pottery has, so far, been debunked, but archaeoacoustics covers more than just recording sound. It's pretty fascinating, and I encourage all you readers to look it up! And definitely give Benford a read. He's brilliant.

Lastly, I always talk about music in my contemporary

fiction. I *always* listen to music while writing. So, if you want a window into my mind for this book, here you go. For the original version of *Residue*, I listened to Silversun Pickups for the majority of the book. But for the prom scene, I exclusively listened to Disturbed's *Asylum* album. For subsequent edits and for this author's edition, I also listened to Kamelot, and Dance Gavin Dance.

The music I choose tends to fit—at least in my author brain —the genre of the book. For example, when I write cyberpunk, I try to find stuff that's kinda '80s metal, or where the lyrical themes are about technology. For *Servants of War*, which I co-wrote with Larry Correia, I listened to Sabaton, Epica, and Tremonti. At the very least, I hope you find a few new bands to listen to!

Anyway, I hope you enjoyed *Residue* and are looking forward to the sequel, *Parasite*, in which Jack and Alex take on a psychic parasite let loose in Sacramento!

If there are characters or events I allude to in this novel that you would like to hear more about, let me know!

PREVIEW: PARASITE

Alex

Heart pounding, Alexandra Courtney shut the server room door behind her, the small lock on the handle her first and only form of defense. She wiped a bead of sweat from her forehead, knowing she had to make a choice, whether she wanted to or not. Another chance to access this room wouldn't happen again for another six months.

A quick look at her MTM Silencer watch—her favorite non-firearm accessory—told her she had only five minutes before the next security rotation entered this room.

If they enter before I've finished...

Six months of effort, all leading to this moment, and it had nothing to do with shooting anything. If she was honest with herself, Alex felt a little let down by the lack of gunfire. Of course, if the hacking program she'd purchased—for an ungodly amount of money—didn't work fast enough, she'd have more bullets flying around her than she ever wanted.

It was now or never.

She flipped up the small screen attached to the server input and plugged a USB drive into the access port on its side. The program engaged automatically, filling the screen with lines of code and data that meant nothing to her. The anonymous hacker who sold Alex the program online assured her it would find and copy the desired information in under five minutes.

She stared at the screen for thirty long seconds. The lines of code simultaneously crawled by, sloth-like, and sped up like a runaway locomotive. Alex wiped away lines of sweat running into her eyes.

She reached into a pocket and pulled out a candy bar. She didn't know which one, and intentionally didn't look. She blindly ripped off the wrapper and took a bite. Chocolate. Caramel. Some other stuff. Nougat? Milky Way. The candy bar tasted... fine.

One of the deficiencies of being able to read the minds of everyone around her was not knowing what she *actually* liked. Did she *really* like something—soda, music, art, movies—or were her likes just the by-product of living in the heads of the morons surrounding her?

Candy bars. Not even knowing her favorite candy bar galled her. She'd tried to find out, had researched it for months, but had come away with no definitive results. Jack knew his favorite candy bar. Whatchamacallit. He just knew it, just like that, without even a conscious thought.

For Alex?

It may as well have been the internal debate of the century.

She checked her watch again. Four more minutes.

The hacker said the program worked using an AI algorithm that sought out files and folders with specific keywords attached, scrubbing directories and databases for anything potentially related to the search parameters. With only five minutes to do the job, the program wouldn't get everything, but it would still grab quite a bit.

As the data sped by, Alex occasionally identified a word before it scrolled off the screen. *Sentinel. Catalyst. ESP.* Nothing unexpected. All would make for interesting reading later.

The Milky Way wasn't doing it for her. Waxy. Alex forced herself to chew and swallow anyway. Where was a spit bucket when she needed one?

No one was around; no thoughts or feelings were impressing themselves on her. She had made this call on her own. Milky Way was not, and would not ever be, her favorite candy bar. She doubted it would even make her top ten... provided she could decide on a top ten.

Maybe I should try foreign chocolate.

She set the partially-uneaten candy bar on the server shelf next to her.

Three minutes.

She almost reached into a different pocket to pull out another candy bar, then stopped. No more time for experiments today.

Just under two minutes.

The handle to the server room door rattled.

Security had arrived early. Alex cursed herself for not noticing the thoughts of the guard as he got close enough to read. The handle rattled again.

Locking the door had been a good move, but it would only make the person on the other side suspicious. The door wasn't supposed to be locked during normal hours. A fire hazard.

"Hello? Someone in there?"

Alex knew the voice. Tony Battalino, the Sacramento branch's head of security, and her boss.

She focused in on his thoughts, which mostly felt like impressions of emotions at this distance. Curiosity being overtaken by suspicion.

"Hello?" The rattling of the door ceased and was replaced by the sound of a key being inserted into the lock.

Still a full minute remained on the program.

As the door opened, Alex grabbed a feather duster she'd brought in with her, and stepped in front of the pulled-out screen, obscuring it from view. When Tony entered the room, all he would see was Alex dusting away.

"Oh, hey, Alex. What are you doing in here?"

Alex faked a double-take. "Hmm? Oh. Just cleaning up."

"You assigned to be in this part of the building?"

"It's on the schedule. You know me, I just go where I'm told."

Six months ago she'd been the interim head of security at Helix's Calm Waters branch. Now? She'd been buried so far down the corporate hierarchy that being an intern would likely have meant a promotion. No one here knew about her skills. No one knew her history. No one knew Helix's CEO, Arthur Gaines, was her father. Here, she was just another nameless cog in Helix's corporate machine.

Re-prove your loyalty to me and I'll elevate you to a proper position, her father told her in private after the Calm Waters incident. *Until then, you can rot in the basement like a nobody. Like a* normal *person without gifts or powers.*

That was what siding with Jack, rather than her father, got her. A windowless, musty room even the rats shunned.

And she didn't regret her choice for a second.

Well... maybe this particular second. If Tony saw what she was doing, he'd try to subdue her, and then she'd have to keep herself from hurting him too badly. She'd read his file. Watched surveillance video of him sparring and shooting. Knew his weaknesses. Even in her current, diminished position, Alex had ways of getting to the internal Helix files she wanted to see. Being prepared was a way of life for her.

"Why was the door locked?"

"It was locked? Weird. I must have accidentally hit the little lock thingy when I closed it." *Play the stereotype.* She pointed up at her hair. "Blonde moment. Sorry." Not her proudest moment.

She isn't normally this scatterbrained, Tony thought. *Wait. Is that server interface open?*

Alex didn't have much time. Tony was an intelligent guy, and he didn't completely buy her act. She turned and dusted the screen with one hand. "I'm almost done here," she said.

She could feel him walking up behind her. A quick glance at the screen showed the program had finished. With her free hand she quickly pulled out the USB drive while obscuring it with the duster. The screen cleared, leaving no visual trace she'd been up to anything. "Yep. That should do it. Dust-free."

Tony appeared at her side and pointed at the screen. "Why is this open? Were you on the servers?"

Alex looked down at the screen, then back at Tony. "Was

like this when I got here. Don't worry, I dusted it too." She gave him her most helpful smile. "Is there anything else you need me to handle before I leave?"

Rogue monsters? Terrorist uprising? Zombie outbreak? Anything I can take down with overwhelming firepower?

"Uh, I think there's some filing that needs doing."

Idiot server jockeys, Tony thought. *Leaving stuff unsecured. Good thing computers aren't in Alex's wheelhouse.*

He wasn't wrong. Becoming a computer expert would never be in the cards for her. Better to let professionals be professionals. Any time she might devote to hacking and computers meant less time improving her skills with weapons and increasing her capacity for mindreading.

Alex gave a thumbs-up and walked to the door.

"Alex? You forgetting something?"

She froze, but then Tony's thoughts drifted into her mind. Anyone else would have been petrified by the words. Not Alex. The benefits of being a mindreader. She relaxed and turned back. "Hmm?"

He pointed at the candy bar. "You gonna take that with you?"

"Nah. I've decided Milky Way isn't my thing. It's all yours!"

She walked out of the room, casually pocketing the USB drive she hoped contained all of Helix's secrets on Project Sentinel.

Helix had their fingers everywhere. Back in Calm Waters, Alex had access to a good chunk of Helix's projects. If she wanted to learn about Helix's Cold War experiments, she could. If she wanted to look into their database of marked and tagged supernatural creatures, no one saw the issue. And yet, even then, she hadn't known much of anything about Project Sentinel. The few details she'd managed to uncover indicated that the program went back decades, to well before Jack's birth. Jack was hardly the first person to be put through the program —unbeknownst to him—and observed for years. His own grandfather, Wyatt, had been one of the earliest subjects. And as recently as six months ago, the program had multiple subjects, all of them being closely observed.

But that all changed after the Calm Waters incident. Now all the other subjects—all except for Jack—had been removed from the program. Jack's "field test," as the Insider had called it, had bumped him to the top of the list. Jack was no longer a mere part of Project Sentinel. Jack *was* Project Sentinel.

Alex knew that Project Sentinel was her father's top priority. His obsession. What she didn't know was the goal of the program. It seemed obvious that it involved turning Jack into a weapon Helix could control, but a weapon of what magnitude? To use against whom? And why wasn't Helix doing anything about Jack right now? As far as Alex could tell, no one else observed him. Her father didn't ask for reports.

The lack of attention made no sense.

After the murders in Calm Waters six months earlier, she'd been called to a special meeting to discuss Project Sentinel's future. Her father had mentioned the company was already instituting plans for Jack. Working together with Dr. Alexander

Jones—a maniac simply known as "The Doctor" in the upper echelons of Helix—Gaines made it sound like Jack would be a focus over the next six to nine months. Instead... they had done nothing at all with Jack, as far as she could tell.

If not for her paranoia—and her inside knowledge about Helix's more underhanded pursuits—she might have believed they had removed Jack from the secretive program altogether.

In an abandoned parking lot on the other side of the city, Alex pulled out a brand-new laptop and powered it on for the first time. The computer was clean and unconnected to the internet or any other wireless signals. For extra safety, this particular parking lot sat in a dead zone, perfect for her needs.

She plugged the USB drive of stolen data into the computer, opened its file directory, then went straight to folder labeled *Project Sentinel*.

After a few minutes of browsing, she knew she'd hit the jackpot.

It was all here. Everything. And so much more than she had ever expected. Given enough time—which she seemed to have in abundance these days—she would know everything there was to know about the program. After months of spinning her wheels, she finally had some actionable intel to share with Jack. And he needed it.

Alex looked up the names of the other subjects involved in the experiment. She and Jack needed someone they could recruit to their side. More specifically, someone who could relate to Jack, and to whom Jack could relate. Someone who could give them a potential edge. Everything else—all the finer details on Project Sentinel—would still be there for her and Jack to go over together.

She was about to shut down the computer—the sun had long since set, and her eyes burned from staring at the screen—when a document named *Parasite* caught her eye. The file's metadata showed it had been created the day before. She opened it and felt her blood run cold. While the document was mostly redacted, it told of a parasitic contagion of some sort scheduled to be released into the general public. The infection vector looked... fast. It would spread across a nation in a matter of weeks. The goals of this action were listed in only the broadest of terms: money, control, power. The usual.

The initial test release had been six months ago, in an isolated village in China.

Phase 2 would commence this week.

Made in the USA
Columbia, SC
10 October 2024

43449673R00200